C000005120

The Wooden Village

(Rivers of Babylon 2)

by the same author

Rivers of Babylon Bratislava: Archa, 1991, Champagne Avantgarde, 1995 and Koloman Kertész Bagala, 2003 [*in English* Garnett Press, 2007]

Mladý Dônč (*Young Dônč*) Bratislava: Slovenský spisovateľ, 1993 and Koloman Kertész Bagala, 1998

Rivers of Babylon 2 alebo drevená dedina (*Rivers of Babylon 2, or The Wooden Village*) Bratislava: Champagne Avantgarde, 1994

Skazky o Vladovi pre malých a veľkých (*Tales about Vlad for Young and Old*) Bratislava: Filmservice Slovakia, 1995

Nové skazky o Vladovi (*More Tales about Vlad*) Bratislava: Filmservice Slovakia, 1998

Sekerou a nožom (*With Axe and Knife*), with Dušan Taragel, Levice: LCA, 1999

Rivers of Babylon 3 alebo Fredyho koniec (*Rivers of Babylon 3, or The End of Freddy*) Bratislava: Filmservice Slovakia, 1999 [*in English* Garnett Press, 2008]

Posledné skazky pre malých a veľkých (*Latest Tales for Young and Old*) Bratislava: Fenix, 2002

Traktoristi a buzeranti (*Tractor Drivers and Queers*) Bratislava: Slovart, 2003

Recepty z rodinného archívu alebo všetko čo viem ma naučil môj dedo (*Recipes from the Family Archive, or Everything I Know My Grandfather Taught Me*) Levice: LCA, 2003

Peter Pišťanek

The Wooden Village
(Rivers of Babylon 2)

translated by Peter Petro

GARNETT PRESS

LONDON

first published in Great Britain in 2008 by

The Garnett Press,
Dpt of Russian (SML)
Queen Mary (University of London),
Mile End Road, London E1 4NS

typeset in Times New Roman by Donald Rayfield
1000 copies printed and bound in Turkey by Mega Basım, Istanbul

This book has been selected to receive financial assistance from English PEN's Writers in Translation
programme supported by Bloomberg.

This book has received a subsidy from SLOLIA Commit-
tee, the Centre for Information on Literature in Bratislava

ISBN 978-0-9535878-5-8

Introduction

Peter Pišťanek (pronounced *Pishtyanek*) is one of the most talented prose writers to appear after the fall of Communism in Slovakia. He is also a colourful and controversial personality whose many-sided activities were unthinkable in the Communist era. He was born in 1960 in Devínska Nová Ves, a village now swallowed up by Bratislava, the capital of Slovakia. He enrolled in Bratislava's Academy of Performing Arts, but did not graduate. He was also a drummer in a very well known rock group. At the end of the 1980s he began to publish in the literary monthly *Slovenské Pohľady* (Slovak Views). His breakthrough came with *Rivers of Babylon* (1991, English publication 2007 by Garnett Press), a novel that caused a sensation and catapulted him into fame. Followed by *The Wooden Village* and *The End of Freddy* (the latter published by Garnett Press in tandem with this novel), *Rivers of Babylon* has become a trilogy. Since the end of the 1990s Peter Pišťanek has worked for advertising agencies and edited an influential Internet magazine *Inzine*. He has also become something of an expert on brandies and whiskies.

Pišťanek's reputation is assured by the originality, fine craftsmanship and imaginative inventiveness of *Rivers of Babylon* and the rest of the trilogy. This second novel develops the story of the anti-hero of the first, Rácz, an unstoppable idiot of genius, a gangster with no conscience, but centres the plot on a secondary character from the first novel Freddy Piggybank, a sexually troubled car park attendant, who finds his path to happiness opened by the wild freedoms of the early nineties, and a new character, an emigré returning from America to an unrecognizable homeland. Pišťanek's black humour is now tempered with a gentle, only slightly ironic romanticism.

The Wooden Village, a cluster of kiosks in an old car park, chronicles the chaotic licentiousness of morals and commerce in a Slovakia where corruption and opportunism is masked as 'democracy'.

Today's Slovak readers acknowledge Peter Pišťanek as the country's most flamboyant and fearless writer, though many are shocked by his iconoclasm. A literature that once showed the Slovaks as a nation of wise bee-keepers and virtuous matriarchs now presents the nation stripped of its myths and false self-esteem. *The Wooden Village* carries on a process of demythologisation.

Some guidance for the British reader...

Time and place

The novel is set in 1992, when the Slovaks are breaking away from the Czechs to achieve independence, and anything goes. Most of the action takes place in the capital, Bratislava, then the capital of a Slovakia which was still part of Czechoslovakia. Other scenes of the novel are in Nová Ves, a village, now a suburb of Bratislava, and on the Hungarian-speaking countryside from where the dreaded Rácz and the unhappy Bartaloš couple originate.

The currency is the Slovak crown, then worth 50 to the pound sterling.

Some characters and how to pronounce their names

We have decided to keep Slovak spellings of characters' names, but here is a guide to pronouncing the more problematic and important ones. All names are stressed on the first syllable:

Rácz, Businessman of the Year *pronounce as*	Rahts
Junec, a Slovak emigrant in the USA	Yoonets
Mešťánek, Freddy Piggybank's real name	Meshtyanek
Kišš, the village butcher	Kish
Eržika, his daughter	Air-s[*as in pleasure*]ika
Bartaloš, Eržika's husband	Bartalosh
Šípoš, a gypsy stoker	Shiposh
Mozoň, ex-secret policeman	Mozogne [*n as in Boulogne*]
Šolik, ex-secret policeman	Sholik

Peter Petro and Donald Rayfield

For Maria and Tomáš Kaluba

Those of my dear readers who happen to have read my novel *Rivers of Babylon* have a right to wonder if this book might begin by not mentioning Mr Rácz. They are right: Mr Rácz is not going to be the subject. At least not as much as any reader spoiled by the first book might expect.

But perhaps I may be allowed to reveal a thing or two about Rácz's private and professional life.

Mr Rácz is pleased with life and is happily married. He is proud of his healthy son; he is doing well, and wants to use this opportunity to say hello to all his well-wishers. Both his hotels, his line of restaurants, his investment fund Oxford Captivate & Consumption, his real estate company X-Racio and his private security service Sekuritatia are all prospering. Quite recently Mr Rácz acquired a large hangar on two hectares of land in the grounds of the commercial port, where he intends to open a duty-free warehouse. All of this will depend on the internal convertibility of the Slovak crown. Moreover, Mr Rácz has founded a new division of his Sekuritatia firm, specialising in recovering difficult debts.

For example: you're a businessman. A company owes you money. You send them an invoice, a reminder invoice, a final reminder etc, and they still won't pay. So you contact the people from Sekuritatia and they buy your debt. Clear now? Other businessmen buy goods and stocks, but Rácz buys debt, too — just to keep business turning over. For an apparently irrecoverable debt of, say, half a million crowns, he will give you in cash a full four hundred thousand, that is, eighty per cent of the sum due. You go away satisfied and you light a candle in the nearest church praying that the Great Benefactor Rácz will live at least a hundred years.

While the candles are burning, Šolík and Tupý, employed by Sekuritatia ever since it was founded, do fieldwork to find out about the debtor's company: what the owner's or owners' names are, where they live, what cars they own and where they're parked, if they have a family, children and their ages and schools, if they have pets (a dog or a cat is ideal — we haven't reached the stage of a severed horse head on a pillow) and where they walk them. When they have this information, they go back to the Sekuritatia office and give a detailed report to their chief, Mozoň. A meeting then takes place. Afterwards, as they say, they get going.

The whole operation usually proceeds on identical lines.

Like this: a beautiful eight-year old little girl, angelic, with long blonde hair, a daughter of the owner of the company in debt, is walking home from school. A huge car stops by her and a nice uncle offers her sweets. She's asked if she'd like to be taken home, to such and such an address. The little girl is surprised that the nice uncle knows her address. The uncle laughs. The nice uncle is an old friend of Daddy's. The little girl gets in the car; her movements already give an embryonic, but very lovely hint of the charm with which she will one day get into other uncles' cars.

The nice uncle asks about the dog: do they still have the same dachshund?

The girls nods, yes, they have a little dog, he's called Satchmo.

"And here we are, Miss," the nice uncle says, as he stops in front of her house. "This is how to open the door. You can take all those sweets, they're bad for me, I've got diabetes," says the nice uncle. "One more thing," he adds, "I almost forgot: please give this to Daddy and say hello to him from me."

The little girl takes the envelope and sweets, says thank you nicely, with the charm we have described, and gets out of the car. She waves to the nice uncle and then vanishes in the doorway.

"A real woman," Tupý says, then puts the car in gear, and the Mercedes speeds up the street.

In the evening the little girl will excitedly tell her parents about riding in a huge car, and so on. Her horrified father, the debtor, will open the envelope. The note reads:

Dear debtor,

Kindly note that on such and such date, such and such company has passed onto us the collection of the due amount... (blah, blah, blah)... we enclose the invoice... (blah, blah, blah)... Please pay upon the receipt of this letter, or come personally, or send your representative to arrange new terms... (blah, blah, blah)...

We remain respectfully yours: our motto is:
'First we try the nice way!'
CANISTRA, a Division of Sekuritatia, Ltd.

Almost everyone pays. If not, their car will be mysteriously torched in the middle of the city. If the debtor still doesn't pay, an unknown perpetrator will wreck his office. If he still doesn't pay, somebody will nail the little dog to his front door. If he still doesn't pay, then...

That's how Mr Rácz makes his living. But in this book we shall not be concerned with his respectable business activities. Although, on the other hand, never say never, as they say. Possibly, Mr Rácz will make a few brief appearances; perhaps only because we shall sometimes be in the same time and space as this dynamic entrepreneur pursuing his adventurous career.

For example, in the Hotel Ambassador-Rácz.

* * *

At four in the morning the Hotel Ambassador is dead, submerged in darkness when nothing moves, just like the street in front of it. The trams aren't running yet; a car might pass by from time to time. One of these occasional cars is a taxi with Viennese number-plates. A well-dressed and young-looking forty-year-old man with an American's white teeth and thin wire-framed glasses steps out.

"Suitcase!" he shouts to the old porter Torontál, who runs out of the lobby in livery and hat. "My suitcase!" he adds in English.

He no longer cares about his luggage. He throws a hundred-dollar bill to the taxi driver and enters the cool semi-darkness of the lobby.

"The name is Martin Junec," he tells the receptionist, speaking half in Slovak, half in English. "I'd like a suite; a big one. For how long? My boy, I don't know myself. For a month, six months? Let me spell it for you. M-A-R-T-I-N J-U-N-E-C. Martin Junec. Got it? Atlanta, Georgia, USA. Here's my US passport."

The foreigner looks round the lobby.

"Is the Ambassador Bar still open?" He asks.

"Yes sir, it is," says the receptionist. "For another hour, till five."

"Just as it used to be," says Junec. "Nothing's changed. A long time ago I used to play here," he boasts. "I was, what's the word, a musician. I played saxophone."

The foreigner performs a pantomime of playing a saxophone.

"It's almost twenty years ago," he adds.

Junec takes the hotel card and thrusts a ten-dollar bill into the hand of the receptionist, who is amazed.

Torontál stumbles in, his spider-like fingers gripping the handle of Junec's crocodile-skin suitcase.

"Okay," says Junec, "let's go!" And, panting like an old dog, Torontál follows Junec into the lift.

"Here you are, grandpa," says Junec in his suite, giving Torontál a ten-dollar bill. "Life is hard," he admits, looking at Torontál's shaking hands. "Why don't you think about retiring, getting a pension," he adds.

* * *

The nights are still cold, but the sun rises up quite high in the day. The tin roof of the snack bar warms up and then cools down long into the night, making popping noises. Feri Bartaloš sleeps with his bedclothes kicked off. He never remembers to zip up his sleeping bag. He turns over, smacks his lips a few times and then sits up: he's thirsty. Eržika sleeps with her back turned to him. Feri gets up, steps over her, and drinks straight from the tap. Again, he steps over her and his inflatable mattress as well. He unlocks the door and steps outside.

The sky is clear. The stars are shining where they should be. The trams aren't running yet, but their approaching rumble can be heard in the distance. Feri walks around the wooden kiosks, thanks to which the snack bar has by general agreement been called the Wooden Village, and he screws up his eyes. On the roof of a tall building behind the Hotel Ambassador-Rácz is a brightly lit digital time and temperature display. It's four twenty, and ten above zero. Feri shivers. Somewhere in the distance dogs are barking. They can often be seen: a motley pack of roaming wild beasts with bared fangs and lolling tongues.

Feri crosses over to the car park. Behind the fibreboard wall of Piggybank's trailer, a fat body turns over with a sigh. Feri clears his throat and spits. He doesn't feel sleepy any more. He bangs on the door of the parking attendant's trailer. From inside come sounds of movement, muttering, searching for shoes, getting up, and cursing. The door opens and the attendant's puffy face appears in the opening.

"What's going on?" asks Freddy Piggybank in a rasping voice.

"Time for a break," says Feri.

"Bugger off!" says Freddy who wants to get back to his burrow.

"Got a light?" asks Feri and a pack of cigarettes appears in his hand. He taps on it and gives the attendant a peep of the filter ends.

Piggybank has time to read the brand name. *Sparta*. Stinginess overcomes sleepiness and bad temper. Inside his lair he digs out some matches, takes the proffered cigarette and joins Feri outside.

Bartaloš interrupts this moment of calm meditation; between puffs he complains of his boss, the snack bar manager. Feri and Eržika work like mad: everything is spick and span. Freddy can see for himself: doesn't everything look tidy?

Piggybank absentmindedly nods and coughs in the chilly morning. He's not used to smoking.

Feri is resentful and feels right to be angry. Their manager is a swine: he gives Feri and Eržika shit for everything they do, for no reason. The toilets are always clean, after all! People shit, piss, and vomit there. Feri and Eržika, needn't give a shit about the manager, either: but they keep it clean. It's completely spotless. And what happens? The manager shows up and doesn't even glance in the toilets, just stands there, like this, behind the corner and gives Feri and Eržika shit. But he and Eržika know what's going on. Feri makes a secretive grimace and smirks. All of this must be Four-Eyes's fault. Clearly, the manager is on Four-Eyes's side. Feri doesn't know what those two are up to. But there must be something. Maybe Four-Eyes knows something about the manager and is blackmailing him. Or maybe the manager is simply afraid of Four-Eyes. No matter, Feri will get to the bottom of it. Feri blows the smoke out. It's clear: Four-Eyes wants to push Feri and Eržika out of the Wooden Village. Four-Eyes is greedy. Nothing is good enough for him. Feri adds up on his fingers. Four-Eyes makes a hundred a day collecting the glasses. His wife sits outside the toilet, and that makes two or three hundred crowns a day. And all they have to do is to buy toilet paper, cleaning powder and occasionally some soap. That's all. Four-Eyes and his wife both get free food and drink. They can save money. So they get four hundred a day. This makes twelve hundred a week. Five thousand a month! Five thousand they can salt away! Feri's voice cracks when he realizes this; he forgets that he and Eržika make the same money, since they do alternate shifts with Four-Eyes in the snack bar. He concludes: Four-Eyes and his wife are trying to push Feri Bartaloš and Eržika out of this job. Feri pauses, his face expressing determination and anxiety, as well as resentment.

The fat parking attendant quickly interrupts, taking advantage of the momentary pause. Freddy Piggybank is also worried. Everything that is happening has happened before. Two years ago, in the middle of winter Freddy was thrown out of his car park. Of HIS car park! He has had to put up with enormous ingratitude. They said it was because of the Christmas Market. But those wooden kiosks stayed there till spring. He got so upset then that he fell seriously ill. It was his nerves. At the same time he mustn't get worked up, because a vein in his head swelled up when he was a child. They were all after him. First the gypsies: they wanted a third of his takings for protection. But Freddy was brave; he wouldn't pay. And what did they do? They hit back and hurt him badly. The attendant puffs his cigarette. Luckily, there are no gypsies around now. Rácz the hotel owner kicked them out of the city centre. Freddy, an honest businessman, feels safer now; nobody threatens him. But he still has to pay. Half his takings. For security. Shit! What kind of a businessman is Freddy Piggybank now? He's a beggar. Half a beggar. Just look at this Wooden Village! There is no space for cars to park, but nobody cares; the point is that the city centre is full of wooden kiosks. And one day that bitch from the town council showed up with a decree cutting the parking spaces by half and using the other half for the Wooden Village. But Freddy's rent would stay the same. While his income is less than half what it used to be. And Freddy is not even mentioning medical insurance and crap like that.

Bartaloš nods absent-mindedly, but without sympathy. If the snack bar were demolished, Feri and Eržika would lose their bread and butter.

The first tram rumbles down the street. They both take it as a signal. They say good-bye and go their separate ways. Freddy submerges in the warmth of his den which smells of hydrogen sulphide and ammonia, and Feri goes for a walk, waiting for the grocers to open. He fancies a beer.

The self-service shop opens, as usual, at five. Feri is one of the first customers. He buys two bottles of Bratislava beer, the sort that makes you crap, and stands, looking miserable, at a counter in the corner near the cashier. He opens the paper and reads his horoscope. Feri is a Cancer. *A creature of the opposite sex will fundamentally change your life this afternoon.* Feri cackles hoarsely and turns to the sports page.

The customers come staggering in, still half asleep. Nobody takes any notice of Feri; he sips his beer with his eyes half closed and studies the football results. His face jerks to attention when Four-Eyes appears. Four-Eyes enters the store. He deliberately ignores Feri. His bony figure, tall despite a hunch, moves towards the shopping baskets. He's wearing black spectacles. Ever since he lost an eye, they've become an essential accessory to his face.

Four-Eyes isn't on duty today. Feri and Eržika are. Four-Eyes wears orange overalls and a blue quilted overcoat. It is the work clothing of the City Transport road crews. He was sacked from there about two years ago, but he still feels he belongs to the big cheerful family of bus and tram drivers. Even today, Four-Eyes deliberately avoids the pavement: he walks along the tram rails in the middle of the road, his eyes focusing under his feet as if constantly checking the condition of the track. Now and then he bends down to pick up a stone. The tram people know him and give him a friendly ring when they see him. When not on duty in the Wooden Village, he often mingles with the crowd entering the transport employees' cafeteria. He gets as much soup and bread as he wants.

Four-Eyes can still recite by heart any regulation that he memorised during the many years he drove trams. When they knocked his eye out in *The Albanian* pub, he was no longer able to judge distance and was made an inspector. He was too stupid to be a controller.

When he stole the money he collected in fines and got drunk, they moved him to a digging crew. He wasn't much use there. He still considered himself a tram driver on leave. When the track was damaged, instead of digging with the rest of the crew, he would chat with his ex-colleagues waiting for the repair to be finished. The track master nearly had a stroke. When they started laying people off, Four-Eyes was the first to be sacked. He had two years to go before his pension, so he found a job in the Wooden Village. But in his heart of hearts he was still a transport worker. To this day he can recite all the regulations in a hushed but strict voice. He dramatizes each regulation really well: Yevtushenko, reciting his poetry at a packed stadium, has nothing on him. An example of Four-Eyes's robotic memory is accompanied by firm gestures of his right hand; he acts out each and every memorised sentence.

By now, Bartaloš has opened another bottle of crap beer. Four-Eyes turns up with a plastic bag full of bread rolls and milk and stands at another counter. He's bought beer, too. They stand with their backs turned to each other.

Feri can't hold out. He smiles when he sees Four-Eyes in his transport worker outfit. "Going to work?" he asks ironically.

The lanky man ignores him on purpose, and calmly pours the beer down his ageing mouth.

"I said, going to work?" Feri repeats.

Four-Eyes swallows the crap beer, wipes his chin with the back of his hand, takes a good look at Feri and then lazily turns his round, almost bald head with its striking aquiline nose. His eye is concealed by the dark lenses.

Feri takes no notice of the warning signals. "What would they do without you in City Transport?" Feri says, as if to himself. "Without you they might as well give up."

In an instant, Four-Eyes is on him. His sinewy hand grips Feri's neck. Feri's eyes pop, and he falls silent. He is two heads shorter than Four-Eyes. The tall man keeps gripping him and won't let go. He is quick-tempered. He beats his wife, too. Sometimes he beats her even in the snack bar, right in front of the customers.

The cashier starts to screech in her piercing voice. "Always the same thing," she says, all worked up. "They knock it back first thing in the morning and then they fight. But nobody's going to fight in this super-market." She's going to call the manager right away. And he can call the police.

Four-Eyes gives her as much attention as he would to a buzzing fly. He still grips Feri by the neck and won't let him breathe.

Feri tries to gather his last ounce of strength, and his fading eyes search around in panic in the hope that one of his beer-drinking mates will show up: bearded Honzík, his colleague from the snack bar across the street, or the murderous Fraňo Fčilek who collects the beer glasses at *The Hunter*. But there's nobody around. In the corner near the pillar, stinking Majerník, who is never sober and who eats leftovers from other people's plates, laughs at him; he won't help.

Feri Bartaloš gathers his last remnants of strength and knees Four-Eyes hard in the crotch. Four-Eyes immediately releases his grip and grabs the painful spot.

Feri catches his breath and his face recovers its normal colour. Vengefully and slyly, with a coward's cruel smile, he gives Four-Eyes two or three more kicks and runs out of the shop. He doesn't even finish the crap beer. Weaving between the slow-moving cars, he looks back to see if there is anyone in pursuit.

Four-Eyes is crouching by the counter. His shrivelled hands are clutching his balls and his belly; he can't decide what to do next.

In the chilly morning air Feri is followed by wild cursing, but he has now reached the other side of the street, laughing and grimacing under the influence of his victory.

* * *

After a brief sleep of less than an hour, Martin Junec wakes up in his suite, wondering for a while where he is. Once things are clear, he sits up in bed. In the Louis XV chair his former brother-in-law Žofré is sitting.

"Fuck that fucking motherfucker!" Junec bursts out in English.

Žofré's expression is unhappy. His fat body fidgets in the chair. Martin should speak Slovak, he says. Martin must know, after all, that Žofré's never learned English.

Martin grabs a slipper and hurls it at Žofré.

Žofré dissolves in the air for a moment but, as soon as the danger is over, he reappears in his chair.

"Yes," Žofré says, "Žofré doesn't speak English and Martin has forgotten his Slovak. What a shame," he says, resentfully shaking his head.

"That's right," says Junec. "And it was bound to happen that way because, while I worked twenty-four hours a day, seven days a week, and was in regular contact with Americans, you were boozing in the Slovak Club with our fellow countrymen!"

"And what did that do for you?" Žofré laughs. "Soon you won't know how to buy even a bread roll in Slovak."

"What did that do for me?" Martin Junec repeats, and gets out of bed. "This is what it did: I used to be a Slovak-trained electrician and former idiot, and now I control seventy-five per cent of the stock of Artisania Lamps, which I founded. And when I feel like having a bread roll, then I can buy it and the whole bakery, too. And what did drinking do for you? You've been dead for the last three years. That's what!"

Martin goes into the bathroom. Žofré dissolves above the armchair he was sitting in and instantly rematerializes, standing in the bathroom doorway.

"A long time ago, when we still lived here," says Junec, his mouth full of toothpaste, "there used to be a TV series: Randall and Hopkirk (Deceased). Do you remember?"

Martin turns to Žofré. Žofré shrugs.

"Randall was a private detective, you know?" says Martin. "He had a friend who was a detective, too. He got killed. But he stayed on earth and helped his friend investigate. Never ever would I have believed that such a thing was possible and that I'd be involved. Fuck this fucking life!"

"You talk like an idiot from a school for the subnormal," says Žofré. "Baťa has spent fifty years in America and still switches to fluent Czech at a moment's notice."

"Like hell he does, Žofré," says Martin and starts getting dressed. "You always were a dirty motherfucker and you still are. even now you're dead. The only thing I regret is the moment that I let Hruškovič persuade me to have you in the band. That's when it started. When you drank yourself to death in the US, I told myself, maybe it was a good thing. But who could have known that you'd appear a week after your funeral? But don't worry, buddy! This isn't going to last very long. Don't you worry!"

"I know you've phoned Hruškovič," Žofré says reproachfully. "I know very well what he's up to now! You want to get rid of me, but it will take a fucking good psychic to make me leave you in peace. When I was dying, I promised Edna to keep an eye on you."

"Leave Edna out of this!" Junec orders him. "She couldn't understand a single word you said!"

"That makes no difference," the ghost retorts. "Promises are promises."

"Suddenly!" Martin shouts at the mirror, as if calling on it as a witness. "Suddenly! You hated her and all the time you were as jealous as a wild boar, and now we have these promises. Just don't take it too far! And scram!"

"Yes," admits Žofré sadly. "I hurt her a lot. That's why I have to atone for it."

"Oh, shut up," says Junec wearily and stretches out on the bed again.

"Besides, it's not fair, anyway," Žofré continues. "I've always tried to help you. Didn't I give you advice?"

"Oh yes, you did," Junec admits. "You advised me. But it was all crap advice. Like recommending carved plywood chandeliers for the concert halls. *The Phantom of the Opera* is a piece of shit compared to what happened in Atlanta when one of those chandeliers dried out and fell into the auditorium. Lucky it was empty at the time! And, like an idiot, I went on listening to you for a while. I really should have realised that if someone was stupid when alive, then even after death he wouldn't get any cleverer. You, on the other hand, got even more stupid!"

"Well, yes," Žofré admits, self-critically. "Mistakes happened. But they won't happen again."

"You can bet on that, buddy!" Junec says. "They won't. And now get lost!"

"Nothing simpler," announces Žofré judiciously and with a grin of condescension dissolves in the air just in time to prevent a projectile, Martin's slipper, from hitting his astral body.

* * *

The little girl was very small; she'd been born very recently. She peed into nappies that absorbed everything. She ate instant creamed wheat, she smiled happily when rubbed with baby lotion. She was regularly washed with baby soap and made happy goo-goo sounds.

In no time she reached the age of dolls with limbs that bent and fairytale ponies with fairytale manes. The little girl talked about them, her eyes wide with excitement. She smiled and her front teeth were visibly bigger than the rest. This was thought to make her attractive. Her teeth had no trouble biting into good quality chocolate. The little girl brushed them with fruit-flavour toothpaste. She kept brushing them and around that time, without being aware of it, she had her first period.

Very quickly, right before our eyes, the little girl turned into a young lady. The young lady started to menstruate regularly into good quality sanitary towels and tampons; she washed her hair with shampoo and conditioner, and banged the metal door of the medicine cabinet. She began to shave her legs. She chewed good minty chewing gum. Whenever she arrived somewhere she'd be offered a bottle of cola right away. The cola would be served from an ice bucket. The young lady would gladly drink her fill. Her teeth didn't break and fall out only because of the good-quality toothpaste she used all her life.

Then she met someone. He was just like her. He smiled with his white teeth, looked a bit silly, but wasn't really. His head was bit smaller than it should have been, but he did have a nice muscular body. He moved in a vigorous, manly way.

The young lady was becoming more and more lady-like. She learned how to walk elegantly, like a model. While walking, she would put her left foot where the right one should be, and vice versa. She moved a bit slower, her figure was rounded. Her hair hung loose. She wore tights. She was drinking champagne now. A bit of foam would always be left on her lips. Her boyfriend — maybe the same one, maybe a different one — watched her admiringly. They bought the same denim suits and resembled each other.

Soon the young lady got a job. We don't know where and what she studied, and we shan't even find out what she did afterwards. Dressed in a miniskirt and top, surrounded by flashing computer screens, blinds, and colleagues scurrying about in suits, underneath a slowly rotating fan, she was constantly on the phone. Maybe she'd become the manager of a successful company.

She and her co-worker seemed to have found each other right away. He was like her boyfriend, except that he wore glasses, was a few years older and had a softer face. The young woman began to wear glasses, too. Thin wire frames did not detract at all from her youthful charm. She and her new boyfriend would go to the theatre and to concerts. The former boyfriend did everything he could to hold on to her. He even showed up on his motorcycle and rode through the office where she worked. The young woman gave in to his charm for one last time, accepted the jeans that he brought along, put them on, and hopped on the back seat of the motorcycle in front of her colleague's sad eyes.

The very same evening, drenched by the rain, she rang the doorbell of her colleague's cosy bachelor flat and fell into his arms: she had come to stay.

She introduced him to her parents. They were always smiling, youthful and immortal. Her father offered him non-alcoholic beer that he used not to drink, but now had a liking for.

Then there was a wedding.

After the wedding both spouses felt fine. They lived in a nice family house. The young woman left her job and became dull. From then on her only intellectual effort was to drive out to do her shopping and to listen to the advice of older ladies about the quality of detergent. She would use lotion on her face, put on some perfume, and cook, menstruate, and wash. She was always staring in wonderment at something. A dull life and staring improved her eyesight so much that she threw away her glasses. Her husband would go to work dressed in a burgundy suit and carrying an attaché case. Occasionally he would invite his boss home for dinner. The young woman would take a pre-cooked dinner from the freezer, and the boss would eat it, thinking she had cooked it. The next day her husband got a small raise in his salary.

From time to time, they invited friends home. The friends looked just as nice as the young woman and her husband. They sat properly in their armchairs and smiled at each other. They always drank coffee and knew all the brand names. Occasionally, the husband would open a bottle of golden-coloured brandy or whisky. Oddly enough, they always poured from the same bottle, but the level never seemed to go down. The same went for the sweets and biscuits.

* * *

By the time Feri gets back to Eržika, everything has been tidied up. Inflatable mattresses, blankets, and sleeping bags are stowed away in the hut at the back: they're not needed. Snack bar customers with bursting intestines can use the front hut. It will have to do. The shitters often nervously fidget as they wait in a long queue, but Eržika copes with the crowd without batting an eyelid. If someone takes too long, Eržika gets off her chair and firmly knocks at the door of the cubicle. "Hey, what's going on?" she shouts. "Get a move on!" she adds. "What's the hold-up?" Then she returns to her post with dignity. Advanced pregnancy invests her with courage as well as dignity. She wouldn't have dared before. A shitter once gave her such a punch that she fell under the sink. He didn't like being charged two crowns for relief. Eržika then ran in tears to get Feri, but he was shopping in the supermarket. She wasn't pregnant yet. Now she is pregnant and charges five crowns for a shit, and nobody dares to touch her, the Madonna of the Toilets.

As if a magic wand has been waved, the bedroom changes into a men's lavatory with all its requisites: a burbling flushing system, two urinals and a smell of ammonia permeating the air.

Feri pauses for a while inside and checks the men's cubicle. Then he goes to check the women's lavatory. Afterwards, content with Eržika's work, he goes outside, in front of the snack bar. Meanwhile, Eržika sweeps cigarette butts, discarded paper cups, broken bottles and plastic trays with remnants of yesterday's mustard from under the tables of the Wooden Village. Her movements are graceful; she is wearing high heels, so high that she has to bend forward when walking.

Freddy Piggybank brought the shoes. Yugoslav women threw them away behind their parked bus when they changed into new shoes they had bought. Feri bought the shoes from the parking attendant; he got the asking price of three hundred crowns down to the equivalent of a can of sausage and beans. The parking attendant bought the can, warmed it up and ate it, and now Eržika walks around in sexy shoes. They're Yugo-slav, Feri reminds himself from time to time, watching her with pleasure.

Feri sits down on a bench and gets immersed in the paper. In the meantime, Eržika carries on sweeping around him. She moves quite awk-wardly, like a duck, but for Feri, her walk has a certain charm: the shoes were really cheap.

People show up around seven. They ask the same question every day: "When does the snack bar open?" Every morning Feri gives the same reply: "Eight." To emphasize his importance, he puts on a white coat. People think he is the manager and he maintains this not unflat-tering misunderstanding by turning round and shouting peremptory orders at Eržika as she cleans. When he finishes his paper, he puts it into his coat pocket and gets up with a sigh. The working day has begun. Standing in the middle of the Wooden Village, a proud Feri Bartaloš directs Eržika's activity.

The snack bar staff arrive. They unlock the snack bar and enter. The barmen tap the beer barrels and the kitchen girls switch on the grill.

Soon the bastard boss shows up. He parks his Ford on the pavement, opens the boot and summons Feri with his finger. Without saying a word, he points to the boot, which is full of frozen chickens and a few five-litre jars of sour pickles. Feri nods and starts carrying them into the snack bar. He tries not to show how livid he is: proud Feri Bartaloš has to obey the orders of a midget, instead of the midget following proud Feri Bartaloš's orders.

The bastard boss is a classic example of the animal species *Jerkus normalis*, not just because of his crooked behaviour and the way he treats the Wooden Village employees, but because of his unprepossessing appearance. The bastard boss is between thirty and forty years old, about five feet four inches tall, has a fairly big rounded head with extremely blond hair. His blond hair is cut short and parted in the middle like the heroes of the comic strips by Jaroslav Foglár. Over-developed incisors dominate his face. They are so over-developed that the bastard boss can't close his mouth properly. These incisors arouse in everybody, even strangers, but especially in proud Feri Bartaloš, an almost irresistible desire to knock them out with a powerful, well-aimed blow.

The bastard boss moves quickly in the gait that, on the basis of the most recent archaeological evidence, we ascribe to a dwarf dinosaur of the *Compsognathus* family. He wears shoes two sizes too large, stuffed with newspaper. The bastard boss manages to take long strides unsuited to his stature by standing on his toes in order give an optical illusion of height. But even this optical illusion fails, and the bastard boss's efforts have only reinforced his image as a little jerk, which is now his nickname. The bastard boss's round head is proudly held high. His half-open mouth sucks in air. After qualifying as a cook and waiter and successfully graduating from secondary hotel school, he was still spoken to by people in the street as if he were a boy, so he decided to grow a moustache. Now the bastard boss looks like a child who has glued on a moustache from a fancy-dress hire company.

He is still spoken to by everybody as if he were a small boy.

Feri has unloaded all the goods; the bastard boss gets in his car and vanishes. Lucky for him, thinks a humiliated Feri. Otherwise, Feri Bartaloš would have to give him a couple of whacks...

Soon the first customers show up. They wait. Some of them stand at the counter with a Pilsner, but most of them queue for the crap beer: it's five crowns cheaper.

Among the first impatient customers is a stoker from the nearby Hotel Ambassador-Rácz, the fat gypsy Šípoš, wearing a torn Hawaiian shirt. He impatiently bangs his hard-working fist on the unresponsive counter. His impatient dark eyes are buried in his fat olive face. They give him his beer free because he has influence. He works nearby.

The beer may have been given to him as a favour, but it was sour. The snack bar barman left an unfinished barrel of the crap beer to oxidize during the night.

Šípoš doesn't mind. He pours the yellow piss through his black moustache and down his gullet. He ignores the envious looks of impatient customers still waiting to be served.

"I'm local," he explains proudly and wipes his moustache. "This was a director's beer!"

He takes out of his overalls a twenty-crown coin and gives it to the barman. Then he shows him his thumb.

"Another director's beer?" the barman asks. His voice is content. He doesn't want problems with any of Rácz's people, not even his stoker, but he'd like to draw the soured beer as fast as he can, so he can tap a new barrel.

* * *

Silvia feels like a cigarette, but she suppresses her desire for nicotine. No, she will never again do anything in her life to harm herself.

Instead, she opens a pack of sugar-free gum and puts a piece in her mouth.

The queue of cars at the border crossing moves a little. Someone behind her honks their horn.

"Just take it easy, you fucking arsehole," says Silvia into her rear-view mirror. "I'm not blind."

She presses the accelerator and her Passat automatic meekly moves a few yards further.

"Happy now?" asks Silvia, looking in the mirror, but the driver behind her is looking somewhere else.

"Home at last," Silvia muses. This long-awaited moment has come after four years spent working in Austria. She is returning home richer in experience and with a bit of capital. If she's clever, she'll increase her capital. Silvia knows that the best way of making money is by sex. It always was and always will be. Bratislava is full of massage parlours, brothels and prostitutes. At first sight, you might think the market was saturated. But Silvia knows that people usually get quickly sated by ordinary things and start to want something unusual, unnatural, strong stimulants. Nobody is interested now in a prostitute you just lie down on and screw. Clients will ask for something special. And here Silvia's an expert. For over four years she has slaved in a brothel called the *Perverts' Club*, and she's seen things. Nobody can teach her anything.

For three years she was an ordinary sex-worker and then she was promoted. On a small stage attached to the club she performed various unorthodox forms of lovemaking. It was foul, but at least she didn't have to satisfy six or even ten times a night very bizarre sexual requests from beastly and comically stingy clients who, at the moment when they turned into a piece of quivering ejaculating jelly, were still carefully ensuring that they got everything they'd paid for.

All pluses have their minuses: during that year on the small stage of the *Perverts' Club* Silvia copulated in front of an audience with every-thing except perhaps a child's corpse or an extra-terrestrial.

* * *

Freddy Piggybank was born and raised in an impoverished brickyard settlement, in a jumble of dilapidated buildings put up some time in the previous century right next to the brickyard. The whole family lived only for the brickyard: his father was a master brick maker, his mother was a cashier, one grandpa helped out in the warehouse and the other grandpa drove a miniature diesel locomotive that brought clay from the clay-pit. Uncle Alex was the manager of the company cafeteria and an aunt was in charge of the company library and the recreation room.

As a little boy, Freddy loved to go down to the clay-pit. He would take grandpa his lunch. The clay-pit was a huge open-pit mine. All around were towering greyish slopes, scraped by excavators moving round them. On one side, the slope was covered in thin acacia scrub. At the bottom of the pit ran a railway track, so narrow it seemed like a toy.

A miniature green diesel engine, blackened by oil and age, pottered along the track: it pulled the tipping mine wagons. Sitting behind the engine, sideways to the track on a perforated metal seat, was a man dressed in overalls. This was Freddy's grandpa. He would stop the en-gine and help Freddy up. Then he accelerated and the train sped up along the crooked rails.

"Nice?" asked grandpa.

Little Freddy would blush and nod. He liked his grandpa, but was a bit afraid, too: grandpa occasionally got drunk, and then turned nasty.

"When you grow up," grandpa told Freddy "I'll be very old and weak. I'll stay home with grandma and you'll take over the engine. What do you say?"

Freddy nodded. His eyes shone.

They rumbled on towards an idle excavator. Grandpa stopped so that the last wagon faced the excavator bucket. He opened the driver's cabin, sat down and moved the levers and started the electric motor. The cogs began to move. The grey clay dropped into the little wagon. When it was full, grandpa pushed a lever and the excavator moved a few feet along the parallel track. Freddy admired everything: his grandpa who had mastered these mighty machines, the engine that pulled the wagons, the track, and even the clay-pit's huge grey and seemingly dead expanse.

Grandpa would drive back at full speed. He held the accelerator with one hand and Freddy with the other. The crooked track threw them from side to side and the wind dishevelled their hair. Grandpa's overalls reeked of sweat and mould.

Grandpa stopped in front of a hut knocked together from boards and covered with tarred paper. Freddy took the lunch-tin and got down from the engine. Men in overalls, Slovaks and gypsies, came out of the hut. Grandpa uncoupled the wagons and signalled to the brickyard, less than two hundred yards away. Soon a steel cable suspended over the wagons began to move. Grandpa, together with other men, would push the wagons along the track. Each wagon had a hook that caught the moving cable pulling them, one after another, up the straight gentle slope. Starting from the pit, they moved through a narrow gap between the two halves of the settlement, and then along a gently rising wooden structure.

Freddy shaded his eyes with his hand, watching the first wagon until it became very small and vanished at the top, where track ended, into the dark brickyard hall. Soon it reappeared empty and, pushed by the cable, came down along a parallel track. Another one followed, then others. The men stopped work.

"Let's go inside," said grandpa.

Little Freddy followed his grandpa into the tiny hut covered in tarred paper. Inside was a long, rough table covered in newspaper, and two rough benches which were worn smooth. There was a big cast-iron stove in the corner.

Grandpa found a spoon somewhere and opened the lunch-tin. He started his lunch.

Freddy sat opposite, watching him stuff himself. Around sat men with dark or lighter faces and huge, dirty hands resting on the table.

Some unwrapped a snack, others smoked. The hut smelled of tar, diesel, cigarette smoke, onions and sweat.

Freddy didn't feel good here; his grandpa seemed remote. In this hut he belonged to other people, as well as to Freddy.

The boy blushed as he answered the workmen's kindly, jocular questions; he stubbornly kept his eyes down, looking under the table.

Finally, grandpa finished lunch. He closed the lunch-tin and handed it to Freddy.

One of the workers took out some grubby cards and made a show of banging them on the table.

"Go now," grandpa told Freddy gently. "Grandma will be worried if you stay too long."

Freddy left the hut, but not by the crooked slippery path up from the pit: he went in the opposite direction, round a huge mound of coal dust and then along a path lined by reeds, which led downhill.

The tall reeds, taller than Freddy, opened out, and in front of the boy appeared the surface of a lake that covered the bottom of the pit. Freddy paused for a moment and then ran to the water. His shoes were sinking into the soft clay, but Freddy watched the water with excitement. Near the shore the lake was shallow, less than ten inches deep, and the crystal-clear water revealed all the mysteries hidden beneath the surface. A water spider was building a nest of bubbles, a shoal of fish flashed by just under the surface, and a frog, its head camouflaged by vegetation, was taking a breath of air.

Freddy longed to have his own water creatures, he badly wanted an aquarium like his friend Edo's: Edo also lived in the workers' settlement. Freddy's aquarium was a one-gallon pickling jar.

Freddy opened the lunch tin, took out one of the pots, rinsed grandpa's tomato sauce out; then he took his shoes off, rolled up his trousers and got into the water. Soon he had a few black tadpoles in the bottom of the pot. Freddy took them home and poured them into the gallon jar. He could watch the black creatures for hours.

A few days later, all the tadpoles were dead. Father took the jar and poured its contents down the lavatory. He didn't notice that some live water snails perished with the dead tadpoles.

Freddy felt sorry for the snails. His eyes full of burning hot tears, he cried so loudly that his usually passive and eternally tired mother gave him a few smacks.

Some time later Freddy visited his friend Edo and, when nobody was watching, he poured into his aquarium a phial of grandpa's lighter fuel.

* * *

The young woman is shopping. She feels like having an iced cola. She puts her shopping in the boot of a small car that only she drives, looks around and heads for the snack bar. Freddy Piggybank watches her admiringly. His X-ray eyes can see through her clothing and he knows she is wearing expensive lace underwear regularly advertised on television. "Wow!" thinks Freddy.

The young woman goes up the snack bar. She takes a look at the stinking down-and-outs surrounding Majerník; she thinks they look picturesque. Whenever the young woman is bewildered, she smiles. As she does now. Her inner light lights up her wretched surroundings.

"Have you got cola?" she asks the bartender with a radiant smile.

"Yeah," the bartender nods.

"Is it chilled?" the young woman enquires.

The bartender spreads his arms apologetically.

"I'm sorry, I don't get time to chill things."

He gives her one from the fridge, but adds that it hasn't been there long.

The young woman gives up her dream of ice-cold refreshment straight from a bucket of crushed ice: she drinks the warm slop. She's never had warm cola before. Her body reacts to it in an odd way. Something stirs inside her belly. The pretty woman puts the empty bottle on the zinc counter and, barely concealing her haste, heads round the corner, guided by the radiant liberating sign: WC.

Eržika is already waiting there with a two-inch length of toilet paper and a bowl for five-crown coins that she eagerly holds out.

"Both ladies' cubicles are occupied," she says. "You'll have to use the men's. Don't worry, I'll make sure nobody bothers you."

The young woman, holding the piece of toilet paper, enters a narrow cubicle with a constant stream of burbling water and a penetrating stench of male urine. She has never smelled that odour; all the lavatories in her life have been clean and fresh-smelling. Her head spins for a while, but then she sits on the lavatory. The smell of ammonia gets up her nose, her ears, and all her other orifices. The outside door opens. She instinctively grabs the door handle, even though she has locked herself in. She hears steps. A man approaches a urinal, opens his fly and urinates with a sigh of relief. The young woman imagines a mighty stream pouring from the man's big veined member and feels a thrill running through her body.

Never in her life has she felt such a strong thrill, if we discount the excitement of drinking chilled cola, or trying a new soap powder or washing-up detergent. Her long, carefully manicured fingers unwittingly make for the place where she sometimes introduces good quality tampons. Her crotch has a delicious sharp spasm.

The man stops urinating, farts, shakes his member and leaves the lavatory.

Soon the pretty woman also leaves the men's lavatory. She stumbles like a drunk and her eyes burns with passion that hasn't been even one-tenth satisfied. The smell of urine has awakened a demon in her. She looks around. Dirty, uncouth beer drinkers stand at the counters, drinking the Bratislava crap beer, smoking cheap cigarettes. The stinking and eternally drunk tramp Majerník, who eats other people's leftovers, sits on his own; he has in front of him a glass he has filled with beer from others' unfinished glasses, and he's singing a Russian ballad.

The beer-sozzled eyes of the rough-looking, evil-smelling drunks radiate an innate magical charm which rivets the pretty woman's atten-tion. If she were to lie down here and now and they all urinated on her while she rubbed her crotch...

The young woman knows that she is not going to go home to her technicolor husband. This Wooden Village and, above all, its lavatory will be her world from now on.

She goes up the snack bar and the barman asks her if she wants another cola.

No, says the young woman. She needs Dutch courage. "A whisky," she says.

The bartender laughs and replies, "We don't stock it."

"Cognac, then," says the pretty woman. She instantly remembers the brand she usually drinks with her husband by the blazing fireplace. "Hennessy."

The barman shakes his head. "Rum, vodka, gin," he says impa-tiently; the young woman is holding up a queue of eager beer drinkers clutching the sweaty ten-crown coins in their palms.

"Rum, then," says the young woman. "And another cola."

She takes her rum and cola to the table. She takes a sip. The taste of rum takes her by surprise. All the alcoholic drinks that she has so far tried with her husband have had the bland taste of expensive products. The rum is strong and has an acrid, vulgar smell. She chases it down with a cola and feels a pleasantly mangy warmth rising up from her belly, and her muscles and bones feel a sweet prickliness. Some of this warmth descends to her crotch and makes it eager and ready to be penetrated by big, solid flesh.

The pretty woman goes to talk to Eržika. Eržika is sitting on a chair in front of the lavatories; her hands rest in a dignified pose on her big belly. She is resting. On the chair next to her is the bowl full of five-crown coins.

"What is it, ma'am," Eržika asks seeing the pretty woman standing next to her, looking embarrassed.

"Tell me," says the pretty woman, "you wouldn't need an assistant, would you?"

Eržika ponders. She takes the young woman to be some busybody of a journalist, or a bored, petulant married woman out to make trouble.

"Well, if you think this is a gold mine, you can start right away," she says aggressively.

The young woman's face lights up with a smile. She has fine perfect teeth cared for by toothpaste recommended by the dentists' association.

"Right away?" she asks.

Eržika now realises that the madam really means it.

"FERI!" she shouts at Bartaloš.

The proud Feri comes from outside the snack bar. He looks dignified and busy in his white coat. He assesses the situation in a flash. Trouble. He puts on a threatening and harsh expression.

But Eržika calms him with a wave of her hand. "There's no problem. The lady here would like to work for us," she says.

Feri looks at the lady. He noticed her earlier, when she was having her rum. Women like her have always frustrated him; they are out of his league. He looks at the lady's long legs.

"If you think that we're raking it in here, you're wrong," he says cautiously.

"I don't care about money," says the young woman.

Feri exchanges glances with Eržika. The woman is mad.

"And what would you like to do here?" Feri asks.

The pretty woman shrugs.

"I don't know," she says. "I don't know what there is to do. Cleaning?"

This is Eržika's chance. "There's a lot of work here. You have to clean the urinals and bowls all the time. People are pigs." Eržika is pregnant. She's now seven months gone. She feels sick all the time. She breathes in fumes from the cleaning fluids and that makes her sick all day. If madam would like to do this, she's welcome.

"Cleaning the urinals?" asks the young woman. "That would be fine. When can I start?"

Eržika and Feri are pole-axed.

"How much do you want for doing that?" Feri asks.

"Nothing," says the young woman. "It would be nice if you gave me a place to sleep."

"A place to SLEEP?" Eržika is puzzled.

"She's run away from her husband," Feri tells Eržika in Hungarian, so the lady can't understand them.

Eržika nods knowingly.

"We'll see," she says in a good-natured way, gets up, goes to the men's room, opens a closet with cleaning equipment and takes out a wire brush and disinfectant. "Go and clean the lavatories now," she tells madam. "We'll sort out somewhere for you to sleep."

"What was all that about?" Freddy asks a rhetorical question, when the pretty woman goes off, carrying a bucket.

Eržika taps her forehead.

Feri is smiling. If madam doesn't want to be paid, all the better for Feri and Eržika. Though madam won't last very long.

"The real problem is where she's going to sleep," she reminds him.

Feri thinks seriously. "Yes," he says. "Maybe we could make the entrance to the second lavatory a bedroom for the night. We sleep in the first lavatory, she sleeps in the second."

"If she agrees to that," says Eržika. She can lend her blankets, no problem. But would that be good enough for a fine lady like her?

Feri reflects. "What about Freddy Piggybank?" he asks.

Eržika doesn't understand.

Feri explains: why not put her up in his trailer?

Eržika shakes her head. "That won't work."

Looking like a group of statues, they reflect.

The young woman stands above the urinal and takes deep breaths of the ammonia fumes from men's urine. Her right hand can't help slipping under her miniskirt, into her crotch. Her excitement knows no bounds. Behind her back the door opens. A beer drinker smelling of cheap cigarettes comes in to have a pee. When he sees the pretty woman he stops in amazement. The young woman drops her bucket, turns to face the drinker, her hand still on her crotch. Her eyes are those of a wild animal let off its chain. The drinker closes the door behind him. Lady's every gesture offers her to him. The drinker clutches her. The pretty woman wraps her leg, clad in smoke-coloured tights, around him, as if she were climbing a tree. They lock themselves in a cubicle. Lady puts the lid down, sits and spreads her legs to the drinker. The drinker opens his fly with shaking yellow fingers. In the cubicle's artificial light appears a huge member, darkened from disuse. Lady gasps. She has never in her life seen a member like that. Her technicolor husband's is half that size, and even so he rarely gets it up, since he's always sitting in his burgundy suit and tie at a computer screen.

The young woman sighs and moans loudly, as if she is about to die. The drinker kneels down between her legs. He enters her and moves wildly. After a few seconds, the young woman is drenched in a pulsating stream of white liquid. The drinker sighs. He quickly pulls his member out of Lady, gets off his knees and leaves without so much as a glance at her. In the front of the cubicle he urinates into the urinal for a long time and when he finishes, leaves.

The young woman rearranges her clothing. Her fire is still burning; it hasn't been quenched. She gets up and staggers. Something is pouring out of her, so she uses the toilet paper. Then she picks up the cleaning fluid and begins to clean the bowl.

When Feri finds out from the satisfied beer drinker what he'd just been up to in the cubicle, he is dumbfounded. It takes a moment for his brain to get to work. He goes to see what Lady is doing in the lavatory. He watches her mopping the ever-wet floor.

"Everything all right?" he asks.

The young woman smiles and nods. Her hand reaches for his fly. Feri looks around in embarrassment as if he's afraid of Eržika seeing, even though the door is closed. He's a faithful husband. The city hasn't spoiled him. One day, when they're rich, Eržika and he will go back to the village in the south where they were born, and they will leave the lavatory and Lady behind them.

"You want a man?" Feri asks and immediately corrects himself: "Men?"

Lady nods.

"I can send you someone," says Feri.

Lady runs the tip of her tongue over her lips. She nods.

"Just wait for me here," he tells her and goes back to Eržika.

They haggle quietly for a while.

"How much are we going to ask each man for?" Eržika asks.

They can't settle on a sum. A hundred is too little, two hundred is too much. They finally agree on a hundred and twenty for intercourse. One hundred will go to them, and twenty will be for her food and, if need be, for accommodation in Freddy's trailer.

"Do something," Feri orders Eržika, pointing to the men's lavatory. "Give her a blanket," he specifies. "So it looks a bit more cosy. I'll go tell the men and then settle a price with Piggybank."

Piggybank has his hands full. There are lots of cars. Feri guards them, collects the money, and asks for money already owing. Proud Feri Bartaloš in his white coat approaches and stands by him quietly for a while.

"What do you want?" asks Freddy.

Feri can't find the right words. "Listen, I have a bit of a problem. We have this Lady, you know? The woman assistant. She's run away from home and is working in the lavatory. She has nowhere to sleep."

Feri eyes Piggybank.

"So what?" asks the fat parking attendant.

"So, Eržika and I were wondering," Feri says, "whether she couldn't sleep for a few nights at your place…"

Feri firmly shakes his head. Piggybank now lives in the car park. It's the start of summer, high season. He doesn't go home. He needs a bit of privacy. He works here, eats here, and sleeps here. By midnight he's happy if he can shut his eyes for a few hours. Soon, in the morning, the whole thing starts again. By eight the car park is full. No, no, Freddy, doesn't need some old bag in his trailer.

Bartaloš twists his face into a grimace, pretending to be surprised. WHAT? Has he heard right? Old bag? Well then, Freddy'd better come with him right away and take a look at what he's calling an old bag!

Freddy Piggybank cautiously frees his shoulder from Bartaloš's firm grip. Freddy is up to his neck in work. The car park is full; cars are constantly coming and going. That's Freddy's money. He's not on a salary. He's in business. He has no time to look at old cunts.

If Freddy gives Lady a place to sleep, says proud Feri, she may let him screw her.

Freddy pauses, but then just waves his hand. Freddy Piggybank doesn't need to screw some old fossil. He's got better contacts.

Bartaloš bursts out laughing: "You mean Five-Fingers Annie?"

Again he grabs the fat attendant by the shoulder.

"Come with me, if you don't believe me," he insists. "At least take a look, you don't have to get close."

They both cross the car park so they can see the entrance to the lavatories. Feri motions to Eržika to call Lady out. Eržika gets up and with a dignified gait enters the men's lavatory.

Lady has by now made herself at home in one of the cubicles. A patterned blanket has been thrown over the lid of the pan, turning the cubicle into a love nest. Lady is sitting there, waiting for another drunk. Eržika takes her outside.

Freddy gawps. The young woman's beautiful slender figure in an elegant two-piece takes his breath away. He can't believe his eyes.

"Well? You want her?" Feri asks, noticing Piggybank's amazement. "A fantastic woman, isn't she?

A drunk turns up at the lavatory entrance. He gives Eržika money and disappears with Lady into the men's lavatory.

"That's the Lady you'll be having," says Feri. "All night long. And fifty crowns into the bargain. Agreed?"

Freddy nods. "When does she come?" he asks impatiently.

"As soon as we close, I'll bring her to you," Feri promises, winking at Freddy and, pleased with himself, strides over to his Eržika.

Meanwhile Lady is kneeling on the seat of the bowl, holding the cistern with both hands, and the drunk, thrusting hard, is entering her from behind. He wants to get it over as soon as possible. Beer and gin is waiting for him outside.

* * *

The ambulance came all the way to the clay-pit to fetch Freddy's grandpa, Freddy was told when he got home from school. It was a stroke.

Sunday was visiting day. They all put on their Sunday best and took a dirty train. The train spat them out in the city. Then they took a tram and after a few stops got out at the hospital. While father asked the receptionist where grandpa was, Freddy gazed round the dark, repulsive corridor, which stank of chemicals and death and was full of patients waiting for visitors.

Then they entered a large ward with a row of beds separated from each other only by white screens.

"Keep it short," the doctor told them.

Grandpa was lying on a bed with his eyes closed; he looked odd.

"Mr Mešťánek, you have visitors," the nurse told him.

Grandpa opened his eyes, one eye, to be precise. The other stayed closed and, anyway, the whole left side of his body seemed somehow bigger, powerless and odd, horribly odd.

Freddy's new Sunday shoes pinched him; the pain had started in the train, where they had to stand all the way. It seared his soles and insteps and absorbed all his attention, so that he had little energy for noticing what was around him.

Grandpa was looking at him with his one eye. It was an eye without expression, that was void of any thought, or pain, or fear, or anything: an eye from the other shore.

Freddy touched the old man's hand, which lay listlessly alongside grandpa's huge body. He felt a slight pressure, but perhaps he only imagined it. Grandpa tried to say something, but his lips vented just an awkward sigh. Freddy thought that grandpa was trying to sing. He was puzzled. But grandpa fell silent and closed his eye in tired resignation.

After they left grandpa, Freddy's father and brother, Freddy's uncle, stopped to talk to the doctor. They quietly discussed grandpa's condition in the corridor, next to a bin for cigarette ash. Father and uncle were not the kind of people the doctor would invite into his office for a chat. Grandpa was an ordinary brickyard worker, one of many. Famous actors or artists die differently. Their relatives look different, as well.

Freddy, his mother and grandma waited nearby.

Then they took the tram to the railway station.

They had missed the train and waited for an hour for the next one. Freddy was thirsty, but his father wouldn't buy him a raspberry drink, nice-tasting red water in a plastic bag with a straw.

"We have running water at home, and it's free," Freddy was told. "A raspberry drink costs as much as half a brick for the new house."

In the end, Uncle Alex bought him the raspberry drink. Freddy drank it greedily, but guiltily; he rightly sensed that his father would rather his brother gave him the money instead, to spend on half a brick.

* * *

Later that evening, after eleven, Feri brings an exhausted Lady to Freddy Piggybank. Lady has had it, she just wants to lie down and sleep. She reeks of semen: you can smell it a hundred yards away.

"This isn't what we agreed," Piggybank protests, disappointed when he sees Lady sleeping like a log the moment her head hits his pillow.

Proud Feri takes out a pack of *Sparta* cigarettes and offers one to the fat man. He lights up. Then he gives him a hundred crowns.

"You can screw her any time you want," he consoles him. "Wake her up early in the morning, if you want, but leave her alone now. She's had a hard day. You know, our cleaning assistant Lady's a bit delicate."

They say nothing for a while, watching the decreasing night traffic by the Hotel Ambassador.

Feri clears his throat. There's something else he wants to say. Tomorrow is Four-Eyes and his wife's shift. Freddy knows they do alternate shifts. Feri Bartaloš doesn't know what to do with Lady. He'd like her to take on clients, but it can't be done in the lavatory. Could Freddy let him have the use of the trailer? He spends all day outdoors anyway, he only goes in to get new parking tickets. Otherwise Lady will be idle all next day.

Freddy considers. "But this is going to cost more than a hundred," he says finally.

"Of course," Feri agrees. "You'll get twenty crowns for each customer. That'll make a thousand, judging by today. Agreed?"

They shake hands on it.

Proud Feri Bartaloš goes back to the lavatories. Before she left, Lady cleaned everything and mopped the floor dry. Eržika has now managed to turn the men's lavatory into a comfortable bedroom. A thick blanket over two soft inflatable mattresses covers the floor. Two sleeping bags are ready to receive Feri's and Eržika's bodies into their downy warmth. The bags are rolled up nearby, under the sink.

Feri and Eržika sit on the edge of the mattress and count the money. First the lavatory money, then the money they got for Lady: four hundred for the lavatory and five thousand five hundred for Lady. In total it makes almost six thousand crowns. Feri and Eržika silently look at each other: words fail them.

This would come to forty thousand in two weeks. Eighty thousand a month. And in a year? Feri gulps. The unbelievable income from Lady has completely upset their value system.

"I hope she doesn't run off tomorrow," says Eržika, reading Feri's mind.

"She won't," Feri says, "She liked it."

"We won't make her do any work," Eržika decides. "She can do just this."

Feri agrees. They have to make Lady's life easier.

Feri takes a hundred as always and goes to the snack bar to see the bastard boss. The bastard boss expects everyone to give him a third of their takings. But he hasn't the slightest idea how much they make. That's why everybody cheats him. So do Feri and Eržika. But this time the bastard boss is smiling.

"The usual hundred?" he asks Feri. "I think you did better today."

Feri doesn't know what to say, so he chooses to say nothing.

The bastard boss fills his glass with Pilsner. Standing behind the counter makes him look even more like a little jerk. Proud Feri Bartaloš watches, with a mixture of contempt and hatred in his eyes, the manager's skinny little hands reach for the tap.

"Even the birds on the roof are singing about your new trade," says the bastard boss casually. "I don't mind if you want to run a brothel in my snack bar," he adds in a conciliatory tone.

Feri sighs in relief.

"But you have to pay," orders the bastard boss. "Give me a thousand, or else you're out. Four-Eyes can work every day, if it comes to it," adds the bastard boss threateningly, and then smiles amiably at Feri.

A humiliated Feri goes to the lavatories to fetch a thousand crowns for the bastard boss. His lips mumble wild curses in Hungarian. He goes in noisily.

Eržika is reluctant to hand over money that she now considers to be hers. "Why?" she shouts at Feri, as if he were lying.

Feri gives her a slap. "You making a scene now is the last thing I need," he chastises her, becoming conciliatory when he sees the imprint of his five fingers on her face, and the tears rolling down her cheeks.

Eržika is snivelling; pregnancy makes her very sensitive. She reaches into her bra. She mumbles unhappily. The bastard boss can come here, if he thinks it's so easy. People are pigs, they shit and piss and vomit all over the place. And she has to go and clean up after them. Is it dirty now? Feri must say: is it dirty now? "No," she replies when she gets no answer.

Feri mutters something under his breath, takes the thousand and goes back.

The thousand warms the bastard boss's heart. "You know," he explains, as if to make amends, "I'm responsible for everything here. If anything goes wrong, I'll get you out of trouble. But why should I do it for nothing? I have a wife and children. What use will I be if I end up in prison because of you?" He gives Feri Bartaloš a comradely slap on the shoulder: "You'll soon find out what it means to have children."

Demeaned, proud Feri Bartaloš goes back to the lavatory, and a sense of injustice gnaws at his soul. He couldn't give a shit for the bastard boss, get it? Nor for his effing children. He should go to the men's lavatory and spread his legs all day long to see what life's like. A feeling of social empathy awakens in Feri's heart.

Eržika is asleep by now. Her pregnant belly sticks up happily. Feri gets into his sleeping bag. He is pissed off and doesn't even kiss Eržika good night. But the bedding's sleep-inducing warmth calms him down. If nothing else, tomorrow at least he can afford to eat and drink as much as his heart desires.

* * *

Freddy's grandma survived her husband by less than half a year. Losing grandpa deprived her life of all its meaning. She caught a fever. Her mind went, and she saw parrots and palm trees everywhere. This was something she had secretly dreamed of all her life in the bleak workers' settlement, just as others long for a fireplace, or a good record player. Grandma Mešťánek's dream came true and she left this world with a smile on her lips, surrounded by the rustle of palm trees and the screeching of parrots.

Grandma's death didn't affect Freddy as deeply as grandpa's. He loved his grandma, but, because he admired grandpa, he despised her a little for being so meek and gentle.

All the brickyard workers were puzzled at grandma Mešťánek loving her useless husband so much that she followed him into the grave. There were times when he binge-drank, times when he had mistresses, and times when he beat her. Sometimes all three things coincided. When he got back from the front, he went too far and was sent to prison for a few months: he'd almost killed someone in a pub near the station. In his youth, grandpa Mešťánek was a dangerous and unpredictable drinker and troublemaker. His wife was a saint for putting up with him all her life.

Freddy learned all this after his grandparents' death from what he happened to hear adults saying in his presence.

A new employee with a family soon moved into the grandparents' old flat, and the fairytale was over. Freddy didn't like the new tenant; he had an egg-shaped head, he was bald and wore glasses. His children had egg-shaped heads, too and his helpful, cheery wife, who wanted to be friends with everyone, was annoying. Her desperate efforts to fit in with the brickyard community made everyone avoid her. Freddy looked at the newcomers as enemies: people who had taken away his grandparents.

That was when Freddy was about seven or eight years old. During his lonely walks in the brickyard neighbourhood he met a woman who worked in the brick-drying hall. Her name was Tera Sziládyiová; she was about thirty years older than Freddy and lived in the workers' wooden houses, right inside the brickyard area. She had the answers to all Freddy's questions and never made him feel that she had no time for him. She liked this lonely boy with an adult's thoughtful gaze.

Freddy's parents didn't mind Tera looking after him sometimes. Nobody forced her. At least they could get on with building their house.

Freddy loved it best when she took him in the evening to the showers in the community block that was next to the brick-making hangars. The huge room with lots of showers on one side and washbasins on the other was always overheated and the hot steam in the air took their breath away. The women's showers smelled different to the men's showers where he used to go with his father.

At first, Freddy was shy of undressing completely in front of Tera, but soon he got used to it. Tera undressed in front of him. She had a firm muscular body and powerful breasts with large aureoles around her nipples. The bruises and scars all over her body were proof that her life was tough. She had a prison tattoo on her buttocks. She locked the shower-room with a key she took from the porter's lodge and turned on the hot water.

Freddy felt hot steam all over his body and he found it very pleasant.

Tera took him under the shower and then soaped him. Freddy never understood why she spent so much time on scrubbing his genitals so carefully and with so much love. Then he used the soap on her. Tera showed him where cleanliness was most important: between her muscular thighs. She showed him how to wash that spot with a soapy sponge and then slowly and precisely rub it with his fingers. After a while, she closed her eyes and sighed. Then she smiled. She took Freddy's soapy tail in her hand and massaged it. Freddy soon had a special feeling of relief. It was like someone, after prolonged hesitation and denial, finally having a drink of water, or urinating, but much nicer.

"Nice, wasn't it?" Tera asked, took him under the shower and thoroughly washed the rest of soap off him. "When I'm not here any more, you can do it yourself any time you want. All men do it. Girls, too. But promise to keep it our secret!"

"Scout's honour!" Freddy promised, as he was taught at school.

Then they dried themselves with towels and went home. Tera turned off to the singles' dormitory, a wooden building. Freddy went on to the porter's lodge, gave back the key and, his head wrapped in a towel, ran into the first apartment building opposite the porter's lodge. He had to cross a dark section between the lamp over the lodge and the illuminated entrance to the building. Freddy always tried to get across this section as fast as he could, with bated breath and eyes opened wide. In the darkness around him were hidden mysterious creatures, madmen, Dracula, and aliens from UFOs. He clearly felt them poking out their cold bony monstrous fingers. He managed the stone stairs, worn smooth by a century of use, three steps at a time, and he breathed with relief only when he reached the kitchen, at home, filled with his father's suffocating cigarette smoke. His heart beat with anxiety; the excitement of the frightening journey home was stronger than the indefinable bliss under the hot shower.

"When I grow up, I'm going to marry aunt Tera," he said one day in a solemn voice at some family celebration at his maternal grandpa's house.

His declaration caused great hilarity. They all knew Tera and they knew about her wild love life. They laughed so hard they had to hold their aching bellies.

Freddy's father, however, had never had a sense of humour.

"Tera Sziládyiová is a tart," he said. "A loose woman. Mentally retarded. Starting next week, you're going to the school cafeteria. And no more communal showers. You're a big boy now. Boys don't go to women's showers. From now on, you'll come with me, or with Uncle Alex, to the men's showers."

And that's what happened.

Tera Sziládyiová soon vanished somewhere else, another factory, another single worker's dormitory, driven by her hot blood to corrupt other little boys.

New experiences erased the memory of Tera from Freddy's mind. No wonder: he never attached any importance to the peculiar manipulation of his member in the women's showers.

However, he began to practise regularly what Tera had taught him in the shower in the communal building and is still doing it to this day.

* * *

The days when Four-Eyes is on duty in the snack bar are for Feri Bartaloš and Eržika rest-days. They have nothing to do, so they spend the whole day sitting in the snack bar. They know lots of people.

Early in the morning the slamming of lavatory doors wakes up Feri Bartaloš and Eržika. "Wake-up call!" hollers Four-Eyes through the door. "Wake up, parasites!" Four-Eyes adds without a grain of humour.

The morning calm is immediately ruined. Feri and Eržika jump out of their makeshift beds. While Feri washes, Eržika puts the beds away in the unused rear cubicle.

When they come out, Four-Eyes's wife is already sitting in front of the toilet. She eyes them like a madwoman; they hate each other. "The people who sleep in the lavatory," is how Four-Eyes's wife refers to Feri and Eržika.

However, Feri and Eržika are smiling today. They have tons of money and will not have to eat those typhoid-infected fake sausages; they can even afford trout. Their heads held proudly high, Feri and Eržika sit down on a bench like a king and queen. With vague benevolent smiles, they observe what is going on inside the snack bar hut. They feel on top of the world.

The day has hardly begun, but behind the window the busy figures of the snack bar staff are moving briskly. The barman is tapping a new barrel of Bratislava beer; he managed to finish the old one yesterday, even though he had to shut up shop a quarter of an hour late. The cooks are now frying pork schnitzels. Fake sausages are roasting on the grill. Another cook is sliding larded chickens onto a rotisserie spit. Impatient beer drinkers are already gathering in front of the window where the crap beer is served. They are mostly stokers from the nearby buildings, among them the gypsy Šípoš: this time he's brought his colleague Berki with him. They are decent gypsies, hard-working ones. Berki even goes to school in the evenings, I believe.

Feri says a few words to Eržika, gets up and goes to the bar. The queue is moving; beer is being sold. When it's Feri's turn, he doesn't order beer, but asks for two coffees with rum, and for several kinds of chocolate wafer, too. That's what rich people have for breakfast.

Four-Eyes observes Feri and Eržika mistrustfully. His white coat makes him stand out in the Wooden Village. But he can't do a thing. Feri and Eržika are as much a part of the snack bar as he is.

After a good breakfast, Feri gets up to have a word with Freddy Piggybank.

41

* * *

As a child, Freddy Piggybank saved up to buy a rubber boat. That was his life's dream. The idea of navigating the clay-pit lake, in relative safety and staying dry, so as to watch the water creatures, almost made him dizzy. That was why, when he saw the rubber boat in the Magnet mail-order catalogue, he began saving up for it. When he had saved up the sum required, his parents broke his piggybank and, instead of the rubber boat, bought him a suit for his First Communion.

Freddy raged like a madman. In floods of tears, he roared in a tantrum. A vein burst in his head and from then on he began to put on weight and lurch into periodical fits of rage. He also became a little backward; blood leaked into his brain and affected some glands, or cells, or something like that. His wise adult eyes were buried under an inch-thick layer of fat.

He used to play with friends and, even though he wasn't much liked because of his obesity and the clumsiness that went with it, they still accepted him as an equal. Freddy was happy. Boys and girls played games of Red Indians and soldiers and went on long rambles round the brickyard settlement. Afterwards, more and more of his friends started to ride bicycles. The radius of their activity grew considerably. Suddenly, they could easily get to Vápenka or Polimlyn in a few minutes. Mysterious adventurous expeditions extended to the distant surroundings of the village. The original group split into two. One half owned bicycles, the other didn't. Those with bicycles rode to Devín, Devín Lake and Stupava. It only took them a while. Those without bicycles continued to play in the clay-pit and near the settlement. Their numbers diminished. They gradually got bicycles and moved into the cyclists' gang.

One day Freddy Piggybank found himself the last person without a bicycle. He came out of the house and watched all the others getting ready for some new exciting trip to the woods behind the Devín Lake. Nobody paid any attention to Freddy Piggybank, who was more excited about the trip than any of the others.

As far as he could, Freddy ran after them. He longed for friendship and adventure so much that he managed to run for a long time. However, when the bikers gained so much speed on the dusty road along the railway track that they looked like mere pinheads, Freddy, worn out, the veins in his brain pulsating wildly, stopped. It took him a long time to catch his breath on the strip of land separating the track from the field, but then he decided to keep moving and to find his friends in the woods behind Devín Lake and take part in their games.

After an exhausting trek he arrived in the woods, all dusty and sweaty, with thorns sticking in his body. He walked through the trees, looked all round and shouted his friends' names. Nobody shouted back. The woods responded with a mysterious rustling silence. Suddenly Freddy thought he heard far-off children's laughter filtering through the barrier of greenery. He was so worked up that he had a stitch in his groin. His heart beating fast, he ran in that direction, but found nobody. It took a long time for him to turn back, disillusioned and frustrated.

It was almost evening when he got back to the brickyard settlement. Outside the buildings was a pleasant smell of simple but delicious food cooking. The children in his gang had come back a long time ago. They were sitting in front of an apartment building, smelling of the campfire that they had lit in the forest behind Devín Lake. They talked excitedly all at once about the new adventures they had had. Freddy realised that his friends, without whom he couldn't live, had become estranged from him. If he didn't get a bike, he would be lost.

He found a frame in the attic, but the other components were harder to get. After the incident with the rubber boat and his fit, his parents had, as a precaution, stopped giving him pocket money, so he had no way of buying the wheels, chain, or brakes. He depended on presents. That was why it took him an interminable time to build an entire bicycle. It took him practically the rest of his childhood. As he lay in his bed with his eyes shut, he could clearly see himself one day hopping on his bike and joining his friends as a regular member of the gang. His desire for a vehicle was painful. If he'd wanted, his hand could have touched that desire in the middle of his chest. He often dreamed that everyone was off somewhere and he was rooted to the ground and couldn't follow them.

Freddy's parents noticed their son was spending entire days in the tool shed, working on something. They were glad that he was showing technical inclinations and decided to enrol him in secondary technical school. The truth was completely different: Freddy Piggybank had no technical inclination and passionately hated his endless work on the bicycle. Only one aim existed for him: to ride a bicycle with the others. If he could have bought one, he would have never picked up a screwdriver.

Obsessed with finishing his bicycle, he didn't even notice that times had changed. The gang broke up. The girls became young women and stopped being interested in military-type adventures. The members of the bicycle gang would gather behind the football stadium to smoke their first cigarettes and drink a first bottle of beer. Freddy Piggybank didn't notice: he was stuck at home, or hunting for components, or building his bike. Time passed him by without his noticing, and when he emerged with his new bicycle, the children outside were completely different.

Children his age were smoking their first *Mars* cigarettes, drinking beer illegally in *Vašiček's* pub and riding down the village road with their heads turned aside on newish, polluting *Pioneer* and *Jawa 21* motorbikes, which they had bought by doing odd jobs in the brickyard. Freddy didn't feel like working, he was as lazy as a dog. Besides, he had realised that he could never catch up with his contemporaries. He threw the bike on the rubbish tip, getting a beating from his father who didn't like his son's lack of respect for things.

With no bicycle and no motorbike, Freddy was tied to the brickyard settlement and its immediate surroundings. So he made friends with children who hadn't started to cycle yet, and he declared himself their leader. They were the younger siblings of his former friends. They were all five to six years younger than Freddy. This didn't bother him at all; he felt at ease with them. They respected him. He initiated them into all the mysterious adventures that he had experienced with his contemporaries. The younger boys and girls liked him: when they had an older boy with them, they weren't afraid of gypsies or children from hostile parts of the village beating them up.

After a time the company of children of a younger age group stopped amusing him: bored, he began to torment them. For example, he took children on a long trip into the fields behind the clay-pit and then ran away from them. The children came home crying, hungry and tired by the long trek over the fields. Another time, Freddy took his gang deep into the acacia forest, and then ran away from the group with two girls. He took the girls into a bunker made of straw bales left in the field after the harvest. By the light of his pocket torch, the girls had to show him all sorts of things. If they didn't, Freddy threatened them, he would set fire to them and the straw. The girls didn't mind. They thought it was fun. They knew Freddy's threats weren't serious. He ended up showing them all kinds of things of the sort Tera Sziládyiová had taught him.

Freddy demanded unconditional obedience from his children's gang, but despite his severity he was much liked. He constantly kept inventing new combat situations. They all acted as characters in the East German Wild West movies based on Karl May, starring Gojko Mitič, or in the Romanian-French film series *The Leather Stocking*, or a series about four tank drivers and a dog, or a war film *Liberation*. In combat situations they communicated only in Czech, to preserve the magic atmosphere of their favourite films, which the cinemas then showed dubbed into Czech.

Sometimes the boys in the gang couldn't understand the somewhat secretive and conspiratorial relationship between Captain Freddy and the girls in the gang, but since they were very young, it didn't bother them.

One day Freddy and a few girls ran away again from the rest of the gang. They went to a forest near the railway between Nová Ves and Devín Lake, north-west of the clay-pit. There he showed them what his former woman friend taught him. The little girls gladly let him massage them in places he chose; it gave them a pleasant dizzy sensation. Freddy pulled down his underpants and let the girls stimulate his genitals.

While they were engaged in this pleasant activity, they were caught by Mr Forgách, a pensioner, out cycling, intending to cut grass for his rabbits. The girls screamed, pulled up their knickers and ran away. Freddy got his underpants twisted and was bemused and paralysed by the last throbs of his bliss.

Pensioner Forgách broke off a willow branch and whipped him like a horse. Then he grabbed his ear and marched him back to the brickyard.

The whipping from pensioner Forgách was just a friendly rebuke compared to what awaited Freddy Piggybank at home. His mother broke her wooden laundry paddle on him and his father broke the carpet beater. They both clutched their chests and assured each other that it wasn't their fault; they were after all busy building their family house, their new future, their new life. They had no time to deal with their pervert of a son. It was all Sziládyiová's fault.

Pensioner Forgách lived in the workers' settlement, too. He knew everyone who lived there. He didn't keep anything to himself. The result was a general beating, followed by a gynæcological check on all the girls in Freddy's gang. Luckily for Freddy, the result was negative; all the girl gang members were still virgins.

In any case, Freddy was fifteen when this happened and had just been accepted into the Brick-making Technical school in Hodonín. He went there right after the summer vacation so he saw no more of the members of the children's gang whose captain he used to be, nor of their furious parents.

"They'll show him what's what in boarding school," Freddy's parents consoled each other.

* * *

Feri Bartaloš crosses the car park, which is packed chaotically with cars blocking each other's exit. Other cars forcing a way into the car park from outside contribute to the chaos and stop the cars trying to leave from getting out. Freddy Piggybank is not there.

Proud Feri Bartaloš bangs on the fibreboard wall of the attendant's trailer. From inside comes the noise of wheezing and squeaking. Feri bangs again. The trailer door opens and through a narrow crack Piggybank's moon-like face appears.

"Give it a break, will you?" Feri insists, "It's broad daylight!"

"Shut your stinking trap," a disgusted Freddy tells Feri through the crack in the door.

Proud Feri Bartaloš laughs. It's Piggybank's mouth that stinks, not his. Freddy must have bad digestion: he must be constipated from arse to mouth, that's the only explanation Feri Bartaloš can think of. Piggybank shouldn't hoard up so much and should occasionally wash the stench down with gin or vodka, Feri helpfully suggests through the crack.

The crack widens and the parking attendant's corpulent figure fills the doorway. He feels like a man. He woke Lady up around four in the morning; but he hadn't closed an eye all night, gazing on this creature's sweet repose and sexy curves; his jaw had dropped with excitement and he had to use all his will-power to fight down the temptation to masturbate. By early morning he could take no more: he woke her up and tried to have sex with her. Lady woke up, but soon afterwards went back to sleep, uneasily, but asleep all the time, even when Piggybank was moaning loudly. Piggybank was so excited that he couldn't get it up. He tried to introduce his useless, flaccid piece of flesh into Lady's tired crotch. Freddy Piggybank's superhuman effort to get at least some tumescence made the veins on the forehead swell and turn blue, but this resulted only in a sudden eruption of semen that sprayed the sleeping Lady, the bed, the floor and the opposite fibreboard wall. So all he could do was to lie down on the other bunk and fall asleep.

With a look of an experienced debauchee, from the height of his doorway, fat Freddy sizes up Feri Bartaloš.

Feri peeks under Piggybank's hand which is holding the trailer door open.

"Come out, Lady," he tells the woman, who is sitting on the bed and looking haggard. "You need breakfast," he adds.

He looks at the attendant.

"We've got an agreement, right?" Feri reminds him.

The attendant nods. He is looking for his clothes and hat.

Lady comes out unsteady on her feet and follows proud Feri. The day and night that she has been through has somewhat raddled her carefully nurtured beauty, but she still arouses male interest among the beer drinkers clustering round their tables. Today they all know what's in store, so they express their passion and impatience in restless muttering and occasional eager shouts.

"What will you have for breakfast, Lady?" Eržika asks.

Lady turns her gaze to her. She smiles. "A big bowl of muesli and milk," she says. "A big chilled glass of fruit nectar. And a cup of delicious aromatic coffee," she adds.

Feri's and Eržika's mouths drop.

"Wouldn't sausage and mustard do?" Feri asks uncertainly.

Lady says nothing. As always, when she doesn't know what to do, she smiles.

"Of course," Eržika agrees on her behalf. "Lady must have a good breakfast if she's going to face a hard day like that." Eržika will even order coffee for her. "But the snack bar doesn't stock that mussels and tar." Eržika once asked for those things once, she knows all about it. She, too, comes from a good family, just like Lady, Eržika makes it clear. She gives Lady a sidelong glance: Lady sits on the rough bench very stylishly, with one leg crossed over the other. Eržika's father is a butcher, Eržika goes on in her weepy, querulous voice. Eržika was once engaged to none other than Rácz. If Lady is a city girl, she must know who Eržika is talking about.

Lady shakes her head and smiles. No, she doesn't know who she is talking about.

Eržika raises her voice insistently. How can Lady not know about Rácz? Didn't she see on TV the ad for the Oxford Privatisation Fund when Rácz was sitting there talking about it? That Oxford belongs to him. He is the biggest crook on earth. Oxford indeed! Actually, he only graduated from two-year agricultural college! He transferred there from the sixth grade of primary school. That's all his Oxford. He's a tractor-driver, for Christ's sake.

Proud Feri interrupts her. This can't be of any interest to Lady, he tells her gently in Hungarian.

Feri knows Eržika pretty well and understands her disappointment over the broken engagement to Rácz. She only just missed having an easy life in an enormous high-class villa above the city, while being with Feri Bartaloš has meant being in the lavatories down here. That's why he is not too hard on her; he feels as if it was partly his fault.

Eržika calms down. Then she goes back to the original topic. Sausage and mustard will give Lady more energy than any mussels and tar, Eržika says with authority. She signals to Feri to get Lady's food.

Feri crosses the Wooden Village with dignity. Four-Eyes' single eye, hidden by dark glasses, makes his stare hostile.

While Lady finishes her food and drinks her coffee, the first client, a youthful drinker who took three turns yesterday, shows up. He clutches the money in his hand. Soon he vanishes with Lady into Piggybank's trailer.

"A good start," says Eržika, putting the money in her bra.

Feri is pleased, too. He rubs his hands. "This calls for two cognacs," he suggests.

Eržika doesn't mind.

They drink cheap brandy from plastic cups and watch the trailer barely perceptibly wobbling on its springs. The rhythmical motion of Freddy's trailer is easiest to see from the regular sinusoid oscillation of the electric cable hanging between the trailer and the hotel.

By the time the beer drinker is satisfied and finished, Eržika has put away money from two more interested clients. They patiently wait their turn with their beer and gin and ogle Piggybank's trailer. When the door opens the client whose turn it is strides over to the car park.

"How was it?" Eržika asks the beer drinker and smiles. "Are you having three goes today, too?"

The beer drinker shakes his head. "It was better yesterday," he says. "No comparison." He blushes; he feels awkward talking about these things with a woman, even if she is a pimp.

He finally confides in Feri, in a friendly way: "Lady just lies there like a corpse, no passion, no spark. Her fire's gone out, as they say."

"Is she asleep?" Feri asks.

"No," says the beer drinker. "Her eyes are open and she's thinking about something."

Neither the second, nor the third client is happy. Feri waits for the fourth one to leave Piggybank's trailer and then enters.

Lady is lying on the attendant's messy bed with her arm under her head.

"What's wrong?" Feri asks her. "Are you in pain? Tired?"

Lady shakes her head.

"Well, what's wrong then?" Feri enquires. "You wanted men and I've sent them to you. And now you don't seem to like it any more."

Lady says something, but so quietly that Feri can't understand her.

"WHAT?" he asks, his head bent towards her.

"That smell," says Lady. "Yesterday. In the lavatory."

"In the lavatory?" Feri is stunned. "You mean the men's lavatory?"

Lady nods imperceptibly and covers her exposed crotch.

"I need that smell," she says categorically.

Feri grabs his head in a panic. "Jesus Christ!" he says. He sits down on the bed and looks blindly in front of him. What is he to do? He gets up and looks round. Freddy Piggybank is arguing outside with a customer over payment. Proud Feri unzips his fly and urinates in a corner of the trailer.

"Is that what you want?" he asks Lady. "Will that do?"

Feri doesn't even want to imagine the weird form Piggybank's anger will take later that evening, when he finds out that someone has pissed in his trailer. But business is business.

Lady takes a deep breath and nods her head contentedly. Fully roused, her hand reaches for Feri's fly. Feri backs out of the trailer in horror.

* * *

And so Piggybank began his studies in the Brick-making Technical School in Hodonín, returning home only for weekends and holidays. Around Christmas, Freddy and his parents moved into their new house.

His old school friends had lost interest in him and members of his old gang were forbidden to mix with him. Freddy had no option but to push his way into another children's gang and declare himself its captain. This time the children came from village areas called Little Hill and Mansion. They were all boys.

Freddy missed the inquisitive intimacy of the girls in the brickyard settlement, but, anyway, the girls had stopped playing with boys of their age. They were becoming young women and, after their first periods, they kept to strictly segregated girl groups bonded by various secrets, and so on.

Interacting with his contemporaries and elders, Freddy came across as insecure and taciturn; he was more stupid than most, but had enough self-awareness to know that the more he spoke, the more obvious was his stupidity. He did not have this problem with younger friends; he was still cleverer than the cleverest of them and that ensured his status as leader.

At that time a phantom attacker was terrorising Nová Ves and its surroundings. He attacked and raped women going home on their own in the evening. The children gave him the name of Strangler. The Strangler was supposed to ride a *Jawa 21* motorcycle with the number plate hidden. He was supposed to wear a long coat and nothing under it. He had military style boots. According to some rumours, he had a wall-eye. He was said to be hiding in the woods around the Nová Ves.

Freddy Piggybank felt he was the protector of his native village. His greatest ambition was to track down the Strangler, catch him and parade him in front of the chairman of the People's Council. In a word, he longed to be a hero, for it upset him that nobody took him seriously.

So, every weekend he and his gang would comb through the thick groves and scrub around Nová Ves, but they couldn't find the Strangler, no matter how hard they tried. One day, above the heart-shaped quarry they discovered a sort of camp. There were two dugouts covered by branches, a campfire site surrounded by blackened rocks, and a totem pole. The totem pole looked scary: some wild beast's big, popping eyes, with a beak, wings and a long tail with scales wound around the entire pole. It inspired fear.

The smaller boys wanted to get away as fast as they could: they sensed evil, and kept making for the camp exit, which was hidden by a dense hawthorn thicket. Freddy, however, felt this was his chance; he had almost no doubt that he had just come across the Strangler's hideout. His nostrils flaring, he inspected the dugout and failed to hear the quick but cautious steps of several pairs of slender feet on the forest floor.

The gang fled in all directions and Freddy was left to face the fury of the girls from Sida Tešadíková's gang. The girls were a bit younger than him. Dressed like boys, they were members of a Young Border Guards Squad as well as a Young Fire-Fighters Squad. Their movements were short, hard, and brusque, obviously copied from the same films that inspired Freddy. They hated boys and all their free time was spent in a semi-military organization called the Daughters of Death. Here, above the quarry, they had their secret headquarters. Now Freddy Piggybank had found it and polluted it by his presence. They would have to look for another camping site. What he'd done cried out for revenge.

Freddy had no idea how he ended up tied to the totem pole. He felt an icy fear that emanated from the Daughters of Death. He looked around, but he knew these Amazons only by sight. None of them was from the brickyard settlement or the pond area, the places known to him. These girls were from Grba, Slovinec and Podlipové, that is, from alien, enemy areas. Freddy was afraid, but at the same time an intoxicating thrill invaded his groin. Knowing that he was tightly bound and left to the mercy of the wild fantasies of the Daughters of Death filled him with a bliss he had never known before.

"How shall we torture him?" Sida Tešadíková, whose hair was cropped, asked the other gang-members.

They discussed it quietly for a while.

The torture began. Yelling and screeching, they started to tickle his face with clumps of grass, pricked him with thorns, and whipped him with stinging nettles. Freddy tried to move his head, but couldn't. He moaned with pain and closed his eyes in exaggerated anguish. He let his body hang on the ropes that bound him and cut into his body. His tormentors' closeness vaguely excited him. He was almost driven mad by the subtle aroma of girl's sweat coming from Sida's boyish chequered flannel shirt.

"That will teach you to spy on us!" said Tešadíková after the torture was over; she stubbed out on his chest the cigarette that she had chewed on for an hour to denote her leadership status. Freddy was hanging helplessly on the ropes; his head had fallen to one side. He raised his blank eyes, clouded by torture, to look at his tormentor.

"We'll let you go now, but you'll have to run the gauntlet!" the leader of the Daughters of Death continued.

The Amazons cut some springy switches and formed a corridor. Freddy felt somebody cutting his bonds from behind. Soon he was free, his face, arms, and neck and chest reddened by the nettles. He started to run through the corridor. The switches rained down on him and his entire body vibrated with stinging pain. He ran as fast as he could and suddenly his groin was flooded by such pure, blinding, intoxicating bliss that he slowed down for a moment and let the switches of the Daughters of Death hit him longer than necessary. It was like showering with Tera Sziládyiová, but somewhat better and more penetrating.

"And if we see you here again, you'll get tortured so bad that you'll wish you'd never been born," Sida Tešadíková shouted after him.

Milada Macháčková, her deputy, added in a hoarse voice: "You'll beg us to finish you off."

But Freddy was running down the wide path as fast as his fat legs could carry him, slipping on the black humus and fragrant fallen leaves, and didn't hear the threats of the Daughters of Death, who were furious at having to move their secret camp.

* * *

Martin Junec enters the Ambassador bar. He's in good spirits; Žofré has vanished somewhere and hasn't manifested himself for two days now. Martin sits at the bar and orders bourbon on ice.

Silvia is sitting at the back, near a window with a view of the busy street. She's given up dressing provocatively. That was then. Today, Silvia wouldn't wear a black leather jacket and an elastic miniskirt of the same colour. Apart being out of fashion, it looks ridiculous. And suede thigh-long boots? Silvia has to laugh. They're for peasant girls. In Austria girls wearing those outfits are unmistakably Slovaks.

Silvia now wears a discreet, but very expensive grey mini suit. Mini, but not up to the arse. Her legs, still beautiful, are clad in shiny radiant nylon stockings that look like translucent hoar frost. Her feet are shod in simple black pumps with low pointed heels. She sits with her legs crossed. Her skirt, modestly riding up, shows the edge of a lacy elastic stocking top that covers the upper part of her thigh, nothing more. The fingers of her right hand, with its long, manicured nails, hold a glass of juice. Her other hand props her face. She is engrossed in watching the traffic outside the Ambassador.

"Who's that lady?" Junec asks the barman.

The barman glances discreetly in the direction which Junec has pointed with similar discretion.

"No idea," he says and, for want of anything better to do, wipes the counter with a wet cloth. He's bored and doesn't mind chatting to a guest for a while, particularly one like this American.

"She comes here every day," he tells Junec. "She interviews all the local hookers. Could she be from Social Affairs?" he wonders. "Or maybe the Tax Office? Police?" he shrugs. If it were the police, then the boss, hotelier Rácz, would be bound to know something about it.

"Hotelier Rácz?" Martin asks.

"Yes," the bartender says. "The owner of this hotel, Mr Rácz."

Martin Junec's attention focuses again on the unidentified woman. He takes a quick look at her neat profile and legs.

"She's local, is she?" he asks the barman.

"Yes," says the barman. She'd spoken to him in Slovak.

"I'd have thought she was Austrian," said Junec, a little surprised.

Silvia is an experienced hooker — a sidelong glance tells her that she is the centre of attention. Her intuition tells her that she is the topic of conversation. A professional reflex unwittingly starts working: her seated body begins to move: it seems to become more slender and languid. She slowly lifts the glass of orange juice, takes a sip, and puts the glass on the table, but does not let go of it. She gracefully tosses back her mane. Her left hand slowly runs over her shiny thigh and rests on her knee. She gives Junec a brief, inconspicuous glance. Her built-in computer goes to work. Judging by his clear complexion and carefully groomed hair, he must be a Westerner. His suit and shoes are Anglo-Saxon. To judge by what he's drinking, he's American.

Silvia lowers her long eyelashes and inwardly smiles. She hates men. They have hurt her terribly. In the *Perverts' Centre* they tormented her for four years. Or let her torment them. Pigs. Silvia has to avenge herself. She will torture this man, too. She has seen him here twice now. He deliberately comes here when she does. She will torment him for a while. She'll be a promise on legs but, in the end, she won't let him have her. She will drive him insane. He'll cut his prick off himself. And if not, she'll do it for him.

Silvia lifts her eyes and for a fraction of a second meets Junec's. She smiles. "Just you wait, sweetie," she thinks. "You asked for it."

"Is she really local?" Junec asks yet again, as if he finds it hard to believe. He has had experiences with the local women; he was married to one. And it's nice to discuss a pretty woman like this stranger.

* * *

Apart from the beer-drinking regulars, namely the local stokers and the ill-smelling and eternally drunken Majerník's wild parasitic gang, the Wooden Village has quite a variety of other customers.

Among the frequent guests are three long-haired bearded poets. They always sit with their beer, looking tragic. Sometimes they show up in the company of one or two elderly and ugly bitches who pay for their drinks. Sometimes, especially when they've had too much to drink, they recite their poems in hysterical, unpleasantly high-pitched voices and try to trump each other as if they were playing cards. Other, less artistically oriented beer drinkers gawp at them with their mouths hanging open, switching their gaze from one poet to another one, according to whoever is reciting at the moment. One of the customers reacts: "Stop fucking around, boys, you're Slovaks, aren't you! Have a drink instead, for God's sake!"

But when the poets get too noisy, proud Feri or Four-Eyes, depending who happens to be on duty, brings a bucket of water and splashes it over them. The wet poets fall silent. They're cowardly and afraid of being hit. They're scared of Four-Eyes, who's like a bean-pole, and even of the slightly built Bartaloš. But they don't want to leave, they're not that proud. Wet, with wet rucksacks on their backs, they humbly keep silent and look into their beer glasses. But their heads generate colourful poems filled with opposition and resistance, courage and combat.

The poets disappear in summer. They leave for Germany or France where they hire themselves out as slave labour. They clean lavatories, hose down slaughterhouses, collect rubbish and sweep streets: whatever they can get. When they return, they turn their backs on the Wooden Village and its ignorant and uncouth customers. They prefer to lounge about in the snobbish Writers' Club. Now, young slender girls with big eyes accompany them. The poets down one Scotch after another and with condescending voices shout clever lines about the dirt, stink, and repulsiveness of this world. The girls ogle them and the Club's stylish furniture. They want to be part of the big world. All around them sit old writers, whose angular bony behinds are sunk in the plush furniture, tremulously sipping delicious cheap soup. The long-hairs make a mental note of their profound utterances and later, at home, make poems out of them. The poems meet a generally positive response. The critics have even found a label for them: they call them the Bastard Generation. If the bastards, when they travelled abroad, worked in pastry shops, their poems would be filled with whipping cream, chocolate and vanilla. But we have to take them as they are.

But the money from abroad is soon gone. The head waiter in the Writers' Club will put the bottle of whisky back on the shelf. The hairy bearded poets sit there drying out and occasionally cadge a beer or a cigarette off someone. When they drank whisky, they were too proud to know anyone; they only talked to each other and their pretty companions. The pretty companions have vanished somewhere, and the poets recall their ugly older bitches. If their stupid and naïve colleagues won't buy them drinks, the old cows will. If they won't help them of their own free will, they'll do it without knowing. The bastard poets will somehow get hold of a gold ring, a brooch, or a necklace.

After the second-hand dealer, the poets' next stop is the Wooden Village. They'll order Bratislava crap beer, sit round a wooden table and take refuge in meaningful silence. They are set up for one more year.

* * *

No, Freddy Piggybank didn't fall in love with Sida Tešadíková, the leader of the Daughters of Death. He loved only himself, and even coming events would change nothing. However, memories of the strange intense pleasure he experienced when tortured by the furious Amazons were retained somewhere in the middle of his skull, and in his mind he began to plan how to relive this experience.

Nothing could have been easier. The legend of the Strangler had fallen into oblivion, but Freddy found a way of recharging his gang: a new campaign. For several Saturdays they combed the hills from the Sandhill to the Limestone Pit and from Glavica to Mare Mountain, until they finally discovered the carefully camouflaged entrance to the new camp of the Daughters of Death.

"Burn it down!" ordered Freddy Piggybank, nonchalantly leaning on his stick like Rescator, a character from the film about Angélique. "Burn the lot!" he repeated, and a thin fibre of spittle ran from his mouth.

He silently watched the dugout's burning roof and the burning totem pole. He knew that the smoke over the Limestone Pit would bring out the Daughters of Death, and they would come running like furies. That was why he kept delaying the departure of his gang of arsonists. His younger friends saw what the fire had done and took fright.

"All right, leave!" Freddy commanded them. "I'll stay for a while," he added. "I want to make sure that everything has burnt down!"

He sat down on a rock and paid no more attention to his underlings. The thought of being tied up again made him go red in the face.

The girl avengers didn't show up. The Daughters of Death were probably all doing their homework. Their camp burnt down completely and none of them noticed. When the camp was reduced to ashes, Piggy-bank got up, and slowly, reluctantly walked home, occasionally looking over his shoulder.

He didn't escape vengeance, though. The Daughters of Death am-bushed him in a neglected and abandoned little park near Nová Ves train station, as he took a short cut home, which he always did on Friday when he took the train from Hodonín for the weekend.

A silent group of adolescent tom-boys in heavy military boots surrounded him, jumped him and began to tear his clothes off. Nobody gagged him, but, in any case, Freddy uttered only quiet moans of com-plicity. Everything happened as if by unspoken mutual agreement. When Freddy stood as naked as a worm, the girls took some rope and bundled him up, so that his wrists were tightly bound to his knees. They stuffed his clothes into his sports bag, which was the first thing they had grabbed. Later they threw it into the fish-pond.

Freddy lay on the damp earth, which constant shade and wild vegetation had turned acid, and again felt the excitement he had enjoyed before. He lay naked, bound, and defenceless as his furious tormentors watched. His tiny little penis, typical of most obese males, started to swell with passion and soon hung between his thighs like a stallion's. The Daughters of Death didn't miss this transformation. Sida Tešadíková laughed diabolically and spat on it.

There are two kinds of stinging nettle. One grows on sunny slopes and its potential for causing pain is largely imaginary. Quite different is the fleshy stinging nettle that grows in humid shady copses. A blow with a bundle of this kind of nettle is like a burn from a red-hot iron. Those were the nettles that grew in what used to be the little park beneath the railway station.

The Daughters of Death put on heavy leather gauntlets and grabbed the nettles they had already gathered. They threw themselves with yells at Freddy, and soon his screeches drowned their shouts. His member was as erect as a small, but thick telegraph pole. Soon a white fluid spilled from it and Freddy closed his eyes under the strain of a penetrating torment and pleasure that ran through his entire body. The tormentors noticed nothing. Their rage was quenched and they left him in the park.

Freddy Piggybank lay there naked until late in the evening, bound and beaten with the nettles until he was bleeding. He found the suffering quite tolerable. Only when his unnaturally twisted arms and legs began to hurt, did he begin to sigh: with the fingers of his tied hands he blindly groped for a carelessly tied knot. He could hear the voices of passengers waiting for a bus at the nearby bus stop, the sound of their spitting, and the noise of buses coming and going. Obviously, the Daughters of Death had taken his bag. His joints ached and stretched tendons hurt unbearably. Luckily, the Daughters of Death, like most women, lacked thoroughness. Despite being tortured, Freddy had little trouble freeing himself from his bonds. Then, tired, he stretched out on the wet moss.

Darkness came over the village, then the last few drunks from *Jack's* pub passed by. Some time later, the last bus rumbled by the abandoned park on its way to the city and then silence spread out, interrupted only by the nightly Morse signals of the village dogs.

Freddy summoned up all his courage, covered his genitals with his hand and emerged from the shrubbery. The memory of the torment he had experienced still excited him mildly, but even more exciting was the thought of avenging himself on Sida Tešadíková and Milada Macháčková. Pondering the things he would do to the naked and bound bodies of both leaders of the Daughters of Death gave him another erection. Still excited, he rang the bell at the gate of the newly built family house by the pond, where they had recently moved to. His member drooped only when the window opened and his father angrily barked: "WHERE ARE YOUR KEYS, ALFRED?"

He told his parents that he had been attacked and robbed by gypsies; his father got angry and started to scream about concentration camps, the Ku-Klux-Klan and the stone quarry. His Mother burst out crying, took a piece of paper and, swallowing her tears, began to list the rough value of clothing and objects that the imaginary gypsies had stolen from Freddy.

Freddy went to bed tired; before falling asleep he was roused by the vision of Sida Tešadíková naked and bound, her legs spread wide, and tormented in many ways in front of his eyes by an equally naked Milada Macháčková, only to trade places with Sida, while both of them were at the mercy of the cruel ruler Freddy. They were in torment, yet swooning with pleasure. These girls, Freddy's main enemies, underwent some torture, but no marks were left to mar their still slightly childlike, but (as Freddy had one day seen at the pond) beautiful and smooth bodies.

These beautiful images made Freddy's member emit concupiscent mucus, and then both Freddy and his member fell into a deep sleep.

* * *

Junec's ex-wife was called Maria. Martin liked her at first sight. He lived with her in Nová Ves. He worked shifts in the water-works. Despite being a trained electrician, he worked as a greaser: it paid better. In his free time he played saxophone and later started up a group. Junec was a saxophone player, his brother-in-law Žofré played guitar and sang, and a lad called Hruškovič played the organ. They were hired to play at dances all round Nová Ves. Soon they turned professional. Then Maria gave birth to his son Oliver. Martin was making good money, but got very little in return. Maria grumbled at him, and his in-laws treated him like dirt. Martin wasn't going to put up with it. One day he decided to draw a line under his past. The group was just about to return from a long engagement in a bar in Norway. He packed his bags and asked for political asylum. Žofré decided to join him. Martin wasn't too pleased; he was fed up to the teeth with his fat, stupid brother-in-law. Nevertheless, he ended up taking him along. They used the money they had saved to fly to the United States and begin a new life. Only Hruškovič went home. After the Velvet Revolution he discovered he had psychic abilities and is now a naturopath. He fixes spines and casts horoscopes.

As soon as Martin started working, he sent his wife money for their son: five hundred dollars a month. Maria didn't think this was enough and she took him to court. The court ruled that Martin had to send fifty dollars a month. Willy-nilly, Martin had to obey. It had been a long time since he had laughed so loud.

When Maria realized that she had really screwed herself badly, she almost went blind with hatred. She would write long, poisonous letters to him. Her parents occasionally joined in, too. They berated Martin for leading their son Žofré astray. Žofré only laughed at this. Martin always got stomach cramps. Then he stopped opening letters from Czecho-slovakia, and threw them in the wastebasket the moment they arrived. He had no time to waste: he worked like a slave. Finally, they got a divorce and he had peace and quiet.

Then Martin met Edna. She was a thin, leggy American with a smooth complexion and glasses that gave her the charming look of a very intelligent intellectual. She was a feminist, but only up to a point: she still felt that in order to attract men it was still worth using make-up and removing unwanted hair.

She found the phone number of Martin's company (he had by now a permit for sole proprietorship, that is, he was self-employed) in a local daily paper. She called him to change the neon tube in the kitchen. Martin came with Žofré in a small Chevrolet pick-up truck with a built-in workshop. Edna lived in a small rented bungalow on the Pacific coast. She opened the door for them wearing shorts; she had a book in her hand, and she wore reading glasses. She was no beauty, but had a slender, attractive body. When Martin saw her tanned legs he got excited: a long time had passed since he had had a woman.

The kitchen was small and narrow. Martin was changing the tube. Žofré was holding his ladder and running back and forth fetching one thing or another. It was eleven in the morning and he was already a bit high. He would make mistakes and drop tools. In front of customers, Junec communicated with his former brother-in-law only in English and, since none of them had a good command of the language, confusion and misunderstandings occasionally broke out between them. Edna had to laugh a few times.

"Please, don't take it the wrong way, Mr Junec," she said to Martin, "but you two remind me so much of the Marx Brothers that I had to laugh."

Finally they managed to change the tube. Martin asked for eighty dollars, gave Edna a receipt and his card. He didn't know why he added also his private number. ("You can call me any time day and night, I'll come.") Maybe those tanned legs made him do it.

"Well, I had no idea that Marx had a brother," said Žofré in the car.

Junec drove in silence, though, to tell the truth, that was news to him, too.

"Maybe she's confused this Marx brother with Engels," Žofré speculated.

He took a swig of vodka from a hip-flask in his pocket.

"Ignorant American," he concluded with an educated European's superior attitude.

A week later, Edna (she was still Dr Gershwitz to Martin) called again. She needed her fridge mended.

This time, Martin went alone; Žofré had depression and had been spending the last few days in Slovak Hall, drinking with his compatriots.

Dr. Gershwitz opened: she was wearing shorts and reading glasses, and had a book in her hand. She took him to her fridge.

"Will you have a drink?" she asked.

"A glass of water, please," said Junec, and turned the back of the fridge towards him.

"Where do you come from?" Edna asked when she brought the water.

"From Czechoslovakia," said Martin, putting the detached cooling rack against the wall.

"Oh," said Miss Gershwitz. "A friend of mine went there. Prague. Kafka. You like Kafka?"

"Yes, very much." Junec said, red in his face.

Edna was pleased. "This isn't your real job, is it?" she said and pointed to the fridge that was now in bits. "What is your job?"

"I'm a musician," said Martin. "I used to play saxophone. In a bar."

"Oh," said Edna. "Do you like Dexter Gordon?"

"I adore Dexter Gordon," said Martin, getting even redder in the face. "And what's your job?" he had to ask.

"I'm an anthropologist," said Edna. She looked Martin straight in the face. "I study the sexual habits and rituals of indigenous people."

Martin fell that he was turning deep red from head to toe.

"Ah," he said uncertainly, "interesting work."

"Yes, very interesting," Edna agreed.

Junec mended the fridge, finished his mineral water, deliberately undercharged her, and said good-bye.

Less than a week later she rang again. Her doorbell was broken.

Martin came and knocked at the door. Dressed in shorts, wearing her reading glasses and holding a book in her hand, she opened it.

"Come in, Martin," she said and let him in.

"Hello, Dr Gershwitz," Martin said.

"Where's your colleague?" Edna asked.

"He's busy doing something else," said Martin.

Žofré was probably sleeping off a hangover, or working up a new one.

The doorbell had obviously been broken on purpose. Somebody had taken the screws out and disconnected the bell. Martin pretended not to notice. He reconnected the bell and asked Edna to try it. It was all in working order. He got off the ladder and smiled at Edna. Only now did he realise that she reminded him of an American singer and actress, the one with the big nose. His group used to play a song of hers.

"I have another problem here," Dr Gershwitz said. "Maybe you'll be able to solve it."

She took him to her bedroom and pulled out of her bedside table drawer a rubber object whose shape and realistic finish made it look like a man's penis. Martin had never seen anything like this before, except perhaps in pornographic magazines, and he'd never paid any attention to them. Again, he felt himself blushing.

"It doesn't work," Dr Gershwitz said, as she placed it in his hand. "The motor's broken," she added. "Could you mend it?"

Martin's mouth went dry. He knew this was the moment. Clearly, he had got himself into a situation that was neither natural nor spontaneous. Someone had scripted his part and he was supposed to act it, though he didn't know the script properly.

He hadn't slept with anyone ever since he had come to the United States, either because he was too shy, or because he had no time. He worked twenty, twenty-two hours a day, every day, weekend or no weekend. He wanted to get ahead. Thanks to his efforts, three years after his arrival in eighty-six, he was working for himself.

"Why do you use a machine?" he asked Edna in a trembling voice, as if reciting a line he had learnt. He knew there was no going back. "A machine can't embrace you," he said and showed her. "A machine will never take you and put you on the bed like this," he said and showed her what he meant. "A machine will never lay you in bed like this," he continued. With one knee he kneeled on the bed, between her spread thighs. "Do you think a machine can take your clothes off?" he asked Edna, as buttons flew off her blouse in all directions. When he saw Dr Gershwitz's naked breasts, he started taking deep breaths and wrestled with the zipper of his yellow electrician's overalls.

"Take this and put it on," said Edna in a broken voice, handing him a condom fished out from under the mattress.

Martin Junec obeyed and put the condom on his painfully engorged penis.

Dr Gershwitz had also spent a long time without a man and both came the moment their sexual organs made contact. A spark flashed from one to the other and Martin's condom filled with hot white liquid that he had probably brought from Czechoslovakia.

They lay for a while on top of each other, catching their breath.

Edna recovered first.

"That feels good after a long wait," she said with a smile, took the rest of her clothes off and threw them onto the floor by the bed. Then, naked, she collapsed by Martin's side.

"What's going to happen to us?" Junec asked as world-weariness and a shattering melancholy took hold of him.

"What do you mean?" asked Edna.

"Well, what now?" Martin repeated his question. "What are we going to do now? How do you imagine it will continue?"

"First of all, we'll wait a bit," said Edna. "And then we'll do it again. But this time will do it so we get something out of it."

"And then?" Martin asked. "What happens next?"

"Then we'll see," Edna said. "We'll sort something out."

* * *

In 1980 Hruškovič returned from Norway alone. For a while he lounged about spending the money he'd made and visiting the Secret Police, who could not understand why two thirds of the Hurytan trio had asked for political asylum but the third man in the trio had come back. They seemed more puzzled by his return than by the others' defection.

When the money ran out, he got a new group together with young musicians, and, using the old name, Hurytan, he began to play at dances and gigs in the Ambassador's night bar. The young bar musicians didn't stay with Hruškovič for long: for some unfathomable reason he was not allowed out of the country and so the young musicians, who considered playing in the West a pay-off for slavery in the bars, left him. Hruškovič was constantly replacing musicians in the group, since he had no skills except playing music.

One of the musicians who strummed with Hruškovič had major problems with his back. When his back was out, he couldn't play. Several times Hruškovič got him to lie down in the dressing room and relieved him of his pain with one powerful touch of his hand.

"You've got golden hands," the musician was ecstatic, getting off the table and buttoning up his shirt. "You're in the wrong profession."

This was around 1987–1988, when the hysteria around the Russian psychic healer Anatoli Kashpirovsky started. A cassette of his performances was passed round the musicians. Everybody swore that the man was a healer. The base guitar player's daughter claimed her warts had vanished, the drummer's chronic cold in the head disappeared, and he no longer polluted his surroundings with it.

"You see," Hruškovič's guitar-playing back sufferer said, "You could do the same. Of course, you can make a living playing music, but if you switched to being a healer, you'd be rich. You have the ability; I can feel it in my own skin, I mean, my spine…"

Hruškovič shrugged the idea off, but didn't stop thinking about it.

Then came November 1989 and the Velvet Revolution. After the New Year, Hruškovič visited numerous healers whose clinics sprang up like mushrooms after rain. Using imaginary ailments as a pretext, he tried different therapies, took advice, bought various teas, magnetic bracelets, dowsing rods and talismans. Now he knew how to start.

Hruškovič lived in the centre of Nová Ves called The Village, just opposite a former pub, *Vašíček's*. His house had an outside kitchen, used in summer. One day he cleared it of all the junk, painted it, put down carpets and furnished it like a doctor's surgery. In the middle stood an enormous massage table that he ordered from the local cabinet-maker Zielinski. Along the walls stood shelves and cabinets filled with mysterious objects, bottles and tiny glass phials filled with various healing tinctures (mostly ordinary water tinted with aniline dye). People were also intrigued by the sight of the spines of old books that nobody read: they were mere decoration. To a casual observer, Hruškovič's surgery seemed trustworthy and responsible.

In the beginning, Hruškovič decided to see patients only at weekends — he wanted to keep playing with his group in the Ambassador. On Friday, an advertisement was published in the evening paper: Hruškovič offered his healing and psychic services (Hruškovič discovered the term "psychic" in a newspaper article and took a liking to it). On Saturday morning, with his wife's help, Hruškovič donned a brand-new white coat, hung round his neck a metal cross he bought in a sacral objects shop for 150 crowns, and started on his career as a healer.

About twenty patients gathered in the street. Hruškovič was stunned; he wasn't expecting that. Some patients came from afar, arriving in cars with licence plates from various towns: Dunajská Streda, Topoľčany, Trnava, Trenčín, and even Žilina. They parked in the main street, leaving only a narrow passage for traffic. Hruškovič was apprehensive, but he pulled himself together in time. After all, he knew how to handle people: as a bandleader, he often had to get the guests into the mood for dancing at the beginning of the night, or, later on, defuse a potential massacre on the dance floor. His patients were a bent mass of moaning and expectorating wretches whose hopeful faces were focused on him, Hruškovič. He used his strong voice to establish order among the waiting patients, called in the first one, showed him into his summer kitchen and began treatment.

Hruškovič's first patient was a man in his fifties with a displaced lumbar vertebra. Hruškovič was no fool and that was something he diagnosed immediately. He ran a hand down the patient's back and made knowledgeable grunts. He took two home-made wire objects out of the cabinet. They were shaped like something between a children's wire puzzle and a complex astronomical instrument.

"What are you going to do to me, doctor?" asked the man.

Hruškovič, flattered by the title, placed one of the objects on the man's neck and the other on his hips.

"Your spinal cord is blocked, I think," he said. "Have your legs ever gone numb?" he asked.

"No," the man said.

"That's strange," said Hruškovič. "Your thought conception current has been interrupted between the Chutney and the Özall points," he explained helpfully. "If you'd come a few days later, your lower extremities would have been paralysed."

The man was visibly horrified. "Does that mean I'd have been a wheelchair case?"

"Absolutely," Hruškovič confirmed.

"What now, then?" the patient asked in despair.

"You leave that to me," Hruškovič said brusquely and placed on his head a wire helmet that he had assembled himself. A decorative ball from his Christmas tree glittered on the helmet's peak.

"For heaven's sake, what are you going to do?" moaned the patient, terrified by the idea that he really might become paralysed.

"I'll try using this patent mental energy amplifier to disperse the negative Salam energy," said Hruškovič. "Between these two hyper-altruistic receptors an emission of invisible polyrhythmic Övegesh particles will flow and it will charge your spinal cord with positive Khotsmah energy. Do you understand? You don't! Now be quiet! You may feel a lot of heat, but that's fine."

The patient lay there helpless. Hruškovič stood over him and put on an expression of devilish concentration. He was thinking how long it would take him to see to such a large number of patients. Suddenly, he realised that he was in charge. If he didn't feel like it, he could announce that his energy had gone and tell them to come back tomorrow. Once he realised that, his mood improved.

"I can feel that heat already," said the patient after a while.

"Like hell you can," thought Hruškovič. "That's normal," he said. "Energy is flowing. Negative Salam vibrations are being cancelled out."

His sensitive nose caught the aroma of stewed pork and sauerkraut that his wife was cooking for his lunch. He would have to send her to the shop for beer, it occurred to him.

"Well," Hruškovič said after a while, "that should do." He took the wire objects off his patient's back and put them back into the cabinet together with his helmet. "Now we have to disperse the depolarized remnants of negative Salam energy," he added, putting a bit of camphor ointment on his hand (it was in a porcelain dish with a sign saying CHILLI EMULSION that he had inscribed in Gothic script) and began to massage the patient's back. With a practised movement, he pressed the backbone and the displaced vertebra obediently snapped into place.

"Just lie there for a while and let the Chilli emulsion work," he ordered the man.

The patient lay on his belly without moving.

"I'm certain that your bed is positioned over a geopantogenetic zone," Hruškovič said, wiping his hand on a paper towel. "When did you experience the back pain? I'm sure it must have been in the morning, when you got out of bed."

The man shook his head. "No," he said, "It started hurting when I unloaded the eighth bag of cement from my car."

"Quite," said Hruškovič in a voice that brooked no contradiction. "All the same, your spine was weakened by the pantogenetic zone. Radiation comes up from the earth, weakens the good vibrations, and turns them into bad ones. My job is to reverse that. You can get up now."

The patient carefully got off the table, sighing. His face gradually expressed first fear, then mistrust, then surprise, joy and, finally, profound relief.

"Well?" Hruškovič asked, lit his cigarette lighter and theatrically passed the flame under both his palms. "Does it hurt?"

"It doesn't!" said the astounded patient and made a few cautious movements. "It doesn't hurt!"

"There you are, then," said Hruškovič.

"And what about that… zone you mentioned, doctor?" asked the happy patient.

"Well, it would be best if I came and measured it myself," said Hruškovič, "but there's no chance of that in the foreseeable future: too many patients. Take this," he said and gave the patient a one-litre bottle with a label that said AQUA OROASŒUR. This is water that has passed through forty transcription falsettos. Do you have a watering-can with a sprinkler at home? No? Then buy one and fill it with this water. Then sprinkle the floor of your bedroom evenly. Under your bed, too. This water will safely shield the whole bedroom from the geopantogenetic zone. But watch out!" Hruškovič raised his finger. "Before you begin sprinkling, you have to say the word Aehieh."

"Come again?" asked the patient.

Hruškovič wrote "Aehieh" on a piece of paper and gave it to the patient. "Don't lose it," he reminded him. "This word will put you in long-distance contact with me, and with my mental energy I'll influence the creation of the impermeable energy subdominant-conceptual shield," he explained.

The patient nodded. "Thank you, doctor," he said cordially and tried to shake his hand.

Hruškovič stepped back and raised both hands in a gesture of refusal.

"You know," he said, "I don't shake hands. Don't take it badly; seriously, I'm only protecting you by refusing. You see, my hands are powerful energy irradiators," he explained, holding his palms out to him.

The patient couldn't help taking a step back.

"And how much do I owe you, doctor?" he asked.

"For the bottle of Aqua Oroasoeur give me three hundred crowns," said Hruškovič. "As for treatment, I don't take money for it. My abilities are a gift from God that can't be sold, they can only be given to others. However, if you like, you can donate a sum of your choice. Over there."

Hruškovič pointed to a little table under the window with a champagne cooler enthroned on it. In the morning he put in a few five hundred and one thousand crown notes. This was a psychological trick: no patient would dare to put in less.

Hruškovič's first patient was no Scrooge, either: he added a crisp new thousand-crown note.

And that's how it went all morning. Patient followed patient. Hruškovič tried out all his home-made instruments, sold dozens of bottles and phials of his concoctions. All the patients went off home satisfied. Hruškovič was amazed how stupid people could be.

He took a break for lunch. He was sitting in the kitchen, eating his fill of stewed pork and sauerkraut. His body was feeling a fatigue he had never known before. He ascribed it to standing too long in his surgery.

"How many were there?" his wife asked.

"About fifteen," said Hruškovič. "I'm as worn out as a horse."

"And there are another twelve waiting out there," said his wife, pulling back the window curtain.

"Who'd have thought it?" Hruškovič shook his head. "I had no idea there were so many idiots in the world."

After lunch Hruškovič went on with his healing. The champagne cooler was filling up nicely with banknotes. Occasionally, Hruškovič's conscience awoke and he made a gesture: he tried to stop an old granny or grandpa from dropping their hard-earned money into the kitty. The pensioners always resisted vehemently, called him a man of God and shouted in cracked voices until Hruškovič, feigning anger, capitulated.

At about five in the afternoon, a young woman, pretty as a picture, accompanied by her husband, came to see him. Judging by their accent, Hruškovič guessed they must have come a long way. He made them sit in the armchairs and asked about their problem.

The young people began to talk. They couldn't have children. They'd tried everything they could: doctors, healers, prayers, pilgrimages: nothing helped.

"The doctors believe the sperm is fine," the young man said in a lilting Slovak and blushed.

"It's probably my fault," the young woman confessed sadly.

"Well," said Hruškovič, "should we not have a wee look at you?"

He unwittingly switched to the quaint folk language this young couple used.

"May I ask you to leave us?" he asked the husband.

The husband nodded and went out to the yard.

"Well, let's have a look, young lady. There's nothing to be afraid of," said Hruškovič and at the thought that the patient was at his mercy, his heart began to race.

"Take off your clothes," he said and fixed his gaze on the young woman's eyes.

The young woman blinked a few times like a chicken.

"Take off your clothes," Hruškovič repeated.

The young woman, keeping her blank gaze on his, began to take her clothes off.

"Knickers and bra, too," Hruškovič commanded.

"Knickers and bra, too," repeated the patient in a monotonous voice, meekly obeying.

For a fragment of a second, Hruškovič was surprised. A naked patient was standing in the middle of his surgery. Hruškovič couldn't believe his eyes.

"Lie down," he said, "face down."

The patient obeyed.

Hruškovič ran his hand down her spine. "Most problems come from the spine," he mumbled.

"Most problems…" the woman repeated.

Her back was smooth and still pleasantly warm, since she had only just removed her clothing. Hruškovič's hands circled over her peachy skin; he was lost in thought. He waited until something meaningful came into his mind. He reached for her firm buttocks, and something told him to spread its two cheeks.

"Hmm," he said after a moment of inspection, "the problem is in the tailbone. We have to reset your tailbone." He palpated the patient's spine at the point where her tailbone began. "Don't be afraid, it won't hurt," he said. He was shocked at what he was about to do, but something told him that it could and must be done. He put on rubber gloves and smeared Vaseline on his finger from a container with a label saying ACENT-ACER EMULSION, and carefully inserted his finger into the patient's anus. The patient jerked a little. "Relax," Hruškovič said quietly and his index finger completely slipped into the patient. With his palm turned up, he was checking the tailbone. He felt his member beginning to react. He tried to suppress his excitement and focus on the patient's problem. In a second of clear-headedness, he realised what he was doing and was frightened that someone might catch him in the act. The patient was surrendering to his finger and unwittingly, almost imperceptibly, began rotating her hips as if she, too, were getting excited. Hruškovič couldn't remember why on earth this mad idea had come to him. Something in the tailbone cracked and the patient moaned. Hruškovič was overcome by a strange feeling of relief. He took his finger out, ripped the gloves off and threw them into the waste bin. Then he went to the sink.

"Just lie there for a while," he told her, as he washed his hands. He was almost levitating from a seductive feeling of omnipotence.

"You can get up now," he said when he'd washed his hands.

The patient got up.

"Get dressed," he said.

The patient began to dress.

Hruškovič still couldn't believe his eyes. Had he really hypnotized her?

The patient got dressed, put on her court shoes and, with a blank look in her eyes, faced Hruškovič.

"Sit down," Hruškovič ordered her.

The young woman sat down in the armchair.

"You will get pregnant now," said Hruškovič in a masterful voice. "Repeat after me!"

"I shall get pregnant now," said the young woman.

"You will forget what I did to you," said Hruškovič.

"I shall forget…" the patient repeated obediently.

"And now wake up!" Hruškovič ordered and banged the register of patients on the table.

The patient was startled, blinked and looked around in puzzlement.

"Everything is fine," said Hruškovič. "I think you can buy a layette; it will be a girl. There, you can go now. And ask your husband to come in; I need to have a few words with him."

The husband came in, very worried.

"I have good news for you," said Hruškovič. "There was a negative Tnopibui power lodged in the tailbone," he explained. "It blocked the quartol tracks of the uterus and ovaries. I used a dual modal conception and managed to cancel out all the negative vibrations."

The husband sighed in relief.

"Your wife will get pregnant," Hruškovič declared. "It'll be a girl."

A capricious feeling of personal power began to permeate Hruškovič's soul.

"Take three days off, both of you, and spend them in bed."

The young man went red.

"You have to have intercourse at least ten times a day," Hruškovič continued. "And all the way!"

The young man, his eyes popping, stared at him.

"At least ten times!" Hruškovič stressed. "And at least once a day, you have to insert your member in the anus, too," said Hruškovič. "As deep as you can."

The young man began to tremble.

"But before you do that, you must use this ointment." Hruškovič passed him a container full of Vaseline, labelled ACENTACER EMUL-SION. "That will help to destroy any possible remnants of negative Tnopibui force that may be lurking there."

The young man was startled and stared at the ointment for a while. Then he got up and took his wallet out. He was no skinflint.

"And don't forget to invite me to the christening," Hruškovič called after the departing newly-weds.

The crowd in front of his house had thinned out, but not disappeared.

"Please," shouted Hruškovič shouted, waving his hands in impre-cation. "Please, I'm drained now! I've no energy left! Come back tomor-row! We'll continue tomorrow!"

His patients mumbled, but dispersed in an orderly fashion.

Hruškovič entered the kitchen and in his white coat threw himself at the stewed pork and sauerkraut, even though it was cold now, eating it right from the pot.

"Warm it up," his wife advised him, "or else you'll be sick."

Still chewing, Hruškovič turned towards her. Gently but firmly, he grabbed her round the waist and dragged her into the bedroom. There he threw her onto the bed and hungrily jumped on her. The woman moaned loudly; it had been ages since she last had this kind of treatment. Luckily, their daughter had gone to the Community Hall for her jazz gymnastics.

Then the healer slept like a log.

In the middle of the night he woke up thirsty. He lay there and felt as if he were riddled with holes, like a sieve. Through all those holes energy flowed into him from some dark place under the bed. Hruškovič had an uncomfortable feeling, despite being half asleep, as if he had forced his way into a room where something was going on that he was not meant to know about. He dared not move and fell asleep, still thirsty.

In the morning, of course, he remembered nothing. He quickly choked down a brioche and drank milky coffee, incredulously watching the meek crowd of patients that took up the entire pavement.

"People are fucking idiots!" he told his wife and sighed. He was disgusted with himself.

He swallowed the brioche, chased it down with the coffee and, whistling a tune went out into the yard to continue his fraudulent healing.

On Monday, Hruškovič officially disbanded the Hurytan trio and decided to devote himself to healing and psychic work.

He was going to become a famous man, much sought after, loved, feared, and wealthy.

* * *

Every time Martin Junec meets Silvia in the Ambassador bar, he is aware that he is a successful, wealthy man in his prime and that he hasn't slept with a woman for quite some time. Edna is stuck somewhere in the jungle in New Guinea, scientifically studying copulating Papuans, while Junec is assailed more and more insistently by importunate visions.

Whenever Martin recalls making love with Edna, he always gets excited. Edna always liked him ejaculating into her mouth and her sensitive lips noting his member's rapid abrupt spasms which foretold the unstoppable emission of sperm. She jokingly dubbed this "plumbing noises."

She adored it when she could feel Martin's testicles hardening in her hand and almost receding inside at the height of passion.

Junec, too, liked servicing Edna with his mouth. He used to dream of doing this when he lived with his former wife, but she would vehemently refuse him: she considered even a man taking a woman from behind, or touching her genitals, or leaving the light on during intercourse, and so on, to be perversions.

Dr Gershwitz helped Martin make up for it: she loved being roused by his tongue. Martin liked to run his tongue over her passionately welcoming vulva which, after he once shyly asked her, she gladly and regularly shaved. He liked to toy with her erect clitoris that courageously crawled from its bed and provocatively offered its sensitive rosy tip to his gourmand's tongue. Martin liked to dip his tongue as deep as he could into Edna's vagina: he was always excited by the awareness that, a few seconds before, his member had preceded him. He always lingered over the apparently chastely closed entry to Edna's rectum, which was also one of the gates of their shared pleasure, but only from time to time, when its owner was in the mood.

Junec loved Edna's moaning at the moment of climax, he loved the geometry of her open crotch suddenly altering completely, and most of all Edna's inability then to retain her urine, so that a thin stream would spray straight into Martin's obliging mouth.

Martin often wondered what they had in common. They came from two different worlds: she was a Jewish American intellectual and he an immigrant electrician from Eastern Europe.

Although, when you thought about it, Edna's roots in the United States weren't that deep; one day she admitted to him that her great grandfather had come on a boat from Tsarist Russia in the nineteenth century.

They didn't discuss abstract topics much; Martin's knowledge of English was improving, but when Edna occasionally got talking about her opinions, her work and interests, he had to concentrate devilishly hard to understand it all. So they were most at ease in bed, with long hours of shared silence.

And so the electrician Martin Junec and the university professor Edna Gershwitz became intimate friends. The fact was that when Edna wasn't doing research for new scholarly publications, when she wasn't lecturing, or travelling to meet her savages, she was in bed with Junec.

Martin preferred not to enquire how Edna researched the sexual rituals of Amazon Indians in the field. It suited him to see Edna only now and again; he didn't have the time for an intense daily relationship. He owned a little workshop with two electricians and two assistants and he devoted his time to it.

One of the assistants happened to be Žofré. Although he was almost constantly marinated in alcohol and his work contribution was pretty well zero, Martin put up with him for personal reasons and out of compassion and didn't sack him. He regularly tried to make him return home, to Czechoslovakia, but had no success; Žofré liked it in America where he didn't have to do anything, since Junec looked after him. Besides, he was also afraid that the Communists would punish him.

That was when Martin started to develop his entrepreneurial idea. In the long evenings, when he sat watching television, waiting for a call from a customer, he took up an old hobby that had absorbed him a long time ago, when he still worked in Czechoslovakia, in the Water Works: making lamps out of plywood. He would do a drawing, buy plywood and set to work with a jigsaw. He used these lamps to decorated the humble flat and workshop that he shared with Žofré. The entrepreneurial idea came from a neighbour who dropped in to make a phone call and was moved to tears when Martin gave him one of his lamps. Two days later, the man was back, asking Junec to sell him four lamps: for his brother in New York, his parents, in-laws and a brother-in-law. He offered Martin fifty dollars a lamp. He left two hundred dollars poorer, but happily clutching to his chest four carved, decoratively burnished, stained and varnished little lanterns. Martin sat down, opened a can of beer, got paper and a pencil and started calculating.

Edna was leaving soon for Brazil. Martin drove her to the airport in his Mustang banger. When she returned, two months later, he met her in the arrivals hall and helped her with her luggage. In the car park he opened the door of a brand new Mercedes: the first batch of plywood lamps had been sold in two days to the mail order department store Sears & Roebuck and by the time Edna arrived, there were two hundred employees of Korean origin operating their jigsaws in hastily rented production halls to Martin's designs, burnishing, staining and varnishing hundreds of lamps.

The Americans couldn't get enough plywood table lamps and night lamps, lanterns and chandeliers with the label HAND-MADE QUALITY by ARTISANIA LAMPS. They were a hit, and were so popular that they pushed even the famous Tiffany lamps out of the market.

The Mercedes was on hire purchase, but was good to drive. Martin drove Edna home and then they spent hours making love. Edna was aroused, and not just sexually; she had never believed stories about the American self-made man but suddenly she actually had a role in one.

This newly minted Great Gatsby was taking her unusually roughly, almost cruelly. His once shy and hesitant love was now overlaid by the arrogant decisiveness of a successful man, a winner.

Edna accepted that. She was a feminist, but not in bed. With a woman like that at one's side, a man could even become the President of the United States, Martin bragged; he had plenty of time to work at his career. But he didn't become President of America: he was satisfied with being president of Artisania Lamps, of which he was the founder.

And then Žofré died. He was hit by a car when drunk and passed away in hospital. He was fully conscious by then, having completely sobered up. Although Žofré hated Dr Gershwitz and called her a "Yid" ("that Yid woman of yours") to Martin's face, she was the only one with him when he died: Martin had an important business meeting and didn't get the news of Žofré's fatal accident. Edna was holding Žofré's hand and weeping silently. She accepted this permanently sozzled fat slob as an inalienable part of Martin Junec, a part of his personality, one of the two inseparable Marx Brothers: she still remembered their first visit to her house. She knew very well that in all America she was the only close person Martin would now have. She wasn't quite sure she could play that part. She never found out about the hatred that Žofré felt for her: Žofré was a typical hypocritical Slovak and never let on that he was allergic to her. She, as an American, was used to consistently face-to-face relationships, so she didn't notice anything.

Žofré called Edna by her first name for the first time at the moment that he was expiring. He raised himself up on the bed and said something to her. Edna didn't understand: it was in Slovak. It sounded like a strange prayer or a vow. Then Žofré's head fell back on the pillow and one of the monitors by his head began to emit piercing bleeps. The room instantly filled with people in white. Edna was pushed out into the corridor; someone tried to resuscitate the fat patient with electrodes, but to no avail.

In the evening Martin got back from his meeting. When Edna told him about Žofré's death, he was stunned; then he walked to the bar to pour himself a double bourbon. He gulped it down and poured another. His insides were permeated by a pleasant warmth. For some reason, tears streamed down his cheeks; he didn't wipe them away.

However, paradoxically, he felt nothing in his soul except a light breeze of satisfaction and intoxicating freedom.

* * *

Feri Bartaloš and his Eržika spend entire days keeping a furtive eye on Lady. They are worried. Her sexual insatiability, her weird alienated look, her trembling — everything arouses their suspicions.

"What if she's out of her mind?" Feri asks Eržika in Hungarian over breakfast.

Eržika is also anxiously watching her performing animal, who is being fed coffee cake and hot chocolate. She shrugs.

"Well," Feri goes on, "Lady lost her marbles and came to this car park. We don't know anything about her. Her husband, if she has one, or her relatives, are sure to be looking for her. Perhaps the police are looking for her, too." Feri considers this to be a real possibility; Feri and Eržika don't have television and would be the last to find out. Feri doesn't want to be an alarmist, but what if the police come to the Wooden Village one day and find they've got her with them?

"So what?" Eržika counters. They'll have nothing on Eržika and Feri. They take care of her and help her any way they can. It's simple: Eržika and Feri are good people. They are ready to help. Life is hard.

Feri nods. He can see that. But what if they then find out that Lady is mad, then they'll screw Feri and Eržika for hiring her out to the beer drinkers? And for forcing her to fuck fifty customers a day?

"Hang on!" says Eržika, apparently upset. "What do you mean 'forcing'? Who's being forced? Nobody's forcing anyone. Lady's got ants in her pants, she needs men: just look at her. Didn't Lady begin by volunteering to help clean the lavatories?" Feri knows very well what that led to. Lady doesn't have to be forced to do something like that.

Feri ponders. His wife's arguments seem quite persuasive. On the other hand... He takes a sip of coffee and rum. "Well, yes," he says. "If Lady's mad and not responsible for her actions, then she should be reported to the police. Then the loony-bin is the right place for her."

Eržika doesn't like this argument, either. Why does Feri think that Lady ought to be in a loony-bin? She looks quite sane, on the whole.

Lady has finished eating and drinking. She wipes her mouth with the back of her hand and her searing gaze surveys the drinkers sipping their beer. She's slept with almost all of them. She smiles wanly at the regular customers and nods to them.

"We could end up in jail for that," says Feri in Hungarian. "We'll be locked up and left to rot."

"Why?" Eržika asks. "Because we take care of her? Because we feed her, clothe her and give her a roof over her head?"

"No," says Feri. "They'll say that we're... you know... abusing her. She isn't responsible for her actions; she's insane. Just look at her."

Eržika gives madam a look. She bends under the table to see what Lady is doing with her right hand under the table. Then she sits up, grabs Lady's arm and forces her moist hand back onto the table.

"I think the most sensible thing to do would be to take her to the police right now," Feri continues. He might do it personally. He doesn't want to end up in jail. "This isn't a joke anymore," he adds sternly.

Eržika loses her temper. She's livid. This is typical of Feri. Eržika is trying to earn a few crowns, to achieve something, to get out of this filthy snack bar and lavatories, but his Excellency wants to act the hero. The honest citizen. The good Samaritan.

Feri gets off the bench and slaps Eržika in the mouth with the back of his hand. His eyes are blazing. "That was too much," he says. "You don't use that tone with me, woman! Get it?"

Eržika falls silent and calms down. She didn't mean anything; it's just that...

Lady listens with her blank, distant, alienated expression to this argument in Hungarian. She finishes her hot chocolate and reaches for Feri's *Mars* cigarettes. She has learned to smoke during the long boring breaks between each lover. She puts a cigarette in her pallid chafed lips. In a flash, at least four gentlemen in overalls offer her a light. Lady lights up, inhales the smoke, and smiles invitingly at the beer drinkers.

Eržika returns to her topic. She only meant to say that in the five days that Lady has spent with them they've made twenty-five thousand from the beer drinkers. That's not to be sneezed at. She'd like to suggest that Feri waits until they get a quarter of a million crowns. That will be two months. Then Feri can take Lady to the police. All Eržika wants is for Feri to let her have those two months. If Eržika had wanted to, she would be lolling now in Rácz's mansion. But she chose Feri. So, Feri shouldn't spoil her fun now.

Feri nods. This makes it quite different. The sum Eržika has named cools his Samaritan inclinations. A quarter of a million is big money. For a start. "Very well then, have it you own way," Feri concedes. "But then I take her to the police. So we don't have to worry about a thing."

He goes to the snack bar counter to get another coffee and rum. In the meantime, Eržika takes Lady into the hotel Ambassador boiler room. After a terrible row with the fat car park attendant who didn't like his trailer being pissed in, Lady has to receive her customers in a hovel behind the boiler room on the days that Feri and Eržika are not on duty. They did a deal with Berki and Šípoš: they get a bottle of wine and a hundred crowns each per day, and they both get a free go with Lady.

The hovel is musty and dark, but it is warm and dry. From the stokers' lavatory comes an ammoniac smell of urine. There is a shower, too, which Lady will appreciate, especially in the evening after her fiftieth customer. Besides, she's out of sight there. Customers get there through the boiler room.

Once Lady is naked, Eržika takes all her clothes and puts them in her bag. Later she will wash them and hang them out to dry; they will be ready by morning. Lady will have no clothes until evening. Then Eržika goes to the slot machine between the hotels Ambassador-Rácz 1 and Ambassador-Rácz 2 and buys fifty condoms. That's enough for one day. Eržika has to use alternate slot machines; sometimes they run out. Eržika doesn't like this job: originally, proud Feri was supposed to buy them, but he's too embarrassed. It's up to her, then. Besides that, Eržika has to buy lavatory paper and cleaning fluid for tomorrow's shift. Her feet hurt; in addition to her own person and her shopping, she also has to lump her and Feri's embryo.

Bartaloš sits drinking his second cup of coffee and rum. Soon fellow drinkers join him. They all have a go with Lady and then join him. They get their cards out and play "sixty-six" until noon. Then comes lunch;

Feri and Eržika take their seats. The choice is limited: schnitzel with cheese, schnitzel with garlic, fried ox testicles, grilled chicken, fat pork sausage. This comes with round stuffed green peppers and bread. And beer.

Soon a sweaty Feri, a toothpick in his mouth, takes a break, while Eržika sets out to the boiler room with food for madam. Lady eats sparingly; she would throw up with all that shaking about.

* * *

One day policemen turn up in the car park, open Lady's car, search it and discover a rotting bag of shopping in the boot. Then one of the policemen, wearing civilian clothes, goes up to Piggybank, who has been watching them from a distance. He shows him his police ID and asks how long the Fiat has been parked there.

"About a week," says Freddy truthfully.

Does he know where the lady driver went, enquires the policeman.

Freddy laughs. Freddy has a thousand cars in the car park every day. How could he remember one person?

The policeman shows him a picture of the lady. Freddy takes a look. Lady looks very good in it. She has a confident smile on her face and her eyes and lips are beautifully made up. She doesn't looks so perfect now, Freddy is aware, but she's still quite good-looking. Although, ever since one of the beer drinkers broke her nose, Bartaloš has had to lower the price for intercourse.

"No, I don't recall her," says Freddy firmly. He might be a swine, but he's not a snitch, he thinks.

* * *

Junec's lamps were a huge hit in the United States and soon he was getting orders from Europe as well. Martin had to take on more employees and was, at first, overwhelmed. Soon Europe was taking a third of Artisania Lamps' production. Though transportation by ship was relatively cheap, it still had a negative impact on the price of Junec's lamps in the European market, and a solution had to be found. Martin realised that if he could free himself of shipping costs, he could sell his lamps cheaper and brush the competition aside.

That was when a political revolution happened in Martin's old country, sweeping away the Bolsheviks. Martin followed events taking place
on the other side of the world attentively and was often glued to the
television for hours, watching CNN news. "Good God!" he said, pin-
ching himself. So Martin Junec had lived to see the day, after all!

Edna understood his excitement and held his hand.

"I wonder if the Slovaks will benefit, too," Martin worried. "Let's
hope the Czechs don't screw us again!"

"What do you have against the Czechs?" Edna asked. "After all,
Havel is a Czech. And you're a Czech, too."

"No, darling!" Martin retorted. "I'm Slovak. Slovak, for God's
sake!"

"I understand," said Edna. "Catalans, Castilians, Basques, and
Galicians all live in Spain and they're all Spaniards, aren't they?"

"But I'm not a Czech," Martin explained. "I'm Slovak. I'm from
Czechoslovakia, not Bohemia. Do you see? From Czecho... Slovakia!"

"I see," Edna said. "That means you are Czechoslovak."

"I'm not a Czechoslovak," Martin said. "I'm Slovak."

"I see," said Edna.

* * *

Siegfried Heilig is about forty and lives in East Germany. It's not
surprising: he's an East German. He is a former member of the SED
party, a district agent. It couldn't be proved that he was a Stasi informer,
as the documents, including his letters denouncing people in his workshop, were burnt. He's still a foreman in a dilapidated factory making
pollutants, but soon he'll be unemployed. It's all thanks to Gastarbeiter
and asylum seekers.

After the dissolution of the GDR, Siegfried Heilig quickly changed
politics; he became a right-wing sympathizer: foreigners, especially
Russians, are to blame for everything. Only now has Siegfried Heilig
begun to understand how demeaning it was for him to have to put up
with being vomited over all his life and being compelled to put on a
happy smile. Humiliation is the worst thing in the world when it is felt
after the event; it gives rise to indomitable hatred of everyone around
one: the humiliators and the humiliated, too.

Luckily, Siegfried Heilig was always too cowardly to express his
hatred other than by loud talk and German Nationalist posing. He even
helped burn down shelters for asylum seekers, if only indirectly, by

watching it on television, even though these frantic evenings of arson were happening in his own small town, a few streets away.

In a pompous gesture of disowning his past, Siegfried Heilig even burned his wedding picture: the couple had got married wearing Communist Youth League uniform.

To settle the score with the former Soviet Union after the unification of Germany, Siegfried Heilig, together with his neighbours, big, blond, red-faced men with moustaches and similar psychiatric problems, lurked behind rubbish skips and ambushed Russian soldiers who, when they wangled a permit to leave their base, came to scavenge from the skips (just as dozens of other Russian soldiers scavenged from dozens of other skips). When the starving, frozen soldiers in huge peaked caps and stinking boots put their hands into the rubbish to retrieve leftovers of food, clothing, and other goods, Siegfried Heilig, or one of his compatriots, jumped from behind the skip and slammed the lid down on the Russians' dirty hands. This painful piano-lid effect always scared the Russians so much that, as soon as they freed their mangled limbs from the skip, they ran off, howling with pain, to the loud laughter of those nice merry Germans. Siegfried Heilig always went back to his wife, warmed up by caraway schnapps and a sweet feeling of satisfaction of contributing to a Greater Germany and the coming of a New World Order.

Siegfried Heilig is a big man with a red face. His upper lip bears a blond moustache, not the kind Hitler wore, but the kind every other fat German tourist wears. Siegfried Heilig is a fat German tourist, too. His wife complements him perfectly: she is a dry blonde stick with bleached eyelashes, male facial features and cold light-blue eyes. They used to drive their Wartburg regularly to Lake Balaton and sometimes even to Bulgaria. After the reunification of Germany, they swapped their useless GDR money for hard Deutschmarks, one to one, and in summer, with another friendly family, indistinguishable from them, they went to Spain. For entire two weeks in Lloret del Mar, the former East Germans had to wrestle with their deep-rooted inferiority complex vis-à-vis their compatriots who had the luck to be born further West or South. The men dealt with it by getting drunk, singing choral songs, shouting "Heil!" every night, and pissing through the balcony railings of the hotel Frigola. Their wives did it by bitterly keeping their mouths closed, ostentatiously wiping the cutlery and glasses with their napkins before lunch and dinner and querulously bullying the stupid, dirty, conceited and thoroughly inferior Spanish waiters. The waiters secretly found this entertaining: they could unerringly tell an East German from a West German at first sight. He didn't even have to open his mouth.

After the Spanish episode, Siegfried Heilig and his wife decided to take their holidays in Hungary and Bulgaria. They could feel more like lords there than in Spain, where their West German compatriots ruled. In Eastern Europe the East Germans still felt good. Everyone bowed down to the almighty Deutschmark. And when they substituted their farting Wartburg for a Volkswagen Golf with a catalytic converter and changed their licence plates from GDR to FRG, their self-esteem had no limits.

Siegfried Heilig and his wife are childless. A few abortions in her youth mean that Heilig's wife has no chance of conceiving and carrying a baby to full term. Often, but especially now that the grim wrinkles round her mouth have deepened, she reproaches Siegfried Heilig for this, although he is responsible only for the last three abortions. (There was one he doesn't even know about: the result of friendly extramarital relations with a negro from Zimbabwe at the 1973 International Festival of Youth in Berlin. The newly married Heiligs could then easily have had a mulatto, but the embryo ended in the sink, cut up into black pulp.)

This year the ageing Heilig spouses will go to Lake Balaton. From Germany, they'll go via the Czech Republic and Slovakia: they'll save money. Everything is much cheaper towards the end of the season, they don't have children and needn't worry about school holidays and so on.

* * *

Lady's husband was out of his mind with worry; his wife had gone shopping and vanished without trace. He waited anxiously, and when at eleven in the evening she still was not back, he called all his friends to see if she might possibly be visiting one of them. She was not.

His friends had only the obligatory words of comfort for him. "If you need us," almost all of them said, "we're always here for you." This meant: "Don't bother us; leave us alone. Your wife vanishing is your problem. Don't call us; we'll call you."

Lady's husband got the gist, thanked them all and phoned the police.

The police didn't like the fact that Lady had been missing for such a short time. "Why the panic?" asked the duty officer. "She's been missing only twelve hours. She'll be back in the morning. She must be visiting someone."

Lady's husband sat in an armchair; there was no point trying to sleep. The hours passed, one by one, and there was no sign of the young woman. The bottle of whisky was almost empty; Lady's husband was drunk, slumped in the leather armchair. But even drunk, he looked neat and tidy. Towards daybreak he fell into a deep sleep from which he kept jerking awake. The young woman had not come back.

When the husband went to the police at six in the morning, at first nobody paid any attention to him. They were all very busy. It was only around eleven that a tired dishevelled desk officer, wearing a jacket and with a cigarette in his mouth, agreed to talk to him. When he heard the reason for the man's visit, he smiled.

"Twenty four hours is nothing," he said.

He silently listened to the description of the car that the missing woman had gone shopping in and looked at her picture. "Wow," he said, looking at the young woman's face. "Quite a girl," he added approvingly. His attitude softened.

"Go home: maybe she's got your breakfast ready," the police clerk advised Lady's husband in an avuncular manner. "You know what women are like. They get a bee in their bonnet and you don't see them for three days. There's no point getting upset. Women are like that."

"But she has never done that before," said Lady's husband, pondering the policeman's suggestion.

"Every woman does it once," said the policeman loftily. "Any woman can get a bee in her bonnet. Maybe you had a quarrel before she left, maybe you slapped her about, excuse my saying so: did you?"

The husband raised his hands in shock: they never quarrelled.

"How do I know," the policeman hazarded a guess. "Maybe she's found another man. That's what women are like, after all," he started to philosophize. "It's hard without them, but being with them is harder still…"

"We love each other very much," said the man with dignity.

"Take it easy," said the policeman, trying to calm him. "It's just that twenty four hours is too short a time. I'm experienced. I've been in the police for twenty years. And, frankly, I've been divorced three times."

"And what would be enough time for you?" the husband asked.

"What do you mean?" asked the policeman, puzzled.

"I mean, if twenty four hours is not enough, what is?" explained Lady's husband.

The policeman thought it over. "I'd say a month, or two," he said. "There was another man whose wife vanished. He was out of his mind, just like you; madly in love. Two months later, we started a nation-wide search, and she was soon found. And where do you think she was?"

The man shrugged. He had no idea.

"Less than five hundred yards from her home," the policeman said triumphantly. "In the woods. Someone, actually several men, since that could be ascertained, raped her and then hanged her by her legs, gagged, from a tree. According to the pathologist, she probably lived two more days. You know, women. They're always tougher... But we did find her, by God!"

The policeman triumphantly banged his desk, as if to underline the significance of his words.

"I'm telling you, sir, women tend to disappear," he said soothingly. "Particularly since the fucking democrats opened the borders. I shouldn't be telling you this, but the white slave trade is flourishing. Females between eleven and forty-five vanish like anything. And where do they end up? I'll tell you: in secret perverts' brothels somewhere in Asia, or South America. But why do I bother you with this? Go home and wait. If she doesn't show up in five days, come back. And keep calm. Trust us! I know what I'm talking about."

The desk officer got up, hinting to Lady's husband that the conversation was over. Lady's husband made a move and meekly went home.

At home, he changed and went to work. He sat under a fan, his back to the efficient blinds, watching through his glasses his computer's light-blue flashing screen. The secretary brought him his post. She behaved discreetly; the news of his misfortune spread at lightning speed through the firm. Some pitied him; others, people he had been promoted over, were rubbing their hands with glee. The man sat at his computer and asked himself where he had gone wrong.

Yes, recently he'd spent too little time with his pretty woman. He was constantly overworked; just the thought of having sex filled his limbs with devastating fatigue. He got up very early in the morning, to get ready for the working day, and in the evening he came back, happy to throw himself into his armchair for a few minutes with a drink in his hand. He would go to work almost every Saturday and rested on Sunday. To put it simply and briefly, he could no longer get it up. He began to think about the last time he slept with his wife. It turned out that it had been some time last year. When he realised that, he was stupefied. It was terrible how fast time flew.

Lady's husband got up, turned his computer off, and went to see his line manager. In a few brief, well-chosen words he explained the situation, took three weeks' leave and went home.

Three days later, his erection was back, but not the young woman.

He went to the police again. This time, it was a different policeman, a fat grey-haired man with a scar on his temple, in a sweaty white shirt and with a pistol in an underarm holster.

He wrote up a report, searched in his drawer and found the picture of Lady that his colleague had put there a few days ago. He had a good look at Lady's face. "Quite a girl," he said admiringly and looked at the man condescendingly. "Have you have any arguments recently, or any problems?" he asked.

"None at all," said Lady's husband, shaking his head. "We loved each other," he said shocked at himself using the past tense.

"You loved each other," repeated the policeman with an ironic smirk. "Look here," he said. "It's clear to me. Either your wife ran away with a lover, or she emigrated to the West. Don't take offence; it's my personal opinion. It is, of course, possible that she could have been abducted, but she was too old for that. White slave traders go for twelve- and thirteen-year olds. Foreigners have enough of their own old whores, if you'll pardon me. Oh well," concluded the policeman. "We'll begin to search for the vehicle. That will be our starting point."

A few days later they picked the young man up at his house and drove him to a car park in the middle of the city. "Is this it?" a uniformed policeman asked him, pointing to Lady's car, parked by the snack bar wall. The man nodded silently.

"So your wife's trail ends here," said the other policeman. "You can take the car home now. But don't worry, we'll keep on searching," he added reassuringly.

The young man needed a drink badly. He stopped by the counter and bought a double rum. He gulped it down. His insides went into a spasm; for a moment he didn't know whether the rum would stay down, or come up. He chased it down with a lukewarm cola.

"Hey, Herr! Herr!" he was addressed, in a conspiratorial half-whisper, by a smallish man in a white coat, obviously someone who worked in the snack bar. Lady's husband turned round. Since he was well dressed, the stranger had mistaken him for a German or an Austrian.

"Hey, Herr! Gute ficken!" the man continued, his eyes fearfully roaming. His right hand was hitting his left fist in an obscene gesture.

"Für eine Nummer zehn Mark! Eine Nummer hundert Schilling! Schöne Lady, verstehen? Kommen Sie, bitte! Gut Sex!"

That was too much for the husband. "I'm not interested," he said in Slovak, leaving Feri Bartaloš standing there, dumbfounded by surprise and fear in the middle of the Wooden Village, as he left in disgust.

* * *

Martin's parents have passed away; they both died in quick succession, while he was in the United States. His only sister still lives in Liptovská Osada. Martin writes to her sporadically.

One Saturday Martin decides to give this hopeless paper warfare a miss, gets into a rented Škoda Favorit and drives to Liptov.

First he drives to his native village, Liptovská Lužná, and pays his respects in the local cemetery to the somewhat overgrown family grave. He leaves his car parked by the church and takes a walk in the village. He meets a few passers-by, but nobody he recognizes. He stops at the house where he grew up, but strangers are living in it.

He takes a look at the low gate that he remembers from childhood, but a woman wearing gaudy plastic tracksuit bottoms comes out and gives him a stern look. Martin realizes that none of the original villagers are left; all the houses were sold to city people as holiday homes. But where the locals all went to remains a mystery for Martin.

Once in Liptovská Osada he makes for his brother-in-law's house and finds that the ground floor has been turned into something like a boutique; a shop full of dubious unbranded electronic goods and souvenirs, and a video-rental shop that also sells cigarettes.

Jano, his brother-in-law, comes out to greet him; he's recognized him easily. Jano immediately shouts to tell his wife to come out. Martin's sister Naďa comes out and smiles. She hugs and kisses her brother. Jano shuts up shop and they take Martin to their living room. Martin brings the presents that he bought in Bratislava from the car.

Naďa introduces Martin to his two nieces, born after he left for the United States.

Then the discussion turns to money and business. Jano criticizes everything: the government, the Czechs, the Hungarians, the gypsies, and the weather. He is up to his neck in debt and his business is not going as well as he'd like. Both he and Naďa keep shop from morning till night, weekends too, and barely manage to make ends meet.

Martin hears them out with interest and then offers them a job in Bratislava in the future branch of Artisania Lamps. Martin knows that his sister and brother-in-law are reliable, hard-working, honest Slovaks. He is now founding a branch of his firm here, in Slovakia. He needs people that he can trust around him.

Jano and Naďa begin to demur. They don't want to move. Despite everything, they're doing fine. They have a nice house and their children have healthy mountain air to breathe. What would they do in Bratislava? They go there from time to time to buy stock, and that always spoils their entire day.

Martin tries to persuade them for a while, but fails.

Then it's Jano's turn to speak: he wants to ask Martin for a small loan. Something like a bridging loan; he hasn't got the wherewithal to pay his supplier's invoices.

Martin agrees. He won't just lend them money, he'll give it to them.

His sister and brother-in-law are pleased.

Yes, give, Martin continues. It's his share of the money that Naďa got from selling their family house: that's his gift. He is giving up his share in her favour. That's all he can do for them. Even in America, money doesn't grow on trees. He didn't get rich by throwing money around. In fact, if he lent them a million, it wouldn't help. You don't have to be a financial genius to see that the money would be wasted. Martin took a little walk around the village. In this small village he counted six boutiques and four video-rental shops. And two shops selling cheap electronics. He's not surprised business is bad. Motorists passing by on their way north are not going to buy a Walkman for four hundred, or rent a kick-boxing video-cassette.

The sister and brother-in-law pull a long face.

Martin continues: he wants to help them by getting them out of this hole and offering Jano a managerial position in his Slovak branch. That would be a proper job for a man! The branch would start from zero and it will be up to Jano how it looks and flourishes, say, in a year or two. He'll also get a few per cent in shares, to increase his commitment. And Naďa can stay at home and look after the children. Jano will earn enough.

His brother-in-law explains: Martin's firm in Bratislava will make lighting products and Jano knows nothing about that.

Martin laughs. Jano will be working in the sales department where it doesn't matter whether they sell lamps or beef. Someone else will handle production. So what does he say?

Jano disagrees. He doesn't want to be anybody's employee. He wants to be his own man. That way, there's nobody above him, just his customer. Our customer is our boss.

"Tell me honestly," Junec asks, "when did you last see a customer in your shop?"

His brother-in-law shakes his head. No, never again will he work as an employee. And besides, there's the insecurity he'd be taking on. At present he knows where he stands. It's not much, but when Western tourists come back to the Tatra Mountains…

Martin is devastated by this stubbornness. "Why do almost all Slovaks think that being a businessman means buying a hot dog for three crowns, heating it and selling it for seven? The whole bloody nation is shifting the same hot dog person to person! Who's going to manufacture products and goods? Where are all the craftsmen? Where are the skilled workers? Where the fuck did they go? We used to have great workers here. In the States they still remember the Slovak construction men and tradesmen. And here?" On his way from Bratislava he saw buildings so bad that in America they'd take the whole construction crew out, put them up against a wall and shoot them. And they'd put the architect in the electric chair. Damn fucking right!

Martin is sick with rage.

"Keep your hair on," his amiable brother-in-law advises him.

Naďa, on the other hand, tries a softer approach. She doesn't feel like moving, either. Maybe Martin doesn't realize that what he managed to achieve in the United States, and more power to his elbow, he might not be able to achieve in Slovakia. What if his branch goes bust? What will she and Jano do then in Bratislava? Here, at least they have some security. But if the lamp business goes belly-up, what would they do then? Will Martin take them with him to the United States?

"That could be done," Martin admits, now he's driven into a corner.

But they don't want to move anywhere, says Naďa. Not to Bratislava, nor the United States. They're happy here as they are. Their roots are here.

Not a single word is said about the loan. Martin finishes his fruit drink and his open sandwich and quickly says goodbye.

Only his sister sees him out; Jano is offended and stays in the living room.

"Take this," he tells his sister, pressing a few thousand-crown bills into her hand. "Make sure somebody takes care of our parents' grave. I had a look at it in Lužná. It's awful. Simply terrible!" he adds in English.

Naďa blushes. She nods and takes the money.

Martin gets into his car, starts, and drives a few hundred yards before parking at a restaurant, *Janošík's Hut*. He'll have dinner here. He orders potato dumplings with sheep's cheese and fried bacon. He eats eagerly, and with his favourite dish he swallows his bitter disappointment. When he's eaten, he pays and sets out for Bratislava, driving as night falls.

* * *

One day the bitch from the town council appears in Freddy's car park, or rather, what's left of it after all the adjustments and changes. She goes up to him with a victorious smile and puts an official document into his sweaty hand.

"What's that?" asks the fat car park attendant, studying the document with staring eyes.

"It's the cancellation of the lease contract," chirps the bitch from the town council in her sweet voice.

"What?" Piggybank doesn't understand.

"Your contract for the car park was for half a year, right?" the bitch asks. "And today is June 30th. So, I'm sorry." The bitch from the town council finds it hard to suppress a malicious smirk.

Clutching the document, Freddy Piggybank collapses into his wicker chair. His fat body, his attendant's cap, and his sadly puffy cheeks make him look like a little toadstool. The bitch almost feels sorry for him. "It wasn't my idea," she says defensively.

Freddy looks at the document. He has nothing except this job to live on, he says in a tearful voice. This happened once before, a few years ago, in winter, because of the Christmas Market. They brought in carp, Christmas trees, gifts, and so on. Overnight they built the Wooden Village and it's still haunting us. They put up these wooden huts in the middle of a capital city. At the time it made him very ill. He was delirious for a few weeks with fever. He lost weight, a hundred pounds, maybe more. Then they gave him back part of the car park. That was during the first democratic dictatorship. And now they want to take everything he has from him? Is that why he froze, demonstrating against the Communists? Is that why he fought for an independent Slovakia? Well, he didn't think it would be like this. If he'd known, he'd have voted for the communists. "Yes, the communists. They're the only ones, I think, supporting private enterprise and the development of capitalism."

The bitch from the town council clears her throat and looks at her watch. Mr Mešťánek should have reckoned on this, she says. An area like this in the centre of the city can't be left idle. It can't be left to service the few drivers who want to park here. An area like this has to generate its own income. In a few years there'll be a multi-storey McDonald's here and Mr Mešťánek can come and have a hamburger.

As he sees himself queuing for a hamburger in a multi-storey building erected on his car park, Freddy Piggybank's eyes start to shed tears.

"It's unfair!" he shouts. "A man is keen to work, works entire days here, doesn't even go home, and now this! Where's the gratitude?"

"Look," the bitch from the town council says finally. "I'm not going to debate this with you. As of tomorrow, the car park no longer belongs to you. Do you understand? You do. So sign here, and I'll be off."

The bitch from the town council waits for the attendant's childish signature, and then she turns on her heels, vanishing on the busy pavement in front of the hotel Ambassador.

Freddy sits there lifelessly. Only now does he feel the whole impact of his cruel fate. This is the end of Freddy. Life will not be worth living now. Where will he go? What will happen to him? Back to the brickyard? They're laying off workers there. And his parents? What will his parents say? The vein in his head begins to pound dangerously. Freddy should be taking his medication, but he just sits there. I might as well croak, he thinks, full of self-pity. He imagines big headlines in the daily papers: BANKRUPT CAR PARK ATTENDANT DIES ON HIS LOT!.. HE ONLY WANTED TO LOOK AFTER CARS!.. ANOTHER VELVET REVOLUTION VICTIM? Yes, he'll probably die here. The bitch from town council will read the paper and her conscience will bother her until she dies. Freddy wallows in his misery and rather pleasant self-pity. His chest heaves mightily a few times and he sighs with sadness. No, Piggybank realizes, his death will not be headline news. Maybe some paper will have a little piece about it in the miscellaneous section: MENTALLY DISTURBED MISER DIES OF STROKE IN CAR PARK. Or something like that.

Freddy makes a decision. He will survive. He won't allow his tragic death, a number one event for him, to become a source of entertainment for some fool having his morning coffee. No! Freddy will fight. He will have revenge on this fucking government for this humiliation. He will live off crime. He will sink deep into the muck. He will steal and so on, until they catch him and lock him up in jail. And he'll die in jail. As a sort of silent protest. As an example of what this government did to an honest businessman, Alfred Mešťánek, who only wanted to guard cars until his death and earn a modest living. From now on, no wickedness will be wicked enough for Freddy!

With a pathetic expression on his face, Freddy gets up. He hurls his box of medicine to the ground. The little pills that were supposed to bring his slightly disturbed mind back to this planet at moments of excitement spill all over the car park. Freddy goes into his trailer, takes the money-bag off his neck and empties the money onto the table. He counts it and stuffs it in his pockets. Then he locks the trailer and, whistling, steps out towards the Wooden Village. In the corner of his eye he notices two bad gypsies hovering around a Mercedes with a Bratislava licence plate, but it doesn't stir him to action. Freddy Piggybank doesn't give a shit about stupid cars any more.

In the Wooden Village, Freddy stops by proud Feri Bartaloš. He feels a need to talk to someone, to complain. His tragic tone has, in the meantime, vanished; it has been left behind in the car park, together with the money-bag. Freddy's thoughts and expression now have a euphoric note, a feeling of carefree liberty and free will. He is no longer responsible for anything. He will be bad, he'll steal and lie, and join the dregs: it's all the fault of those people over there! They threw him out, but he's glad. It happened once before, in the first volume of *Rivers of Babylon*, and how did he cope? With difficulty; he lost his mind and joined some sect. Not a well-known one; Freddy Piggybank invented his own sect. But that won't happen again. He won't be that mad. He's not going to shit himself. Others don't own a car park, but they survive. They have a hard time, but they survive. And Freddy Piggybank will do the same.

"The gypsies are stealing one of your cars," Bartaloš interrupts Freddy's monologue and points behind his back. Freddy instinctively jerks and turns round. Two bad gypsies are now sitting in the Mercedes with Bratislava plates and fiddling with something under the dashboard. "I don't give a toss about it," says Freddy. He's finished with that car park.

"And what are you going to do?" Bartaloš wonders.

"Whatever turns up," says Freddy in a forced optimistic voice, which is tinged with fierce and tearful self-pity. He'll thieve. What isn't welded or chained down, Freddy Piggybank will snatch and sell here, in the Wooden Village. He doesn't care who sees.

"You won't be able to run away," objects Bartaloš and prods the folds of fat on Freddy's belly. "You're too fat for a thief."

"I'll lose weight," says Freddy with determination, and this thought, added to his suffering, gives him the idea that he should get something to eat. The grilled chickens in the snack bar window immodestly display their juicy roasted thighs, the giant bread rolls, wrapped in grey paper, sprinkled with shiny crystals of salt smell of the bakery and the giant bursting hot peppers, sweetly pickled in jars, call to him: "Buy us, Freddy!"

Freddy Piggybank, his mouth full of saliva, joins the queue. His new outlaw's career has inspired him.

When Freddy buys his meal, he takes it to the table and eats greedily. By the lavatories Feri and Eržika are debating something in hushed voices. Finally, Bartaloš approaches Freddy.

"May I?" he asks and sits down with two glasses of beer in his hand. He moves one over to the fat attendant. "I might have something for you," he says discreetly. "It's a sort of job, you could say."

"What sort of job?" Freddy asks.

"You know," Feri says. Feri and Eržika have this Lady. They take care of her. At the moment they keep her in the boiler room of the hotel Ambassador. It's better over there than here, in the lavatory. The bastard boss can't see. But somebody has to take customers there. When Feri and Eržika are off duty, it's OK. But when they're on duty here, in the Wooden Village, it's not. Feri has to be at the snack bar and Eržika is in charge of the lavatories. They could use someone who'd help them; he would be an usher. Not much, just take the customer and lead him across the hotel yard to the boiler room to see Lady. Feri thought that maybe Freddy might like to do it…

Freddy thinks it over. "And how much will you pay?" he asks.

"You'll get ten crowns per customer," says proud Feri. "It's not a lot, but it's not so little either, considering that you only have to walk a few yards." What's more, Freddy can reckon on between thirty and fifty customers per day. That brings in a decent amount. And for no effort. "So, how about it?"

Freddy is quiet; he mulls it over. He quite likes the idea. No effort, no work, and decent money. Besides, the work seems criminal enough for him. As he sinks to the bottom of society he couldn't wish for a better job.

"Fine," he tells Feri. "I'll try it."

* * *

Silvia enters the day-bar of the Ambassador and sits down in the compartment that is practically reserved for her. Ever since she got back, she has always sat there. The waiters are new, and don't know that this compartment was always her favourite place when, before her departure for Austria, she made her money here in the Ambassador cabaret as a dancer and occasional whore.

"Good afternoon, ma'am," the waiter bows. "The usual?"

"Good afternoon," Silvia replies and flirtatiously flashes her eyes at the waiter. Flirtatiously, but not too flirtatiously; he is only a waiter, after all. Silvia keeps tight control over everything.

Soon the waiter returns and on his tray sits a big tumbler of juice with pleasantly tinkling ice cubes.

"Thank you," says Silvia and takes a drink.

For a while she sits there, looking out of the big window. Soon, a young woman enters the room. Her expensive, but quite tasteless dress, her gait and painted face clearly mark her profession. She looks round the bar and, when she spots Silvia, she smiles and approaches.

The two friends greet each other cordially, despite the inequality.

Zuza sits down. She lights a cigarette and nods at the waiter. The waiter needs no prompting to mix and serve her Fernet and tonic, what they call a Bavarian.

"You look good, you old bag," Zuza praises Silvia's outfit and feels the high-quality fabric of her mini suit.

"Thanks," says Silvia.

"And how's Edita doing?" Zuza asks. "Did she stay in Austria?"

"Edita's dead," says Silvia. "Let's change the subject. What's new here?"

Zuza takes a sip of her Bavarian and starts to tell her: "Basically, nothing's changed here. Anča-Jožo finally saved up enough money and went to Italy to have her operation. The operation was a success, they say, and a few months ago she sent a postcard. Wanda and Eva live with Video Urban. He's made quite a career, he's a top politician."

"Who, Video Urban?" Silvia can't take it in. "You mean that long-haired faggot, Rácz's sidekick?"

Zuza nods: "He's on the news on TV all the time. He's had his hair cut. Wanda sometimes stops here when she's out shopping. They're doing fabulously; she is all aglow with happiness. Video Urban is in business; they have tons of money. Imagine, those two bitches are in love with him. Eva is expecting now, so they're buying a layette. Same as those... Morons... in America..."

"And what about Rácz?"

"Well, Rácz," Zuza shrugs her shoulders. "Rácz has bought about twenty restaurants and boutiques in the centre and cruises around in his new Mercedes. He's happily married and has a little boy."

"And what about Zdravko G.?" Silvia asks.

"He used to drive here in a white Porsche," says Zuza, "and take girls to Austria. Then he lost his marbles and went home to fight in a war. We haven't seen him since."

"I hope they shoot him in his stinking Albanian balls," Silvia gets it off her chest.

Silvia knows all about what her old friend is telling her. She asks all the whores from the Ambassador, when she interviews them, about all that. She herself doesn't know why she lets them tell her the same things over and over again. Maybe she wants to create an atmosphere of trust, full of nostalgia and common memories. She nods, occasionally reacts by expressing wonderment, pretending to be interested in what she hears. However, she soon gets down to the matter in hand.

"I'm going to open a new house," she says. "A *Perverts' Centre*, if you know what I mean. Well, not completely, or I'd have the cops on my back. For the time being, no animals and no children, of course. But otherwise, I want it to be something special. It's not going to be a massage parlour where they do a hand job for a hundred crowns. There will be normal women, and transvestites, transsexuals, a sadomasochist parlour, a sauna, a group sex room, a surgical room, enemas, spy holes, the works. Maybe, in future we can have little girls, but first I have to find out what can be done and what can't. Downstairs will be a bar and a small stage. Cabaret. Live show every night. We'll cater to all tastes."

"A house like that must cost a fortune," remarks Zuza.

"I've bought it already," Silvia says, and her voice is not without pride. "It's a pretty big villa. I've got builders working there now. We're opening in a month or so."

"And why are you telling me all this?" Zuza is curious.

"Don't tell me the girls haven't told you yet," says Silvia.

"Well, they did say that you were looking for staff," Zuza admitted.

"Right," Silvia nods. "I've got a job for you. I'm offering good work conditions, pay per client, insurance, and regular medical check-ups. My firm will be for well-heeled customers, you see. For people with high IQs: Austrians, Germans, and Americans. Everyone will use condoms."

"I see," Zuza says, "but you mentioned a *Perverts' Centre*. Where is the perversion? You mean golden shower? Anal?"

"What's so perverse about anal sex?" Silvia smirks contemptuously. "Nowadays in the West that's the only way people fuck, I reckon. What I had in mind was that we'd create a special atmosphere, you know. For example, you'd let yourself be tied up, and…"

"Oh no, no bondage!" Zuza backs away. "I once had a punter when I worked in the Zochová chalet and he kept nagging me to let him tie me to the bed. He screwed me, took off my crocodile skin shoes that cost me seven thousand, and ran away. Don't even ask me how long I was stuck there, tied up like a cunt! And he had plenty of IQ, too."

"Well, that won't happen in my place," Silvia assures her.

"And what about money?" Zuza asks.

"It will be decent," promises Silvia. "Depending how many clients you have a day, what services you give them, and so on. Nobody will screw you; everything goes through the computer. If you work hard, you could make as much as fifty thousand a month."

"That's what I make now," Zuza says.

"Yes, but with me, you'll make it risk-free, safely, in a nice setting and with good fellow-workers," counters Silvia. "And the clients won't be riff-raff; the house will be only for clients who want the best. Albanians and gypsies will be barred." Zuza has Silvia's word on that point.

Martin Junec, dressed in an elegant suit, enters the day bar. He sits down near the wall and orders an alcohol-free Miller beer.

"Sorry, we only have Klausthaler," waiter says.

"Yeah, let's try that," nods Martin who feels full of positive energy after a good lunch. "Bring me a Klausthaler, then."

Martin looks round the room and right away spots the attractive young woman he's seen here several times before. Again, she's with a woman whom Martin rightly identifies as a hooker. Much water has passed under the bridge since Martin Junec played saxophone in a bar band in this hotel, but the Bratislava whores haven't changed. They are just as pretty and just as tastelessly dressed. But the other one…

Silvia feels the stranger's gaze on her legs and turns round.

Martin smiles at her and give her a hint of a bow. He moves his lips silently: a symbolic greeting between people who are strangers, but whose paths have crossed so often that they are no longer total strangers.

Silvia smiles in response and moves her head even more subtly. Then she continues her discussion with Zuza.

"Who's that punter over there, near the entrance?" she asks quietly. "Don't spin round like a windmill, you goose!"

"The one over there?" asks Zuza and points at Junec who, in the meantime, has started perusing some American financial paper. "He's a millionaire from America. I mean it. He owns a factory, or something. He emigrated from here. He lives in the top storey, in a suite, but no luck. Several of us have tried, but he's not interested."

"What's he doing here?" asks Silvia.

"He's trying to do business here," says Zuza. "They say he wants to open a branch."

"What kind of a branch?" Silvia asks. "A branch of what?"

"I don't know," Zuza says defensively. "I only know what the receptionist told me."

"Okay, okay…" Silvia says and turns her gaze away from Junec. "Where were we?" she asks absent-mindedly.

"You were saying that you wouldn't let Albanians and gypsies in," says Zuza.

"Right." Silvia finds her train of thought. "Just don't spend too long thinking about it, or you'll end up street-walking. And that doesn't pay now."

Silvia gives Zuza her hand to show her that the interview is over.

Martin's peripheral vision notes movement at the unknown pretty woman's table, and he takes his eyes off the paper. The young woman is alone at her table. Martin feels that this is his moment. He puts the paper down, gets up, adjusts his tie and, newspaper in hand, approaches Silvia. She raises her eyes to him in surprise, half-genuine, half-feigned.

"I'm sorry," Junec says with a smile. "Almost every day we meet here and we've even begun to say hello, but nobody's introduced us yet. So let me do that myself. I'm Martin. Martin Junec. Atlanta, Georgia."

Martin makes a half-bow.

Silvia quite likes this way of doing things. She appreciates Martin's not pissing about, but coming straight to the point.

"I'm Silvia," she says. "Silvia Hronská. Delighted."

Silvia extends her hand and Martin gallantly lifts it to his lips.

"I've made a bet with myself," Martin says, "that you're not from here. Am I a winner, or a loser?"

"You won," says Silvia. "Originally, I am from here, but I've come from Austria."

"I like winning," says Martin. "I hate losing. May I join you?"

"Please do," says Silvia, but takes care not to sound too eager.

Martin joins her.

"And what have you won?" asks Silvia.

"A bottle of champagne," says Martin. "And since you helped me win, I'll share my winnings with you."

Martin nods to the waiter.

"Isn't it too early for champagne?" Silvia hesitates.

"It's never too early for a glass of good champagne," says Martin.

The waiter runs in.

"What kind of dry champagne do you have?" Martin asks.

"We have Slovak Hubert and Soviet champagne," says the waiter.

"I didn't ask you about sparkling wine," Martin smiles. "I asked about champagne."

"But it is champagne…" the waiter defends himself.

"I'm asking about French champagne, young man," Martin says.

"We don't have French, but we do have Soviet…"

"All right, bring me the Soviet," Martin sighs, "And bring two glasses. And bring your boss, too."

The waiter bows and leaves.

Silvia has to laugh to herself at his male conceit. First he's put down the waiter and now he's waiting to give it to the manager with that typical American big-mouth arrogance, just to show off in front of her.

Soon the waiter comes back with a tray. He uncorks the Soviet sparkling wine and pours it into the glasses. Behind him appears a dark, stocky man dressed in an incredibly expensive silk jacket, with a hand-painted tie round his neck. In an impatient, imperious gesture, he shoos the waiter away and makes a half-bow to Junec. His dark steely blue eyes fix themselves on Silvia.

"Hello, Silvia," he says. His sharp facial features, clearly unused to smiling, are forcibly redeployed in a smile. "Long time no see," he adds.

His eyes run over Junec. For a fraction of a second he assesses him coldly, like a snake.

"I'm Rácz," he says, "and I own this hotel. I happened to be in the manager's office when I overheard you saying that you wanted to see him. Is there a problem? Can I solve it?"

Rácz eyes Silvia. The bitch looks good, he thinks. Maybe he shouldn't have kicked her out in *Rivers of Babylon*. Lenka looks very good, too, but after she had the child, she put on a bit of weight. And this one is still as slim as a tapeworm.

"No problem," says Martin. "Everything's fine. I was just wondering why you don't stock real champagne. It seems odd to me, in an establishment like yours."

Silvia could see Rácz's swarthy face turning first dark and then pale again. His eyes narrowed and took on a yellowish tinge.

"That's our sommelier's job," says Rácz. "I'm very sorry, indeed. The man is as good as fired."

"There's no need for that," Martin defends the absent sommelier, and Silvia can't help backing him up with a few negative gestures and interjections.

She and Rácz again exchange glances.

You look good, you tart, the hotelier thinks.

You've become as fat as a bull, Silvia feels.

"Rácz doesn't go back on his word!" says the hotelier. "Today I'll make the new sommelier order French champagne. The best, of course!"

"Thank you," says Martin, not knowing what else to say.

Rácz fixes his stare at him. Then he moves to Silvia.

"We'll see each other some other time," he says, bows to them and leaves in a slow, dignified manner.

Silvia grabs her glass.

"After all, Russian champagne is not so bad," she says to break the heavy silence and prevent any possible questions about Rácz. "Try it."

"I'm from here originally, too," says Martin. "You wouldn't believe how many bottles of Russian champagne I've drunk in this hotel!"

"You used to come here?" says Silvia sceptically: her innate card-index of faces is in furious search mode.

"I used to work here," says Junec. "As a saxophone player. Down in the Cabaret."

"Then I would certainly have known you," says Silvia. "I used to dance here."

"When?" Martin asks.

"From eighty-seven to ninety," says Silvia.

Martin laughs.

"I played the Ambassador from seventy-nine till eighty," he says. "I've been in the States fourteen years now."

"That means…" Silvia says.

"That means we missed each other," says Martin and raises his glass. "Now's a good opportunity to synchronize," he adds.

Silvia pretends she's missed the clear double entendre. "So you're a musician?" she asks.

"Oh, no!" Junec laughs. "A former musician. Now I have a factory in the USA. Lamps and light fittings."

"That must be very exciting!" says Silvia.

"Oh, yeah!" Martin agrees. "A very exciting business!"

They drink the sparkling wine.

"And you know that gentleman?" Martin asks. "That… Rácz?"

"We used to know each other some time ago," says Silvia and mentally rubs her hands in triumph: the American is jealous. "But it was a long time ago," she adds. She drinks up her champagne and takes a look at her watch. "Thanks for the invitation," she says. "I still have a few things to attend to."

Silvia gets up and Junec gets up, too.

"Nice to have met you, Mr... Mr..." says Silvia, extending her hand.

"Junec," says the American, holding her slender hand in his. "But call me Martin, please. I'll call you Silvia."

Silvia is forced to agree.

"What are you doing tonight?" Junec asks.

"Tonight?" Silvia doesn't understand, or else pretends not to.

"Maybe we could have dinner tonight," Martin suggests.

"I'm busy tonight," Silvia says.

"And tomorrow?" Martin is not easily discouraged.

"Tomorrow..." Silvia reflects. "Good, till tomorrow!" she finally decides.

"What time?"

"I don't know, around eight," says Silvia. "That's the usual time."

"Good, Silvia," says Martin. "So at eight, in the restaurant Ambassador, next door. I'll be expecting you. I'm glad we've met."

"See you later, Martin," says Silvia, takes her bag and leaves the Ambassador bar.

Martin sits down, pours himself champagne and begins to read the paper. Out of the corner of his eye he notices movement at the next table. He is startled. Žofré and his puffy face are now materialising there.

"I saw and heard everything," says the ghost. "Don't think, old boy, that I'm not here when I'm not here. I promised Edna I'd look out for you, so that's what I'm doing."

"I don't want you to look out for me," Martin Junec is losing his temper, but quickly lowers his voice: the waiter polishing glasses lifts his head in alarm.

"Do you want to know something about that woman?" Žofré asks. "I'm a ghost, I know a lot. I took an interest in her, too, so I spied on her a bit. Do you know what she did, and does now, for a living?"

"Shut up, Žofré," Martin hisses. "If I want to, I'll find out whatever I want. Unlike you, I never had problems communicating with women!"

"I never had any problems with women either," the fat ghost retorts. Only I was oriented more spiritually, and the women were more carnal."

"They were carnal?" Martin laughs.

"Yes," the ghost confirms. "Now, I'm truly happy. I'm remote from all earthly physicality and…"

"Just shut your fucking mouth!" Martin loses self-control and bangs the table. "I'm not such an idiot that I'd believe that bullshit. And I'm not a schoolboy who needs supervising, okay? If I want to fuck that blonde, then I will; if I don't, then I won't. But no jealous motherfucker is going to stop me. Get lost!"

"Well, it's not my business," Žofré says, and gets up. "I just thought that you might be interested in what this woman's been through…"

"I'm not planning to marry her," says Martin, "so I don't care!"

"When you're with her, put on two condoms," Žofré advises him, "so you don't catch the clap."

"Get out!" Martin hisses at him and looks around in fear.

Žofré just shrugs with pity, closes his eyes and dissolves in the air.

Junec drinks up his champagne, pays and asks the waiter to call him a taxi.

* * *

Freddy Piggybank quite likes his new job. It's not hard, he doesn't have to run around the car park like an idiot, the sun doesn't burn him and he doesn't get wet. The way ten-crown bills mount up is very cheering. There are lots of customers. As soon as the price is agreed outside the lavatories, proud Feri Bartaloš nods to Freddy. Freddy gets up, and with a calm wobbling gait, which is intended as proof of Piggybank's criminal credentials, he heads for the lavatories. With a fleeting nod he greets the customer. "Come with me," he says through clenched teeth and leads the customer to the hotel yard.

Apart from the steady customers, the beer drinkers who go and relieve themselves with Lady a few times a day, just as they visit the urinal, Feri Bartaloš and Eržika have managed to find a lot of new clients who are seduced by the photographs ripped from Lady's ID card and driver's licence. These clients are quite anxious and curious about what is in store and like to pump Freddy, who comes up to each customer, determined to look like a silent, surly, hardened criminal pimp. But the customer has only to ask a few questions and Freddy's silent mask drops. Piggybank loses his self-control and seconds later regales the customer with everything about his car park, his illness, health problems, and so on.

While the customer is with Lady in the hovel, Freddy sits and waits in the boiler-room. Šípoš and Berki urge him to buy them a bottle of gin just once, but the fat skinflint pretends not to hear. He leafs through an old issue of *Playboy* which he's found on the ramshackle table. After a while he puts the magazine down; the women in the pictures have no legs. All the photographs show naked hookers with their legs cut off half way down the thighs. What Piggybank misses is what arouses him most: perfectly shaped knees, calves and slender ankles. A tiny vein zigzagging across a girl's ankle would excite the fat man more than a look at the artificially blown up tits with aureoles the size of beer mats. That is the result of years spent working in the car park, where he ogled the legs of women walking on the pavement. If there are no torture, whipping or rape scenes in a magazine, Freddy looks for pictures of legs. *Playboy* is crap: it carries none of this. Instead, it features an idiotic conversation with some stupid writer.

Berki and Šípoš make fun of Piggybank. They speak Romany, giggle, and keep pointing at him. Freddy doesn't pay much attention to them. If Freddy Piggybank were in power, all the gypsies would end up breaking stones in a quarry. Including these two. Freddy will never forget the hurt the gypsies did him in *Rivers of Babylon*. They must have been relatives of these two.

Then comes proud Feri Bartaloš, and the gypsies get their greasy cards out. Feri is an almost obsessive card player. Ever since he's made some money, he plays like a man possessed. They play poker, and black-jack. Šípoš and Berki are willing partners; to be sure, it is always one of the two gypsies who wins.

The customer is soon finished and emerges from the hovel, buttoning up his fly. Freddy leads him out of the boiler-room and walks him to the Wooden Village, where another customer is now waiting. Freddy takes him over and everything is repeated: ten more crowns in his pocket.

Around lunch-time, Freddy gets his money from Bartaloš and queues for the pork steak Montenegro, ketchup, and a roll. He washes it down with a beer. Eržika queues behind him; she is buying lunch for Lady.

Freddy sits there, sating himself on this delicious food and wishing that those who turned him, an honest businessman, into a despicable criminal could see him. His own suffering moves him so much that he decides to get another beer.

Soon proud Feri Bartaloš comes out of the boiler-room: Lady has had her lunch.

The lunch break is over: another customer is standing by the lavatories, swallowing his saliva with excitement and clutching in his palm a sweaty hundred-crown note.

* * *

For a long time Martin has been putting off his visit to Nová Ves. Nová Ves is the village where his former wife Marfa and his son Oliver live, together with her parents, and where Hruškovič, a friend and a member of Martin's trio Hurytan, also lives.

In Nová Ves, Martin first visits his former in-laws, telling the taxi driver to wait for him.

The light-blue gate is ajar, as if they were expecting visitors. Martin looks over the fence, but there's nobody there. He gently pushes the gate open and enters the yard. He looks around. Nothing has changed. Everything looks exactly as it did when he, too, lived here.

There is a bell by the door. Martin pushes the button, but hears no sign that the bell works. Martin tries one more time, but he can't hear a bell, or any other sound. He presses the handle and opens the door.

"Good morning!" he shouts cheerfully with a tinge of servility in his voice, but nobody answers.

Martin becomes bolder and enters the hall. First he glances to the right, at the kitchen, but no one is there. The corridor leads inside the house; on the left is a living room, and behind it is the in-laws' bedroom. There is no one there either. At the end of the corridor, Martin opens the door to the room that he used to share with Marfa. The room is now a storage room for old junk and also his father-in-law's workshop. It looks as if not a soul is about. Martin is assailed by the embarrassing feeling of an intruder opening thirteen rooms one by one. He quickly shuts the door to his old room and goes into the yard. He decides to go round the house, pokes about in the garden, but doesn't find anyone. Only when he comes back, does he hear voices from the summer kitchen, a separate building where they used to boil pig swill, slaughter animals and, in summer, even cook. He knocks at the door and enters.

In the summer kitchen Martin finds his in-laws. They are taking jars of preserves from a wicker laundry-basket and putting them on the shelf.

"Good morning," Martin greets them politely.

The frightened old woman drops a jar of preserves. Glass shards and apricot halves explode in all directions.

The mother-in-law looks at Martin. She instantly loses her temper.

"What are you doing?" the old man attacks him. "Look what you've done!"

Martin stands hesitantly in the doorway. "I'm sorry," he says.

His former in-laws look at him with frank hatred and revulsion.

"I'm sorry, I'm sorry…" mutters the old woman, sweeping the glass shards and apricot halves into one pile. "Anyone could say that… Coming in like a ghost and then: I'm sorry!"

"And Marfa isn't here anyway," the old man says triumphantly, as if trumping Martin. "You needn't have come."

"Where is she?" Martin asks.

"She's with her husband," says the old woman. "In Trnava. She remarried. She married a decent man. Or did you think that you were the only man in the world?"

"And what about Oliver?" Martin enquires.

"He's in Trnava, too," says the old woman. "With his mother and father."

"I'm his father," Martin stresses.

"You're shit, not his father," the old woman snaps at him.

"The father is not the one who makes the child, but the one who brings him up," says the old man wisely, holding the dustpan while the old woman sweeps.

Martin is quiet. His silence enrages the old people even more.

"A fine father you are, indeed!" says the old woman. "And who left our Marfa and her child and took off for America? And what about our son? Why did you make him go with you? If he'd stayed at home, he'd still be alive."

"I've never made him go anywhere!" Martin retorts. "He wanted to go. He was a hopeless alcoholic, that's why he died."

"Why have you come here, you monster?" shouts the former mother-in-law. "Get lost! You killed our son and ruined our daughter's life and ours. You'll never get us to tell you where Marfa lives. You'll never ever see Oliver. You want to wreck his life, too? Get off our property, or we'll call the police. Did you hear?"

Martin hesitates for a moment.

"Well, good bye," he says and turns to leave.

"Just a moment!" the old woman stops him. "And what about the preserve? You've ruined our preserve. Apricot preserve! The most expensive one! This isn't America, where everything is free."

Martin wearily takes out his wallet.

"How much was it worth, mother?" he asks.

"A hundred dollars," his former father-in-law picks a sum at random.

"No, two hundred dollars!" says his former mother-in-law. "And don't call me 'mother', you wastrel!"

Martin pulls out two hundred-dollar notes and puts them on a table near the door.

The in-laws hungrily pounce on the banknotes. The old woman still can't believe that Martin has given them real dollars, and she checks them in every way, bending them, looking at them against the light, performing a set of senseless procedures that might resemble a layman's verification of authenticity.

But even after all that she seems no surer than before. She puts the money in her apron pocket and enviously, hatefully scowls at Junec.

Martin takes out his cheque-book, writes out a cheque and hands it to the old woman.

"This is a bank cheque," he says, when he observes her uncomprehending look. "It's for Oliver. But take a close look. It will only be paid after his eighteenth birthday."

The old woman holds the cheque in her fingers; his former father-in-law looks at it over her shoulder. Fifty thousand dollars! The old people stare at it, shaking all over.

Martin pays them no more attention. He goes to the street and gets in the taxi. He feels a bit relieved; he couldn't imagine what meeting Marfa would have been like. He feels sorry that he couldn't see his son, but not too sorry; he never had a highly developed paternal instinct.

"We've got that over," he thinks. "Let's go and see Hruškovič now."

"Let's move," he tells the cabdriver.

He asks to be driven to where *Vašíček's* pub used to be, gives a fifty-dollar bill to the driver and sends him away.

He takes a look around. The village has changed a lot. The communists demolished half of it and built prefabricated apartment buildings there instead. *Vašíček's* doesn't exist anymore. It was simply pulled down. All that was left was the fire brigade quarters attached to the pub. Junec sighs, crosses the high street and opens Hruškovič's yard gate.

The yard is full of patients waiting their turn in a quiet, orderly queue. Junec heads for the house, knocks and enters the kitchen. Hruškovič's wife is at the stove cooking something and is startled by his entry.

"Hello, Veruna!" Junec shouts.

"Martin?" Hruškovič's wife cannot believe it is him and wipes her hands on a towel.

They greet each other. Martin kisses her on both cheeks and gives her a present. Hruškovič's wife, impressed by American cosmetics, flushes bright red. The Levis 501 jeans for her teenage daughter, who is on a course for prospective models, also please her. "I'll call Jano right away," she says. In the hall she pushes an intercom button and says: "Jano, Martin Junec is here."

Soon, Hruškovič appears in the hall.

The old friends embrace.

"Old man, you old fart!" shouts Hruškovič, grabbing Junec's cheek with a show of roughness. How Hruškovič has missed his old mate, by God! Ever since Martin telephoned that he was coming to Nová Ves, Hruškovič has been looking out of the window.

"I can see you're very busy," Martin comments after giving Hruškovič his present, a three-litre bottle of twelve-year-old Jack Daniels whisky. "You seem to have plenty of patients, don't you?"

"Actually, they're only poor suckers who believe in miracles," says Hruškovič, dismissively waving his hand. He goes out onto the veranda and surveys the crowd obediently waiting in the yard.

"You can go home today," the healer shouts at them in a stentorian voice. Hruškovič's energy has just gone. They can come back in a couple of days: tomorrow Hruškovič is concocting his miraculous tinctures.

The crowd begins to disperse humbly and without protesting.

"They're like sheep," says Hruškovič indignantly. "They fall for anything."

Martin smiles. He's read about Hruškovič in the papers, in the Slovak American papers, in the USA. They say Hruškovič can cure even cancer and aids. They say he has miraculous healing powers.

"What shit!" says Hruškovič says. If it was true, he'd be the first to know about it.

He looks at his wife.

"My old mate and I are going to have a beer," he tells her.

They cross the veranda and the yard, and enter the old summer kitchen. Martin admires the room's equipment, the esoteric posters, books, and objects.

Hruškovič takes off his white coat and throws it on the massage table. "It's all fake," he says.

He takes from the champagne cooler a five-hundred-crown bill.

"This is the only genuine thing," he waves the banknote at Junec and puts it in his pocket. "You've got to make a living somehow," he says, as if apologizing to his friend for his profession. "Let's have a drink!" he looks at Junec. "Shit, we haven't seen each other for at least fifteen years. We have to celebrate your return."

"They've demolished *Vašíček's*," Martin notes sadly.

"But we do have plenty of new pubs," says Hruškovič. They can choose one at the bottom of the hill, at the football stadium, or in the village near the chapel, and Virgo has even opened his own restaurant.

"Virgo… Virgo," Martin is thinking aloud. Does he mean the one who worked as a waiter in Vienna?

"Sure," says the healer. "Now he has a Croat restaurant on the road to Devín, near the statue of the Virgin Mary."

"You don't say!" Martin is astounded by the enterprise of the Nová Ves villagers.

Finally, they stick to tradition and go to *Konzum*, the grocer's. Hruškovič orders two bottles of beer and two shots of vodka.

"Just like old times," says Hruškovič cheerfully. "Do you still remember, old man?"

Martin nods. "Those were the days," he agrees. "But perhaps they weren't."

"Do you remember Bulgaria?" the healer reminds him. "When we went there the first time? When Žofré got arrested? And a year later, the second time? And then Switzerland! Norway! My God!"

Hruškovič smiles. "We had cash, booze, and a lot of fun," he says. "You remember when we got the runs after we ate that salad in Bulgaria? Ha, ha, ha! And the girls! Don't even mention them! They crawled to the hotel after us."

"That reminds me of Anča Prepichová," says Martin, "What happened to her? Do you know anything about her?"

"As far as I know," Hruškovič says, "she made it. First she married a man who worked for the Water Works. He had an accident and died. Anča couldn't give a toss about her job sewing parachutes and started to going to the petrol station to fuck lorry drivers. They kicked her out of the Water Works housing. Then she worked as a hooker in the Ambassador. I was still playing there at the time. She went out with this little money-changer. That man made it big-time: he even got into parliament. Anča's now living with him and another girl. Together, in a threesome, you understand."

"That member of parliament is a polygamist, or what?" asks Junec.

"No, he's completely sane and normal," says the healer. "What's his name… Yes, Urban. He represents the Movement of the Democratic Right. It's a political party here. He was supposed to be a minister of something… Yes, our loopy Anča certainly has it made!"

"That's strange," Martin says. "In the USA, any politician would be finished if they found out that he was living with two women…"

"Get used to it," says the healer, "nothing's too odd for Slovakia."

Martin reverts to his topic again. He's sure that Hruškovič has made it, too. He's cured lots of people. He can't deny he's got special energy.

Hruškovič laughs. "It's all in the imagination," he says. People are so desperate that their auto-suggestion tells them that he's cured them. Actually, they either cure themselves, or they weren't ill at all and only imagined they were.

"Fuck off!" Martin says indignantly. Hruškovič needn't talk bullshit. He can tell an old friend the truth!

"That's what I'm doing," says Hruškovič. He wouldn't tell anyone else: he has no healing ability; he's a charlatan. A con man, okay? He's after people's money, that's all!

"Oh, come on!" Martin cannot believe it. And what about the woman with advanced breast cancer? And all those childless couples whom Hruškovič helped? And cases when he cured aids? After all, Martin has read all about it. So don't give that fucking nonsense to his old friend Martin!

But even Hruškovič couldn't understand it at first, says the healer with a sigh. He thinks it was all coincidence. How could an ex-musician, cure anyone? All the medication that Martin saw in his surgery is just tinted water. And the miraculous anti-cancer ointment is just ordinary Vaseline that Veruna used to get in the brickyard when she still worked there. They still have ten kilos of it left in the cellar... After all, Hruškovič doesn't even know how to dress a graze on somebody's hand.

Martin shakes his head in disbelief.

"Why are you cross, old man?" Hruškovič raises his vodka glass in cheers. "Would I fucking lie to you?"

They clink glasses, down the vodka and chase it down with beer.

"Have you been to see the old folk?" the healer asks.

Martin nods in silence.

"Marfa married about five years ago," says Hruškovič. "She found someone in the singles ads, I gather. They live in Trnava now."

Junec nods. "She was right. Why stay on her own? And Trnava's all right." Martin is sure that his marriage still wouldn't have broken up if the old people hadn't kept buggering things up. Martin began to hate Marfa when she became more and more like her mother.

Martin shows the waiter two fingers.

"And how about you?" asks Hruškovič. "Have you married again?"

Junec shakes his head. "Still single," he says. "I've got a... let's say, a girlfriend..."

"Does she let you screw her?" Hruškovič asks, as if concerned.

Junec just grins. He raises his glass and knocks it back. He looks at Hruškovič. "Screw her?" he asks. "Don't ask! She fucks like a mink." She knows such dirty tricks that sometimes it makes him sick. Junec just waves a hand, suggesting that there's no point saying more.

"And what's her body like?" the healer is interested.

"Quite good," Martin says. "Sporty, if you know what I mean…"

"Well, that's no good to me," says Hruškovič. "I like a woman with tits, an arse, and thighs. Why didn't you bring her over to show us?"

Martin explains that Edna has gone to Indonesia and New Guinea. She's an academic. She studies the natives.

Junec tells his old friend his story. He remembers the hard times that they, Martin and Žofré, went through: often they couldn't afford even to get a pizza. How he met Edna. How they started making lamps. How Žofré died. The only thing he was still reluctant to talk about was the problem he had with Žofré's ghost.

He's heard that Hruškovič has also had success as a psychic, Martin finally says.

Hruškovič laughs. That's part of the trade, isn't it? Hruškovič has to pretend that he has psychic powers, too.

Hruškovič looks round and lowers his voice.

He has absolutely no powers, he says. He once read an article about that Russian psychic, Kashpirovsky, how filthy rich he was, and said to himself: "Jano, are you any worse than him?" And so he put an ad in, and the next day his yard was full of patients. People are fucking idiots.

The pub landlord brings another round.

"But the first time you phoned me from America," says the healer, wiping the beer foam from his mouth, "You told me that you had a serious problem. What was it?"

Martin takes a breath and can't help spilling the whole truth about the visitations by Žofré's ghost. He describes Žofré appearing to him a few days after his death and giving him no peace ever since.

"And nobody except you can see him?" asks Hruškovič.

"Nope!" says Martin. Only Martin can see him.

"And is he hurting you in any way?"

"I can't say he is," Junec hesitates. "But I'm fed up to the teeth with him. He sucks, you understand. He's poisoning my life."

"I expect you know what I think of this fucking spiritual nonsense, don't you?" asks the healer. "It's all in the mind. Ghosts don't exist."

"You motherfucker," says Junec, disappointed. Is Hruškovič trying to tell him that he has fucking come all the way from America only to find out from the greatest Slovak psychic that ghosts don't exist? Well, if so, Hruškovič has put Martin's mind at rest in a really big way!

Hruškovič is the greatest Slovak psychic only to his patients, the healer retorts. Hruškovič can't put on an act with his old friend Martin. He just doesn't believe in this nonsense about ghosts, energies and all sorts of zones. He only believes in what he can touch. Like money; he believes in money. The more fools there are in this world, the more patients Hruškovič will have and therefore the more money he'll earn; that's clear, isn't it? After Martin and Žofré escaped to the West, the communists kept him in the country, just like in prison, and wouldn't let him earn money abroad, so he's now making up for those times.

"But even scientists don't doubt the existence of biological energy," the American objects.

"Look, old man," says Hruškovič. "I use energy when I do manual labour and I get energy when I get good bean soup down my mouth. Everything else is fucking nonsense!"

"So you won't help me?" Junec says, with hurt feelings.

"Well, you know, I wouldn't leave you in the shit," Hruškovič calms his friend. "Since you say I'm such a great psychic, then I'll help you. I'll do for you what I do for any other patient. No charge, of course!"

Reassured, Martin takes a sip of beer; his peripheral vision registers that Žofré has joined them at the next table. He turns round. Žofré is sitting there motionless, and his big reproachful eyes are silently looking at Martin. He seems to be eavesdropping on the whole conversation.

"What is it?" Hruškovič asks and sniffs the air.

"He's here," Martin whispers and discreetly points his head at the next table.

"Oh, please…" Hruškovič shakes his head in annoyance. "It's only your wild imagination. Ghosts don't exist."

Martin notices Žofré's fat face shining with an ironic smile.

"What if I swear to you that he is sitting there?" Junec insists, pointing his finger at a chair which, to Hruškovič's eyes, is vacant. "Really: no kidding!" he adds and grabs Hruškovič's hand.

The healer carefully frees his hand. "You must be tired and over-worked, old man," he says. "No wonder, with all your success!"

Martin eyes Žofré with despair. The ghost of his former brother-in-law ironically nods at him, the raised middle finger of his right hand makes a vulgar gesture of ridicule at him, and he dissolves in the air.

Provoked, Junec leaps from his chair with a furious clatter, panting heavily. His glass of vodka spills and the stain from the spirit quickly crosses the white table towards the green ashtray. The American's eyes are goggling and the veins on his temples swell with a rush of blood. "Damn son of a bitch!" he angrily hisses and steps towards the spot where Žofré was sitting a moment ago.

Hruškovič grabs him, calms him and turns round to see if anyone else has noticed the incident. Luckily, *Konzum* is half empty and everyone else is in the front room. "You've got to help me!" Martin says when he calms down. "You've got to help me get rid of that son of a bitch."

Hruškovič promises Martin to do so, just to get Martin off his back.

"When?" the American asks urgently.

"Some time this week," says Hruškovič reluctantly. He won't try and back out any more. If his old mate thinks it can do anything for him, then he can have it the way he wants.

* * *

All next day Martin spends running round government offices, getting the necessary permits. He is looking forward to the evening. He's got everything arranged. After dinner, Martin Junec and his new acquaintance will go dancing somewhere. He'll get her a little tipsy, when they dance he'll work her over, and then he'll invite her to his suite for a glass of bubbly. Then he'll shag her. He's a man. He needs a woman. His girl friend is a long way away; she'll never find out a thing. Anyway, in Martin Junec's opinion, infidelity isn't such a big sin.

At a quarter to eight, Martin turns up in the restaurant. The headwaiter has been warned: he takes Martin to the table he reserved.

"What shall I bring you to drink?" he asks obligingly.

"Well, maybe a dry Martini. With an olive, please," says Martin.

It's not long before Silvia appears. She's wearing a sparkling mini dress, black seamed stockings and dark violet shoes with silver heels, the highest that Martin has ever seen. She is dazzling. As she strides, accompanied by the headwaiter to the table, Martin appreciates that even on high heels she walks quite naturally and gracefully.

Martin rises and takes the hand she offers. He lifts it to his mouth and brushes it with his lips. Then he helps her to her chair.

"What will you drink?" he asks.

"I'll have a Becher," Silvia says.

"One Becher, please," Martin tells the waiter as if he is translating from a foreign language.

The atmosphere at dinner is friendly. Martin tells Silvia what brought him back to the old country. Of course, he doesn't say a word about Žofré's ghost. Silvia, in turn, tells Martin that she's made some money in Austria (how, she keeps to herself), that she'd like to invest in a business (what business, she keeps quiet about). Martin orders *bœuf Stroganoff* with chips and tartar sauce; Silvia chooses a mixed salad. Instead of a dessert, Martin orders a glass of Courvoisier, and Silvia has a chilled bunch of grapes.

"We have excellent champagne," says the waiter in a conspiratorial voice. "French," he adds significantly, as if he'd been told to say so.

"What make?" Martin asks, always eager to drink the very best.

"Veuve Cliquot," says the waiter proudly, "Dom Perignon, Moët & Chandon, Marmot and Monnet…"

"Let's have a bottle of Marmot," Martin orders. "But well chilled."

"Yes, sir." The waiter bows and leaves.

Soon a dew-covered bottle of champagne comes on a silver tray. It is brought by the man who introduced himself yesterday as the owner of the hotel, Rácz. He's smiling amiably.

Silvia is shocked: in all the time of their intimacy she has seen him smile only once or twice.

"So," says Rácz, "I've brought you the best French champagne we have in our cellar. Rácz never talks hot air. We had none yesterday; today we carry five brands. We don't do things by halves."

Rácz puts the tray on the table and shows Martin the champagne.

"I may join you for a moment," he says without a question mark at the end of the sentence.

Silvia and Martin have to agree. Martin points Rácz to a vacant chair. Rácz joins them and loudly claps his hands twice. A waiter carrying three glasses appears from behind the curtain.

"Naturally, this is on Rácz's tab," says Rácz, looking at Silvia. "You are Rácz's guests," he adds: it sounds more like an order than an invitation.

The waiter takes out a special tool to uncork the champagne. He first scrapes the top of the cork, and then loosens the wire. The champagne unexpectedly expels the cork and a jet of foam splashes all over Silvia's sparkling mini-dress. "Oh, I'm sorry," stutters the waiter.

Rácz gets up, clenches his fist and, before Silvia and Martin can react, floors the waiter, who is taller by two heads, with a blow to the chin; the bottle of champagne also hits the ground. "What are you doing, you idiot?" he shouts at the prostrate stunned wretch. But Rácz quickly gathers his wits, puts a hand in his pocket, takes out his wallet, removes a few thousand-crown notes, crumples them and throws them at the waiter.

"Spend that on the dentist, Uličný!" he says, rubbing his fist. "You'll never make a decent waiter. Consider yourself fired."

While the trembling waiter picks the banknotes off the floor, Rácz turns to the table.

"Please excuse my temper," he says, smiling politely. "But this is the only way to treat them. Finding good staff today is almost impossible."

Rácz looks at Silvia.

"Your dress is wet, Silvia," he says. "You should go and change."

"What into?" says Silvia who doesn't know if she is more shocked by being drenched in champagne, or by Rácz's intervention.

"I've got some of your dresses in the wardrobe in my office," the hotelier says. "I haven't throw them out..."

"They are as old as the last government and just as unfashionable," says Silvia, more for Junec's hearing.

"That doesn't matter now," Rácz replies. "The point is they're dry."

Actually, Silvia feels uncomfortable in wet clothes, so she gives Junec an enquiring look, as if waiting for him to accept or reject Rácz's proposal. Martin is surprised at being given so much authority so quickly, but ends up nodding silently: Silvia follows a female waiter to the hotelier's office.

Meanwhile, another waiter brings a new bottle of champagne. Rácz takes it from his hands and deftly opens it himself. He pours two glasses.

"By the way, my name is Rácz," he says to Martin. "Hotelier Rácz."

"Junec," says Junec. "Martin Junec."

"American?" Rácz asks with attention. "You speak Slovak too well to be an American."

"I'm from here," says Junec, "But I've spent a long time in America."

"And Silvia is your significant other?" Rácz asks. "Is she?"

"Why do you ask?" Martin asks evasively.

"Well, because it would be funny," says Rácz. "I used to screw her years ago. I stayed in the same suite as you do."

"How do you know which room I'm in?" Junec asks.

"What a question!" exclaims Rácz. "This is all my territory. Rácz likes to keep himself informed. There used to be people who didn't... but... you know what I mean."

Rácz runs his hand over his throat, throws his head back and shuts his eyes.

Martin nods to show he understands.

"I took her off the streets," Rácz continues, "and made her my mistress. She didn't have to look for punters on the street any more, you see? But then she treated me like shit. You don't do that to Rácz twice. I threw her out so fast she flew like greased lightning."

Rácz takes a sip of champagne, refills his glass and Martin's, too.

"Why don't you say something?" he asks.

"What can I say?" Junec asks, and steals a glance at his watch.

"You might be interested why I'm telling you this," says Rácz.

"Then why are you?" Junec asks, pretending to be bored.

"Just because," says Rácz. "When I kicked her out, I thought that I'd forget about her. I got married and my wife's given me a nice healthy son. I bought this hotel and a few other businesses. I dabbled in politics, too. I have my people everywhere: in the government, in parliament. Do you know what she's been doing since then?"

"No," says Martin.

"She went to Austria," says Rácz "and worked in a brothel. But not an ordinary one, with ordinary fucking, you know. She worked in a special one, where all they get up to all sorts of filthy tricks." Rácz can't even imagine the filthy things that go on over there.

Hotelier fixes his immovable, stern, steel-blue gaze on Junec.

"She's come back now," he says. "She wants to start the same filth in a brothel here. Look, Rácz is no saint, either. But I do go to church from time to time. But her? She doesn't respect anything. Not children, not animals. And she acts the fine lady here. But when I saw her here, I knew that it's still not over between us. I saw it in her eyes, too."

"So what am I supposed to do now?" Martin asks.

"If you want a woman to sleep with," says Rácz, "I'll get you the best-looking crumpet in town. But don't touch Silvia. Rácz is interested in her."

"And is she interested in Rácz?" asks Junec.

"You leave that to Rácz," says Rácz. "Now I'll have to break her a bit, but in the end they all give in."

Rácz has clenched his fists, and his dark gaze is trained on Junec.

"Take my advice and drop her," he says. "And if you listen to my advice, you'll find that Rácz can be grateful."

Martin is bewildered. On the one hand, he finds the hotelier's proposals insulting; on the other hand, he's not all that interested in

Silvia, particularly now that Rácz has told him a few things about her past. Rácz interprets Junec's silence as hesitation, or even defiance.

"You see," he says. "Silvia used to be my mistress and basically she still is. All she ever did was done just shit on me. But I gave her as good as I got, too. We suit each other. All that's between her and Rácz. So keep out of it. But Rácz can make it worth your while. I'm offering you my help."

Martin has a drink and takes a look at his watch. Silvia seems to have been gone too long.

"Maybe you're wondering how Rácz could help you," says Rácz, and gives a muted clap with his hands: from behind the curtain comes a waiter with another bottle of vintage French champagne. Rácz insists on opening it and pours it out.

"I like good food," hotelier admits, "and I don't say no to good drink either. I've become rather fond of whisky. The most expensive and best tasting one: *Heevash Reygahl*. Good champagne isn't bad either."

Martin absent-mindedly nods; his mind is on something else.

"I know what brought you here," Rácz goes back to the previous topic. "But if you keep running round government offices, you'll get fuck-all. The door you have to knock at to ask for a meeting is the one where Rácz is drinking cognac. Why are you looking at me like that? Rácz has his sources. Some time ago I happened to buy a big lot with factory floors, in the middle of the port area. Ideal for you. You'd make your lamps and you'd ship them by Danube direct to Austria and Germany. If you like, we could do a deal. As partners. We'll set up a limited company. I'll put in my land and buildings and you your technology and know-how. What do you say?"

Rácz is getting fidgety.

"If you go it alone, you'll end up as fucked as Poland in 1939, I'm telling you," he says menacingly. "You don't know anyone here, you don't know how to go about it. This isn't America. For example, how are you going to get your debtors to pay? Well? Take them to court? Well, in that case, kiss your money good-bye! And when you get your money, *if* you ever see it, with our inflation, you can only use it to paper your toilet. I have a special firm to collect debts. My own company, Rácz's."

Rácz pauses, takes a sip and loosens his tie. He unbuttons his shirt collar as well.

"Another thing is how well you know our commercial law system. I bet you don't. And I pay — royally — three commercial lawyers who do nothing but look for loopholes in our laws, so that Rácz can walk through them. Nobody will ever screw Rácz!"

Rácz taps his low, bumpy forehead. He takes an aluminium case from his elegant beige jacket pocket, extracts a cigar, bites off one end and lights up.

"We have a lot in common," he flatters Junec. "We both started with nothing. Both of us right here, in the Ambassador: you were a musician, I was a stoker. And we've both made it all the way to the top. So let's join forces. If you like, come to my office tomorrow and we can discuss everything with my lawyer. If we come to an agreement, we'll begin straight away by getting the paperwork over with."

Rácz finishes his champagne and puffs his cigar.

"I think," he says and his eyes turn dark, "that Rácz isn't under-paying you for keeping your hands off his mistress."

Martin nods.

"Well," he says, "it's a lot. But I suppose that you'd offer me this much, anyway, what do you say?"

"Yes," Rácz admits. "I'd have spoken to you even if you weren't seeing my mistress."

"I was thinking," says Martin, "that you'd speak to me even if I don't keep my hands off your mistress, as you put it."

"I can't say if I'd speak to you," says Rácz, "more likely you'd wake up one morning without those hands."

Rácz smiles and Junec silently nods, as if he expected the reply and had been forewarned.

"Well," he says finally. "Tomorrow morning at ten I'll come and see you." He raises his hand to summon the waiter, but Rácz pulls it down.

"Forget about paying," he says. "Today you've been Rácz's guest. It's on the company account. See you tomorrow!"

Martin bows and leaves the restaurant. He doesn't know whether to feel like a beaten dog, or a winner.

Meanwhile, Rácz, cigar in mouth, crosses the restaurant and takes a key to his office from a female waiter. At the entrance to the kitchen he meets the waiter whom he knocked down and sacked shortly before.

"Good work, Uličný," says the hotelier, puts a rolled up banknote in the man's breast pocket and sticks his smoking Havana into his mouth.

"I'm pleased with you!" Rácz says. "I hope I didn't hurt you," he adds with concern and gives his cheek a rough pat.

"I wouldn't like to get fucking knocked down by you every day, boss," says Uličný, blending politeness with a show of male solidarity, and takes a puff from the hotelier's cigar.

"You know, Rácz never does anything by halves," replies the hotelier, who is in a good mood. "Learn that and world is yours."

When Rácz unlocks his office, a furious Silvia hurls herself at him and starts to punch him in his face and chest, although her fists still hurt from battering the leather-upholstered door.

"What's all this supposed to mean?" screams the hooker, gasping for breath, as she tries to punish the hotelier with her enraged punches. "The bloody cheek! You've locked me in here as if I was…"

Effortlessly, Rácz pushes her off, and his immovable metallic eyes dwell lovingly on the dry dress that she has changed into.

"See, it still fits you…" he says, referring to the dress. "You still look good, by God! I knew you'd be back…"

Rácz closes in on Silvia and opens his arms to her.

"Don't touch me, you swine!" Silvia shouts in panic, backing against the desk. Rácz flings himself at her, but Silvia eludes his grip.

"Why are you playing hard to get?" says Rácz in a rasping voice. "In Austria you even fucked ponies and God knows what else, and now you won't spread your legs for Rácz?"

He lurches at her again, and this time he manages to grab her and turn her so she has her back to him. Rácz's weight tumbles Silvia onto the desk. In her panic she finds an ivory letter knife and stabs at random over her shoulder. The knife penetrates Rácz's biceps, which he is using to press her against him. Rácz's eyes pop and he shouts in pain. He doesn't loosen his grip, but he slaps her face hard from behind. In one sweep, he rips her dress from top to bottom. He pulls off her knickers, gripping her neck with his other hand and pushing her against the desk. Then he opens his fly and his erect member is exposed. When Silvia feels his glans brushing her inner thigh, she twists her head in distress and opens her mouth to yell. Rácz's giant manicured hand gags her just in time.

"You'd have screwed that Yank right away, wouldn't you?" gasps Rácz, panting after an exhausting battle. "It's only with Rácz that you play hard to get, don't you? You think Rácz is dirt, don't you? Rácz can be a hotelier a hundred times over, a thousand times over, a million times over, but to you he'll always be that dirty stoker, won't he?"

He thrusts his flanks and, from behind, he pushes his member between her legs and presses it deeper and deeper in.

Silvia's contempt for his passion has enraged him. He comes from a family of simple, rich, but miserly parents. Everything grown in the orchard, or raised in the stalls, was sold. Rácz first ate eggs when he visited his Uncle Endre. Rácz's parents sold all their eggs, milk, butter, and fruit in the market. They themselves ate only dry black bread and drank coffee made from roasted acorn flour. That's how they brought up Rácz and his brother. (Soon afterwards, the brother fell under a train while drunk.) When Rácz wanted to butter his bread, he had to do it secretly, without them knowing. Ever since, he had the habit of eating his bread with the buttered side down. Even at working breakfasts with the president of the country, or the prime minister, members of the cabinet or of parliament. His parents later choked on money. But Rácz is as good as anyone else. He too wants love.

Violated, Silvia still tries to avoid the alien body penetrating her genitals, but her belly is forced onto the desk's hard surface. There's no question of an evasive manœuvre to one side or downwards: Rácz's stocky body has completely immobilised her.

"But I know," Rácz says, once he's inside her. "I know you only came back because of Rácz. You just don't want to admit it."

Silvia summons all her strength and bites Rácz's hand, which is over her mouth. Rácz goes white with pain, but goes on moving inside her. His other hand twists her jaw to free his hand. Again, he slaps her face. He grabs her shoulders and holds her tighter, so that she can't wriggle at his ferocious thrusts.

Silvia has lost all her will to resist. Like a big rag doll, pushed onto the desk, her legs spread, she yields her crotch to the hotelier's ravages.

Finally, Rácz is finished. His face freezes for a second. With a sigh of relief, he withdraws his member from her. His mighty spray wets her buttocks and the papers strewn over his huge desk. He pulls the bloodied knife from his biceps, throws it on the desk and goes to the drinks trolley to mix two drinks.

Silvia's eyes are open. They slowly roam the walls of Rácz's office. After all, she is a former whore. She won't let this sort of thing get to her. She gets up and silently heads for the bathroom. First, she bends over the lavatory bowl and vomits. Then, she throws off what's left of her clothes and steps into the shower cubicle.

Rácz goes to the sink and washes the blood off his shoulder and bitten hand; then he stands in the door, watching Silvia shower. When she's finished, he is waiting for her, a big soft towel in his hands.

"You'll be fine with Rácz," says hotelier. He'll buy her the most expensive gifts: dresses, shoes, fur coats, and jewellery. He doesn't ask for anything in return; she only has to be a little bit nice, and let him sleep with her. His wife is very pretty, too, but she's been no use recently. He gets a good erection all right, but she's not in the mood. She can't do it. After having a baby, it hurts. It's supposed to be a kind of kynological problem. But Rácz needs it every day. Sometimes two or three times a day. He wants to have a good girl friend, so he doesn't have to pester his wife, until she gets over her problems.

Silvia dries herself silently.

"Rácz," says Rácz "will let Silvia get on with her business. That's fine. Even though it involves filthy goings-on that turn his stomach. That's fine. He only wants her as his girl friend. Like her, he's short of time. He's not going to interfere in her life or her business. She should think about it. He could have ten mistresses for each finger, but he only wants her. And he doesn't mind her stabbing him in the arm, though she's ruined an expensive jacket! If he had to shit his pants every time he got hurt in his life, his name wouldn't be Rácz."

Rácz takes Silvia's wet towel, smells it and nonchalantly drops it on the floor. He gives Silvia a cocktail in a glass.

"You certainly won't be any worse off," he says. "You know Rácz has always been very generous. So what do you say?"

Silvia takes the glass, looks into it, revolves it a few times and then splashes the contents in Rácz's face. Naked, proud and beautiful, she walks past the stunned hotelier, puts her court shoes on her bare feet, opens the wardrobe, takes out her old elastic knitted mini dress and pulls it over her naked body.

Rácz wipes his face on a handkerchief. He has been hit in the eye by an ice cube, and it hurts; the eye has started to swell. Only now does his rage slowly begin to burn: first she stuck a knife in his shoulder, then she bit his hand, and now an ice cube in his eye, too? Who does that bitch think she is, actually?

"What do you think you are, bitch?" he roars at her. He clenches his monstrous fists .

"You're a son of a bitch," Silvia hisses and before an enraged Rácz can get her, she slips out of the office.

Rácz hurries down the stairs after her. But despite her high heels, Silvia runs faster than the stout hotelier.

"Catch her! Catch her!" Rácz yells in the lobby. The receptionist and his assistant fly after her across the slippery marble floor. But she slips away from them, brakes sharply for the revolving door, and dashes out into the street.

Rácz pursues her through the glass door, but Silvia is by now in a moving taxi, making an obscene gesture at him through the rear window.

"I'll get you anyway," Rácz says. He turns round and slowly goes back to the hotel to get his arm and eye seen to.

Rácz is a gambler, he tells himself. He can take a loss. Sooner or later, he will turn it into a triumphal victory. This is how it's always been and this is how it will continue to be, too.

At the very least I shagged her good and hard, he thinks, while his old maid of a secretary bandages his stabbed shoulder and puts a plaster on his hand.

* * *

Lady is getting worse and worse every day. A fever is burning her up; her lips are dry and cracked. She has stopped eating; her entire body has shrunk and became translucent. Her eyes have sunk deep into her face and her hair has lost its gloss. She has trouble breathing and has occasional spastic coughing attacks. The change is so sudden that it scares everyone involved.

The boiler-room hovel that Feri and Eržika have rented for an extortionate sum from Berki and Šípoš often looks like a hospital.

Feri Bartaloš would prefer to take Lady to the police, as he originally planned. Now, however, he is afraid that Lady will tell the police all about what they've done to her. The quandary is driving him to despair; he realizes that if Eržika had listened to him then, they would have peace and quiet. But they would have no savings.

The swelling on Lady's broken nose has gone down, but there are still two dark blue bruises under her eyes. Her broken rib has healed too, apparently. Nevertheless, almost nobody is interested in sex with Lady; they're all beginning to find her repulsive. No man is excited by her coughing, her quiet moans of pain and her torpid face's ravaged features.

Only a few steady customers still come to her, among them the killer Fraňo Fčilek who broke Lady's nose and rib. Eržika can't bar him, since he has prepaid twenty sessions and claims them regularly. He is one of the few customers still faithful to her. Before the customers arrive, Eržika tries to improve Lady's pathetic looks, so as not to horrify them. Lady lies apathetically on the filthy bed, and lets them do whatever they want. Eržika covers all the bruises on her face and body by plastering them with a thick layer of make-up, then she puts lipstick on her lips, glues on false eyelashes and finally makes up her eyes. All the while, she talks to her gently as to a baby, but Lady doesn't react. Finally, she proudly shows Feri the result of her work: what does he think of it? Good, isn't it? She looks like a Barbie doll. But Feri is now disgusted and a little bit afraid. His sober and realistic eyes can see Lady's steady deterioration, and he is less self-interested than his wife. Maybe Eržika doesn't realize it, but he knows that both he and Eržika now have one foot in jail. Eržika only shakes her head. They haven't done anything wrong. They took care of Lady and are helping her out. Besides, Eržika is pregnant and can't be jailed

Lady goes on coughing even when Fraňo Fčilek or any of the few faithful beer-drinking customers gets on top of her. She is utterly helpless. Eržika has to feed her with a spoon. She can't even go to the lavatory by herself. Eržika has to take her. Lady has trouble walking, her long thin legs, covered in bruises, collapse under her as she stumbles.

Feri is sitting at a table with the two gypsy stokers. They play cards for money: Piggybank the skinflint can only look on. From the hovel comes the sound of an aroused Fraňo Fčilek, their last customer, whose heavy breathing is drowned out by Lady's heavy continuous coughing. Feri screws up his eyes to assess what his hand is worth and says: "Another card." He wonders if he shouldn't after all take Lady at night to the hospital round the corner. He would only have to ring the bell and then run for it, leaving her on the stairs. But when he realises the things she might tell them about her stay with Feri and Eržika, he quickly changes his mind. He looks at the gypsies, but they don't react to Lady's cough. They don't care; they peer at their greasy, well-used cards. For them, she's just a *gadjo* cunt; she can croak, for all they care. Berki and Šípoš make their money and don't care about anything else. Let the *gadjos* do what they like to their women, they can even kill them; what interest is it to them, they're good gypsies.

"The whole bank!" yells Bartaloš and taps his cards with his nails.

Berki keeps the bank; he slips Feri another card. Šípoš smiles, he passes. Feri takes the card, hides it behind the ones in his hand and slowly uncovers it. You can feel the tension, as they say. Water drips regularly from some joint, and the hot water boiler roars monotonously. From the hovel comes the sound of a squeaking bed and intercourse. Feri's face is bland, but his eyes shine with contentment. "Thanks, I'm fine," he says, and takes one more look at his cards as if trying to make sure for the last time that his eyes aren't deceiving him. The gypsy holding the bank begins to show his hand. He first turns over the first card, the jack of clubs. He adds a jack of spades to it: four. Then queen of hearts: seven. He adds seven of spades: fourteen. Berki licks his finger to gain time and prolong Feri's torment.

"A seven of diamonds: twenty-one," says Berki. Feri silently throws down his cards.

The banker right away tries to add up the cash in the bank. "Two thousand eight hundred and forty crowns," he reports. Bartaloš doesn't have that kind of money to hand. He pays some of it from the till, but has to get the rest from the savings bank. When he wins it back, he will put back all the money in their joint savings account.

Soon Feri comes back with the money. He puts the money he lost in the bank, but since he's taken out more, just in case, they go on with the game. Fraňo Fčilek is still tormenting Lady; he prolongs his pleasure like a gourmet, to make it last as long as possible.

After a few insignificant games, Feri gets a seven of diamonds, a trick card. He sees it as a good omen and goes for the bank. He gets a ten, so altogether he has twenty-one. A feeling of happiness comes over his soul. He will be able to put back at least a fraction of the money into Feri's and Eržika's account. He stacks his cards in his palm and calmly observes the game developing. Berki, the banker, follows him. His first card is an ace of spades and the second is an ace of diamonds. A golden hand! Feri has to run to the savings bank again.

He returns and pays off his debt; his hands are trembling like an old man's. They go on gambling, but not for long. In the next round, Šípoš challenges the bank and has twenty in his hand; the banker has only nineteen. The banknotes and coins pass to the gypsy's wallet. Feri rages inwardly; he is so angry he could cry.

Fraňo Fčilek is by now satisfied; he's finished with Lady and is leaving. Feri asks Freddy to get Eržika: Lady needs to be washed.

Eržika comes to the boiler-room and enters the hovel. She goes up to Lady. Lady looking at her indifferently; she doesn't cough. Her white teeth seem dry in her half-open mouth. One of her artificial eyelashes has peeled off and hangs from a corner of her eye. Her shrivelled breasts and flat sunken belly are covered by a few cooling shots of Fčilek's semen.

"So how goes it, Lady?" Eržika asks. "Was it good?"

Lady doesn't react. Eržika takes a closer look. She notices that Lady's enfeebled chest is not moving. Eržika places her hand below the left breast, trying to feel her heart beat. But the heart is silent. "FERI!" screams Eržika in panic, wiping her hand on her apron.

Feri throws the cards down on the rough table and runs into the hovel. Freddy Piggybank follows him. Eržika is standing terrified, frozen over Lady's corpse. Her eyes shed genuine tears. She turns to Feri. It is as if her best friend has died. Feri instantly understands everything. He quietly draws Eržika to himself.

Freddy looks at the dead woman with interest. He wonders if Fčilek had sex with her while she was alive, or if his pleasure was achieved on a cadaver. This sends him into a daydream. He is trying to imagine what it would feel like to do it with a dead woman. A woman in that state would not laugh at him for having such a small penis.

* * *

Fraňo Fčilek is collecting beer glasses at The Hunter's Inn. When Feri comes and grabs him by his collar, he lets himself be dragged into a storage room. "Have you gone cwazy, Fewi?" he explodes when he hears what Feri's accusing him of. He wriggles free of Feri's clutches: "I scwewed her as usual," he says. "And then she suddenly stopped bweething. Maybe she came. I'm no murdewer!"

Proud Feri Bartaloš sits down: he's had it.

"So she's dead, is she?" asks Fčilek with concern. "So I won't be scwewing her any more. Too bad. But of course," he adds, "I'm not a gwass, I'll keep as quiet as the gwave. But you owe me the money for six scwews; that makes six hundwed cwowns."

Feri tells Fčilek that if he ever opens his big mouth, then he'll be jailed too: he was Lady's last customer. The killer nods. He understands perfectly. But when will Feri give him back his six hundred crowns?

When Feri gets back to the boiler-room, the question arises of what to do with Lady. Eržika suggests that Feri should carry her at night to the *Two Lions* police station and leave her there on the steps.

"You bloody cunt!" rages Feri. "You stupid cunt! What if they start looking for her? They've already been; they called on Piggybank." And you can be sure they'll get round to us, too!" In Feri's opinion the body has to disappear. But how? Feri sits down and props his chin on his hand.

The bewildered gypsies reject proud Feri Bartaloš's suggestion. They register their disagreement by throwing up their hands and their panicky eyes turn into balls in their olive faces. "Can't be done! Can't be done! Not that!" They're good gypsies and won't have it. If they burned the *gadjo* cunt in the furnace, her spirit would stay here forever and haunt them, they're good gypsies who have wives and children, hungry mouths to feed, and they're afraid. Šípoš's lower jaw is quivering and Berki's face seems to be drained of blood. Both shake their heads in refusal, waving the apparent danger away with their arms. Let the *dilino gadjo*, the stupid white man, take the dead *gadjo* cunt's body away with him; they're good gypsies and won't have anything to do with it.

Only a few people go to the secret funeral in the depth of night: Erži-ka, Feri, Freddy Piggybank, Fraňo Fčilek, and a few of Lady's admirers. Lady's body is in a black plastic bag mounted on a metal frame, which serves as a rubbish skip in the Wooden Village. An open skip waits for its booty. They are all silent, looking round to check that no police car is about. Eržika grabs Feri's forearm and trembles as she cries. Fčilek and Piggybank lift up the bag with Lady in it, after Feri gives a silent sign, more a plea than a command. Soon Lady rests on a layer of used plastic trays, cups, old bones, rotten fruit, cans and paper. One by one, the funeral attendants go up to the container, and each one dumps their rubbish over her. Soon the corpse is totally covered. The dustmen will come in the morning and empty the skip. All that will remain of Lady will be a memory. The silence of those present is broken only by Eržika's plaintive cry. Feri, stony-faced, taut-lipped, pats her hand; he understands Eržika's grief. They had both got used to her. The silence almost begs to be broken, but no one wants to say anything. Fraňo Fčilek would like to remind them of his six hundred crowns, but he bites his tongue.

When the dustcart comes, two strong men in overalls and quilted belted jackets dump the contents of the container into its craw, and not a trace will be left of Lady.

* * *

Silvia feels a terrible hatred for Rácz and every other man. She badly wants to avenge herself. She has no time to think about it, however, as soon, one nice Friday, she is opening her perverts' centre Justine. Of course, no mention of it will be found in the daily papers, but this is an important event for the European world of erotic deviants and the pornographic branch of the perversion world.

The two-storey villa that Silvia has bought and adapted, using the money she saved up in Austria, looks impressive; it resembles a comfortable guesthouse. The working area is the ground floor and first floor; Silvia has a comfortable and quite large apartment in the attic.

A few big names in the erotica trade accept invitations to the opening party. For example, the editors-in-chief of the Danish magazines *Pre-*

Teen Sex and *Animal Bizarre*, who are hoping that Silvia's company will help them to find new, cheap models, previously unexposed, for their magazines. After some hesitation, Silvia has finally decided to include among her guests her former boss from Austria, Herr Haslauer and his wife. The new staff of Silvia's company, who only yesterday were on the streets around the Ambassador, are also at the party. Some arrive with friends and husbands. Silvia has understandably chosen for her company only hookers who live an orderly life: married ones and those who live without causing any disturbance. Sexual perverts are very shy people and Silvia will try to create a private club atmosphere where no one is shocked by anything and where any bizarre sexual proclivities will be understood and channelled discreetly and safely. So she needs reliable, intelligent, long-standing employees. The party proves to Silvia that she has got the staff she needs. She can rest content.

Part of the evening's celebrations is a tour of the *Perverts' Centre*. The expert visitors, professionals in deviant sex, appreciate the building's generously designed interiors, the well-equipped cosy torture chambers for sado-masochist sessions, the large bathrooms for water sports and, in the basement, a small theatre stage for a perverse live-sex show and other special events. Also of interest is a tastefully equipped bar stocked with high quality drinks and a projection screen for video films. In a nutshell, Silvia, as they say, has dipped deep into her pocket.

The evening stretches into early hours. A weekend break follows, and on Monday at five in the evening, the city's erotic map is lit up by a new sign: *Private Club Justine*, and later, in the darkness of the night, a neon sign comes on, showing a girl in black stockings wielding a whip.

* * *

A few weeks pass, and Eržika gives birth. Her birth pangs come in the Wooden Village, just as she is lifting a glass of beer to her mouth. She freezes as if paralysed, her eyes pop and she shouts to let Feri know. At the time he is queuing for two portions of grilled chicken, and doesn't want to lose his place: there are only two people ahead of him. Eržika's insistent shout drags him from the snack bar. The asphalt pavement beneath Eržika's bench turns wet in an instant; her waters have broken.

Four-Eyes is on duty: he stands in his white coat in the middle of the Wooden Village. Eržika's insistent shouts wake him out of his lethargy. In the tiny cranium behind the dark glasses connections are made and he starts running to the lavatories to get his wife. Never mind about the past: this time it's serious.

Four-Eyes's wife runs in and she instantly takes it all in. She grabs Eržika by the hand, helps her to her feet and leads her off. "Why are you standing there like a statue?" she goes for her husband. Four-Eyes holds Eržika up on the other side. Feri runs to the snack bar to phone for an ambulance. Four-Eyes's wife looks round. "Let's go," she orders.

Freddy Piggybank is standing calmly in the shade of his trailer, smiling concupiscently as he watches the haughty long-legged beauties cruising outside the Ambassador. He has no work after Lady's death, so he just lounges about. Thanks to his meanness, he has some savings, so he isn't starving. He still has his trailer, so he has a place to lay his head. He enjoys all the benefits of a homeless person who has a home.

When Four-Eyes and his wife come, holding up a writhing and moaning Eržika, and demand to be let into his trailer, he does not like it.

"I cleaned it up last Saturday," he says angrily and bars the trio from entering his den.

With surprising strength, Four-Eyes shoves him aside, and all three squeeze into the trailer. "What the…!" Freddy takes offence, but cowardice stops him from responding to Four-Eyes's shove. Taken aback, he squints into his trailer. Eržika is lying on his grimy bed and Four-Eyes's wife is pulling off her wet tracksuit bottoms. Freddy takes a breath; he is about to swear: not long ago, when Lady was about, someone pissed in the corner of his trailer, and now this. But he is quiet, as the sight of Eržika's bleeding genitals, from which Four-Eyes pulls out a chunk of bloodied meat looking like lungs, keeps him interested. Eržika's moaning and the bloodied hands of the old woman busy round the wide-open genitals even awaken mild excitement in Freddy.

Feri Bartaloš, breathing hard, pushes him away from the door. "The ambulance number is still engaged," he tells the old woman. Four-Eyes's wife sends him to the snack bar for a jug of boiling water.

While the water is boiling, the baby is born. It's a girl. She's all wrinkled and cries with a piercing voice. Eržika, tired and sweaty, smiles happily, and proudly holds the baby in her arms. Soon the boiled water is brought. The baby is washed, wrapped in the layette that Feri and Eržika bought long ago, and put in a pram that one of the stokers brought.

They all swarm round the baby, and even the bastard boss is proud.

Only Freddy Piggybank is pissed off; they've left a filthy mess in the trailer. Full of hatred, he starts to clean up. With disgust, he slides the placenta, abandoned on the floor, onto a shoebox lid, adds to it Eržika's wet tracksuit bottoms and, fighting down his nausea, takes them to the skip. Then he goes to the lavatory to get a bucketful of water and carefully washes his trailer clean of blood, amniotic fluid and other muck left behind. Hatred is eating him up, as it does anyone who feels the whole world enjoying things at their expense.

That is why when, at about ten in the evening, an excited drunken Bartaloš comes and invites him to a small celebration in the Wooden Village, he angrily declines, saying that he has a hard day ahead of him.

* * *

Lady's death has impoverished Feri and Eržika. Reverting to their previous earnings, limited to what they get from the lavatories and from clearing beer glasses, they find it hard, particularly now that they have a child. It is especially hard for Feri. The joint bank account that he and Eržika opened and into which they paid in their hard-earned money every day, has been plundered. Luckily, Eržika knows nothing about it. Feri Bartaloš handles financial affairs; his wife has to do as he tells her. Nevertheless, Feri shudders when he thinks what will happen the day that Eržika finds out that the money is gone.

Feri's immediate aim is to make sure that the money gets back into their account. Feri has no idea how many crowns he has taken out and lost at cards, but he sees clearly that he has to get it all back. To get it means winning it. Feri believes that Berki's and Šípoš's lucky streak must run out sooner or later and that he will start winning.

But if Feri wants to go on gambling, he needs money. If he doesn't have any, the gypsies will gladly lend it to him. "You can pay it back when you win," Berki tells him and Feri is overcome by a wave of ardent gratitude. The probability that he has to win eventually increases when a fourth player, a young, twenty-year-old gypsy in an elegant sports jacket, joins the party. Berki introduces him as his nephew Čonka. "He likes a gamble," he adds. From then on, the games of pontoon are more interesting, but, alas, Feri's luck is no better than before.

* * *

It isn't long before Feri and Eržika decide to have their baby girl christened. They browse through a grubby calendar that Freddy Piggybank had in his trailer and lent them, and look for names. The first name they notice is Nora. Norika. Eržika likes it, but Feri doesn't. Alica seems too simple for both of them. Miriama seems too Jewish. Then Feri's eye falls on the name of Bystrík. He repeats the name in his mind, giving it a female ending: Bystrík, Bystríka, Bystrík, Bystríka.

"And what about calling her Bystríka? Bystríka Bartalošová?" he asks Eržika, but she doesn't like the name at all.

For a while they just sit there, each lost in their thoughts. The beer drinkers walk in and out of the lavatories, buttoning their flies, throwing money into Eržika's bowl. The baby is restless; it's hungry. Eržika sighs and lifts it to her breast. The child begins to sucks hungrily. Feri looks at them silently. On one hand, he feels proud of being a father. He looks at his family with joy. On the other hand, the presence of the child puts him out a bit: the baby at breast occupies all Eržika's mind. She doesn't care about anything but her baby. She skives. She pays no attention, doesn't insist on money from people using the lavatories, and doesn't clean or sweep. Feri is supposed to do all that, but he has no time, either. He is trying to make money at cards. Unfortunately, he hasn't had much luck so far. He's up to his neck in debt. He incurs new debts to pay for the old ones. And it's a vicious circle.

"What was Lady's name?" Eržika suddenly asks.

Feri thinks, but can't recall it.

"I don't know," he says.

"Typical," says Eržika. "She was my only real friend in this bloody city and we don't even know her name."

They sit silently for a while.

"But you had her driver's licence and ID," says Eržika.

"I did," say Feri. "But I threw them out. I only kept the pictures."

Eržika reaches into her bosom and takes out the photograph from Lady's driver's licence. In the picture Lady is smiling: a self-confident young woman.

"You tore out the pictures," says Eržika, "but you didn't bother to look at her name."

"True..." Feri agrees sadly. "I didn't look..."

Feri comes up with the idea of calling their daughter Lady. It takes him a while to confide in Eržika. When he finally tells her, Eržika is quite in favour. "Lady. A nice name."

The registry office people have a different opinion. The woman clerk shakes her head. "Not possible. Can't be done. Here is a book with the list of approved names. Only one of these is permitted. If there were no list of names, people would call their children anything."

Proud Feri Bartaloš is not interested in any list of names. He angrily pushes away the clerk's hand and the book. He has already chosen the name. A nice name: Lady. What do they have against the name? Against Lady? Did they know Lady at all? Then why are they bitching about it?

Eržika gets indignant, too. Is this why they had a revolution? So that somebody could now dictate to Eržika and Feri what name they are allowed or not allowed to give to THEIR daughter? Is this democracy? Is this capitalism?

Feri takes the list of names and leafs through it. "There you are!" he says. "Nineteen eighty seven!" he victoriously points out the pre-revolutionary year the book was published.

The shouting wakes the baby up and she starts to cry.

The clerk is intransigent, though she does waver a bit. She calls on her supervisor for back-up. The supervisor, his powerful glasses shining, listens to the clerk's account of Feri's and Eržika's request and without further consideration shakes his head.

"Not allowed," he says laconically and goes back to his office.

"There, you see," says the clerk. Now that she has shifted the responsibility onto her supervisor, her mood has improved.

Eržika takes a breath and produces her final argument: Eržika and Feri know Mr Rácz very well.

The clerk pauses. "Anyone could say that," she says.

"Anyone?" Eržika goes on the attack. "Anyone? And does anyone have one of these?"

Eržika takes out of her bosom an old photograph, well-thumbed and cracked from being folded, but still quite clear, and hands it to the clerk.

The clerk takes the photograph and looks at it for a moment. Feri is curious and he takes a peek over the clerk's shoulder.

The photograph shows Rácz as a skinny crew-cut conscript in his parade uniform. He looks dignified and gazes rigidly into the upper right corner of the photograph. Underneath is an inscription in a childish hand, in Hungarian; the clerk can decipher only the signature: Rácz.

"What does it say?" she asks with interest.

"Cordial greetings and love from the military swearing-in ceremony to his Eržika, from Rácz," translates Eržika, glancing at Feri out of the corner of her eye and blushing.

"Rácz is our friend," Feri hurries to explain. "We see each other and he often asks me for advice."

The clerk gets up and takes the photograph into the next office.

She is soon back. She wears a friendly smile.

"Well," says the clerk, returning the photograph to Eržika, "you may be right. The list of names dates from the times of so-called totalitarianism; now we have a democracy."

The clerk sits down and takes a pen in her hand.

"How would you like to name your daughter?" she asks.

"Lady," says Eržika. "Lady Bartalošová."

The clerk sighs.

A strong national feeling awakens in Feri.

"But write it down the Hungarian way," he says. "Bartaloš Lady!"

"How?" the clerk is stunned.

"Bartaloš Lady!" Feri repeats menacingly.

The clerk hesitates for a moment, but then Eržika goes for her, shouting about democracy and Feri joins in with his monologue in a monotonous and subdued voice from which words like "minority" and "Feri" surface, like foam from the incoming tide.

The clerk, frightened by the awesome photograph of Rácz as a soldier and by the spouses' raucous voices, concedes defeat and issues the birth certificate.

Bartaloš Lady exists.

* * *

Siegfried Heilig and his wife are on their way back from a holiday at Balaton. It was expensive. It's not that they can't afford it, but they are thrifty and, if they squander money needlessly, it hurts them to the core.

In Bratislava they park by the pavement outside the Hotel Ambassador and check in. The high cost of the rooms takes their breath away: for a twin-bed room with windows looking onto the courtyard they pay almost one fifth, or even a quarter, of what they would have paid for the same room in Germany.

In the room, Mrs. Heilig sniffs the bedspreads with disgust and carefully inspects the state of the bathtub and lavatory bowl.

Siegfried Heilig sits on a bed and sips beer from a can. His blond moustache is wet with bitter-sweet foam. His eyes are dull; this is his second can. Siegfried can't take too much.

As soon as they've unpacked, they go down for supper.

They sit down in the restaurant and study the menu. They leave very upset; the prices are extortionate.

"There's a kind of a snack bar near where we're parked," says Mrs. Heilig to Mr Heilig. "Let's go there. At least we can keep an eye on our car."

The spouses walk past their white VW Golf and, as a precautionary measure, Siegfried Heilig tries all the doors. Then they head for the Wooden Village.

They are too hungry to look with their haughty revulsion at the noisy stokers and the smelly, eternally drunk Majerník; they make straight for the counter and buy a baked trout, marinated peppers and bread rolls. Siegfried Heilig queues for beer and brings two glasses of Bratislava crap beer to the table.

The Heiligs finish the food and chase it down with the liquid laxative. It doesn't take long to have an effect. Mrs Heilig's guts loudly begin to voice their displeasure. She quickly gets up and heads for the lavatory.

Eržika is already waiting there, holding out her bowl and a piece of toilet paper.

"Ein Mark, bitte," says Eržika.

Mrs. Heilig uses the last of her strength to clench both cheeks of her thin German behind and rummages in her purse. Then, armed with the piece of paper, she disappears in the lavatory.

Mrs Heilig soon returns. She feels good. The sudden liberating decrease in the level of toxic products of digestion, together with the inebriating effect of Bratislava's laxative beer, have made her normally grim, desiccated soul suddenly break into a euphoric smile.

Her eyes alight on the baby in the pram next to Eržika. The child has beautiful light blue eyes and blond hair. She smiles like an angel. Mrs Heilig smiles. Somewhere at the back of her brain something moves. Something like a stunted, aborted and impoverished maternal instinct suddenly opens her eyes, takes a breath and comes to life. Mrs Heilig crouches by the child. Her heart skips a beat. The euphoria is gone; only sadness remains.

Mrs Heilig, too, could have had an angel like that. Instead she always had herself dilated and curetted. The little souls of the innocents, five white and one black, have hovered all her life behind her, wherever she goes. Nobody can see them, not even Heilig. Only she knows about them. Occasionally, she wakes up in the night and hears their thin, childlike voices: "Mummy! Mummy!"

Heilig holds little Lady in her hands and tears burst from her eyes.

Eržika is alert, but utterly baffled. She hisses a warning to Feri. Feri comes, his chest puffed out. They both look uncomprehendingly at the gaunt German woman kissing their little daughter.

Siegfried Heilig is on his second liquid laxative. Mrs Heilig joins him and wipes her tears.

"What happened?" Heilig asks.

"Nothing," says Mrs Heilig. "Why do you ask?"

"You're crying," says Heilig.

"Really?" Mrs Heilig says.

"Why are you crying?" Heilig is curious. "Did anything happen?"

"No," Mrs Heilig says. "The lavatory woman has a beautiful baby. I've never in my life seen such a beautiful baby."

"Hmm," says Heilig.

He, too, finds his wife's barrenness hard to cope with.

"A gorgeous little angel," says Heilig.

"Boy or girl?" asks Siegfried Heilig, without any real interest.

"A girl," says Mrs Heilig. "She's got little earrings. Please, get me a cognac."

Heilig sighs and goes to the bar. He quickly comes back with a shot of rum.

Mrs Heilig tosses back the rum and asks for another one. Heilig feels vaguely guilty and goes back to the bar.

"Strange," says Mrs Heilig, after knocking back a second rum, "that the child is so beautiful." She saw her parents; she simply cannot understand how such two puny Dinarian type degenerates could have produced a little angel with decidedly Aryan looks.

"Aryan looks, you say?" Siegfried Heilig asks.

"Go and take a look," Mrs Heilig suggests.

Eržika was puzzled at seeing the gaunt German broomstick again, this time accompanied by her husband. However, Lady in her pram is very happy.

"*Kak zovut yiyo*? What's her name?" Mrs Heilig asks Eržika in Russian.

Eržika, unlike the two East Germans, was never on friendly terms with Soviet soldiers, so she doesn't understand, and shakes her head.

"*Kakoe imya*? What name?" Mrs Heilig asks.

Eržika stares at them.

"A beautiful baby, right?" Mrs Heilig asks her husband longingly.

Siegfried Heilig nods in silence. He, too, imagined his life enhanced by the cheerful laughter of children. Whenever this seemed within reach for him and his wife, they considered their financial resources and Siegfried Heilig sent her to be dilated and curetted, instead. And when they could finally afford it, Mrs Heilig turned out to be infertile.

Heilig turns round. Feri Bartaloš, standing in his white coat midway between the snack bar and the lavatories, is discreetly following them.

Siegfried Heilig felt sharp hatred for the inferior Slavs who can have such a beautiful child whenever they feel like it. This is something stronger than the ordinary racial hatred that Siegfried Heilig feels in his homeland for Russians and similar degenerates. This is the hatred of Heilig's Aryan genes that vainly long to replicate themselves in his wife's Aryan womb. This is hatred felt by sperm desperately wandering for hours through the dark labyrinth of fallopian tubes, looking in vain for the one healthy egg which they could bite through and thus start a new life. Siegfried Heilig looks at Bartaloš and feels humiliated.

Lady calmly lies there, her big blue eyes watching with fascination. Her attention is held by the unusual caressing tones of the strange woman's speech.

"Time we were off," Siegfried Heilig says cautiously to his wife. "Let's go."

They return to the hotel.

Mrs Heilig cries all night.

Next morning, Siegfried Heilig plans an early departure.

"Let's stay at least another day," says Mrs Heilig.

"What for?" Heilig asks, but he knows the answer.

They go to the Wooden Village and have breakfast.

Then they silently walk round the city. Their itinerary circles round the Wooden Village and the angelic baby smiling in its dirty pram.

"If we leave now," Mrs Heilig admits to her husband, "I'll feel as if I've left somebody behind. A piece of myself."

"Are you mad?" Heilig asks good-naturedly, pouring the liquid laxative down his throat.

"Let's have another look at that little girl," Mrs Heilig begs.

It's evening. The neon lights are on. The pavements are full of pedestrians.

Eržika feels out of sorts. Those Germans have been here at least a hundred times today. But Lady just happily stretches her arms out towards the strange lady. The strange lady gives her a present, a plush teddy bear that she bought in the city this afternoon.

"Well, let's go," says Siegfried Heilig and gently but forcefully pushes his wife towards the exit.

Soon they leave Wooden Village and walk towards the hotel.

"You've no idea how unhappy I am," says Mrs Heilig.

Heilig says nothing.

On the pavement, a man in the white coat, the baby's father, runs up to them.

"Hey Herr! Hey Herr!" Feri Bartaloš cries in a muffled voice.

The Heiligs turn around and wait for him.

"*Kaufen Kinder*? Want to buy a kid?" Bartaloš asks them in a whisper. "*Nicht teuer, sehr billig*! Not expensive, very cheap."

The Heiligs look at each other and then at Feri.

"*Meine Kinder kaufen*, buy my child," Feri says. "*Nicht krank, sehr schön kinder. Nur zwei tausend mark! Sehr billig*! Not sick, very beautiful child. Only two thousand marks. *Aber*... But..."

Feri Bartaloš puts a finger over his lips.

"*Zwei tausend*," he repeats. "*Wenn wollen Kinder kaufen, um zehn Stunde hier*. If you want to buy the baby, come here at ten."

Feri shows his wristwatch and points his finger at ten. Then he runs back to the Wooden Village.

The Heiligs are stunned.

"Did you understand him?" asks Siegfried Heilig.

"I think I did," says Mrs Heilig. "Didn't you?"

"I did, too." Heilig says.

They silently pass the façade of the hotel Ambassador.

Heilig gives his wife a close look. Her long silence is getting on his nerves.

"Don't tell me you want to buy that baby!" he blurts out.

Mrs Heilig raises her head and looks at him.

"I'll do anything to have that baby," she says firmly.

"You're stupid," says Heilig. "It's too risky!"

"Risky!" Mrs Heilig says contemptuously. "As soon as I saw the baby, I decided to take it. I knew right away that it was our child. Do you understand? Not theirs, but ours!"

"You're insane!" Heilig says in disgust.

"I don't understand how it could be that our child was born to those two," Mrs Heilig ponders aloud.

"It's not our child," Heilig says.

"Yes, it is," says Mrs Heilig. "Even the baby senses it. It's ours!"

"You need to see a psychiatrist," the husband suggests.

"Pay for the hotel," says Mrs Heilig. "We're leaving right away. At ten, we get our little girl from that man; we'll pay him off, and set off for Prague. Are you listening to me at all?"

Heilig is startled.

"And what's the name of our little girl?" he asks his wife.

"Well, Felicitas, of course," says Mrs Heilig. "Felicitas Heilig."

* * *

Around ten o'clock, Feri sends Eržika to unblock the men's lavatory. When Eržika is out of sight in the lavatory, Bartaloš takes Lady from her pram, taking care that he can't be seen from the snack bar, and hurries to the front of the Ambassador, to the place he indicated to the Germans.

The Heiligs are already waiting for him.

"Bitte!" says proud Feri Bartaloš and hands the child to Mrs Heilig.

Siegfried Heilig motions him to follow them to the car.

The Volkswagen is already loaded and ready to leave. Mrs Heilig takes the baby and sits in the back; Heilig points Feri to the passenger seat; he himself sits in the driver's seat. He takes out his wallet and counts two thousand marks into Bartaloš's trembling hand.

"*Danke schön*," says Feri. "*Viel Glück*, good luck!"

He slides out of the car like a snake.

When he runs into the Wooden Village, Eržika is already pacing up and down, desperately looking for Lady.

"Where is Lady?"

"They kidnapped her!" says Feri says.

"Who?" the horrified Eržika asks.

"Those bloody Germans! I ran after them, but they got in their car and took off."

"What car?" shouts Eržika.

"A white Mercedes," Feri lies.

Without a word, Eržika runs after the policemen who are patrolling outside the Ambassador.

In his pocket Feri feels the four five-hundred-mark banknotes and their silky surface calms him down.

* * *

Needless to say, Lady's kidnappers were never caught.

For some time, it seemed as if the wind had been knocked out of Eržika, but then she got over the loss of her child. Her fickle character reconciled her to the situation, especially as it meant that she had one less thing to worry about.

Proud Feri Bartaloš is broke again; he has lost the lot. The savings account is empty and closed. The money he got from selling Lady was to be used to win everything back. It didn't work. Feri is tearing his hair. He could at least have had a child, now he has shit-all.

The card group has acquired another gypsy, Šípoš's brother. This renewed Feri's optimism and his will to play and win. Šípoš junior seems to have trouble counting up to five. When he plays he sometimes even confuses the jack and the queen. He loses badly. But his brother wins it all. Unfortunately, Feri isn't doing as well as he thought he would. Lately, he's been toying with the idea that the gypsies might be cheating him. He sits in the boiler-room, holding his cards close to his vest and keeping an eagle eye on the other players, Berki, Čonka, and the two Šípoš brothers. No suspicious move could escape him, but the gypsies don't make any suspicious moves. They hardly move at all. When Feri looks at his cards they exchange discreet eye signals.

Eržika now has more work than she can cope with. She is faced not only with the lavatories, but with Feri's work, too. These days he's rarely to be seen in the Wooden Village. He is always off somewhere. "Got to make money," he emphasizes. He wants to take good care of his wife. You can't make any money here in the snack bar. Things have been going from bad to worse for Feri and Eržika ever since Lady died. That's why Feri is looking for new openings.

Eržika says nothing. She's modest, obedient, and hard-working. Because she's working so hard, she has quickly stopped grieving for Lady. The police have got nowhere and the little girl seems lost for good; in any case, Eržika has already got over it.

On Tuesday, Feri and Eržika are off. Feri brings a wooden box from somewhere. He paints it white and leaves it to dry in the boiler-room. He carefully removes from a parked van, a big self-adhesive sign *Algida Ice-Cream* and sticks it on the front of the wooden box.

"What's it going to be, when it's ready?" Freddy Piggybank asks, looking at Feri's enthusiastic efforts.

"Can't you see?" Feri asks. "Ice-cream!"

"What about it?" the fat attendant won't be fobbed off.

"Why don't you bring me your collection bag?" Feri says. "Better, two. Do you have two bags?"

"I do," Piggybank says. He had one for the weekdays and one for holidays.

Remembering the good old days at the car park, Freddy gets soppy and sentimental. The feeling doesn't last long. That's all over; now he has to look ahead. "And what do I get?" he asks Bartaloš.

"A share of the profit," promises Feri.

Piggybank has no more questions; he brings two red leatherette bags from his trailer.

Bartaloš takes off the straps and nails them to the box. Then he tries it on; the *Algida* hangs on his chest like an accordion. "What do you think?" he winks at Piggybank.

"OK," says Freddy. "And what next?"

"I've got a plan," Feri says mysteriously. "But we have to wait until Fraňo Fčilek comes, so that I don't have to explain it twice."

"Is that box part of the plan?" Freddy asks, pointing at it.

"You'll see," Feri Bartaloš laughs.

* * *

On Saturday morning, Feri Bartaloš, Fraňo Fčilek, Freddy Piggybank and Eržika set out from the Wooden Village. From the hotel Ambassador they take a trolley bus to a wooded park outside the city. This is where they separate. Each of them knows what to do. Eržika gets the ice-cream box, slings it over her chest and walks further down the neat criss-crossing paths to the outlying parts of the park.

Feri, Freddy, and Fraňo follow her along a parallel path. Soon Feri signals Eržika with a quiet whistle. Eržika comes to a halt where two paths intersect. Her companions hide in the bushes. Feri presses his finger to his lips: talking strictly forbidden.

Freddy Piggybank is more excited than the others. His path to the lower depths of society will be completed by this act. His longing for a criminal future in order to punish the disgusting city council for beggaring him will soon be satisfied.

Soon they all hear the muffled, but distinct rattling sound of a bicycle approaching. A child on a mountain bike is coming towards Eržika. The mountain bike is big and the child is small: it sits on it like a monkey on an elephant. Feri takes a look at his companions. He gestures to them to get ready.

"Ice-cream for sale, my boy, ice-cream!" Eržika calls to the child from a distance, as Feri has told her. "Delicious Italian ice-cream! Lots of different flavours!"

The little boy stops by Eržika. He takes out a small purse.

"One strawberry cornet, please," he says.

Eržika nervously looks at the bushes behind the child.

The bushes part; Feri, Freddy and Fraňo run out. Fraňo's powerful hands pick the child off his bicycle. Feri grabs the handlebars and hops onto the saddle. For a few seconds he pedals furiously and speeds off. Eržika and her *Algida* box also vanish and Freddy is left alone with the child. His job is to make sure the child they've robbed stays quiet.

"Shut your face!" he bursts out when he sees that the child has now taken in what has happened, is taking a breath and is about to howl.

The child is shocked into silence and submits.

"If you don't stay quiet," says Freddy in a horrid graveyard voice, "I'll poke your eyes out and bury you alive. Nobody will find you here. Give me your purse!"

The child obediently gives the fat man his little purse. Freddy takes a look inside and, disappointed, puts it in his back trouser pocket. His hatred for the child is growing. That snotty little kid already has a mountain bike. When Freddy Piggybank was five or six years older he didn't have a bicycle! No bicycle! Not a town bike, or a mountain bike. That was why he never had any friends. Yes, now Freddy can see the reason why. Nobody had any truck with him, because he was holding them all back. He wasn't mobile. Nobody would give up the pleasure of a swift ride and mobility all around Nová Ves just to keep him company. Only now has Freddy finally found real friends. But first he had to become a criminal. An outcast. Where's the justice?

Tears pour from the child's eyes. He stifles his weeping: fear of this evil and obviously dangerous fat man stops him from crying aloud.

"Now face this tree," Freddy orders him. "Close your eyes and count slowly to two hundred."

The child is too scared to disobey.

"And don't turn round until you get to a hundred!" threatens Piggybank. "Or else I'll torture you to death! Nobody will hear your horrible howling. I've got a cave near here that nobody will ever find. That's where I torture snotty kids like you. Well, start counting!"

The child does as he's told and counts; slowly, on tiptoe, Freddy leaves. Once he's at a safe distance, he turns and runs after his companions.

It's gloomy in the woods under the thick crowns of the old trees. Freddy stops in a clearing. Without thinking, he lifts his head. The trees are beginning to colour up; summer is on the wane. The damp smell of black earth, fungus, and rotting bark and foliage excites his nostrils. The counting child is far away and Freddy feels that he is alone deep in the woods. He can hear voices filtering through the green thicket. His innards are gripped by a pleasant tension. A delightfully arousing feeling of *déjà vu* brushes against his trembling eyelids: he has felt this before. At Devín Lake. Before Freddy can grasp and analyse this sensation, it disperses among the trees.

His former friends didn't give a shit about him. But Bartaloš and Fčilek care. Freddy spots them in the trees and steps up his pace.

"Everything all right?" asks proud Feri, holding the new mountain bike.

"Everything's okay," Freddy confirms: he is overcome by a delirious feeling of rough male comradeship and togetherness.

"Good bicycle, wight?" says Fraňo Fčilek. "In the Wooden Village we can sell it for thwee thousand."

"What? Three?" Bartaloš protests. "We'll get four. That'll make it easy to share it four ways."

"Four?" Fraňo Fčilek is baffled. "Thwee, don't you mean?"

"What do you mean?" Bartaloš laughs and counts on his fingers. Feri Bartaloš makes one. Fraňo Fčilek makes two. Freddy Piggybank makes three. And Eržika makes four.

"Eržika is with you," Fčilek disagrees. "She doesn't count."

Freddy would also like to split the loot three ways, but he is careful to say nothing.

"Eržika takes the same risk as us," Bartaloš says. "Why shouldn't she get her share?"

"Just admit that you want half the takings," says Fraňo Fčilek.

"Suppose I do," proud Feri retorts. "Who came up with the idea? Feri Bartaloš! Stupid Fraňo Fčilek could never think of anything like that."

"Stop bragging," Fčilek responds.

If stupid Fraňo Fčilek, says Feri hadn't murdered Lady, Feri Bartaloš wouldn't have to let his wife Eržika take such a risk.

"You bastard!" Fčilek shouts and throws himself at Feri.

Eržika comes out of the trees with her *Algida* box. As an experienced lavatory attendant, she instinctively sizes up the situation at once. She starts to scream so loudly that the two roosters immediately let go of each other.

Eržika is upset. Just as she thought: the moment they get their loot they start to argue and fight. This isn't going to work. They either stick together, or she will bloody well leave.

Her well chosen words of wisdom fall on fertile ground. Each companion takes a role, according to the tried and tested model, and waits for another prey.

This time there are two boys on BMX bikes. As soon as they stop by the false ice-cream vendor, Feri and Fčilek run out of the thicket, take the bikes from the stunned children, clumsily get on them, and ride away.

Freddy Piggybank holds both boys by their necks. Eržika and her *Algida* disappear in the woods.

"I'll give you a triple scoop!" Freddy shouts angrily and shakes the little gourmands. "I'll give you a triple scoop! Snotty kids with bikes at your age! What if I tied you to a tree and burned you alive? Have you heard of the martyr Jan Hus? Have you?"

The children start to cry. Freddy pushes them towards a gigantic tree and repeats his old trick of making them count to two hundred.

"I'll stay behind you and if you turn round, I'll poke your eyes out with these keys," says Freddy and shows them the keys to his trailer.

The terrified children count in tearful little voices. Freddy listens for a while and then vanishes into the bushes.

The group again meets where they had agreed to.

Proud Feri Bartaloš is pleased. His calm, rich, masterful voice echoes through the woods. His confidence has grown. That was a good idea he came up with.

"We must get one more bicycle, and then we can go home," says Bartaloš. "Everybody take up position! Everybody knows what to do."

In less than an hour, they manage to hijack a fourth bicycle, a racing bike in good condition. Its owner, a youth of twenty, wasn't trapped by the *Algida* box: he passed Eržika without noticing her. That was too much for the killer Fraňo Fčilek; he ran out from the bushes and hit him from behind. The young man collapsed like a sack of potatoes.

"Did you see?" Fčilek points to his fist. "Every blow's a winner," he adds proudly.

"Is he breathing?" Eržika worries, and looks anxiously at the cyclist lying on the ground, his eyes closed.

"Of course he is," says Fčilek. "By the time he comes round we'll be over the hills and far away."

They hide the stunned sports-biker in the bushes. Then they get on their bicycles and head for the city.

Freddy Piggybank is the heaviest of them and gets the mountain bicycle with thick tyres and strong frame. Feri and Eržika are slender and small: they're happy with the BMX bikes. Fraňo Fčilek proudly mounts the racing bike: it's his booty.

They leave the wooded park behind and ride down a steep road into the city. It is a beautiful warm Indian summer's day.

As they go downhill, Freddy Piggybank brakes with the others; the swish of the tyres, the quiet clicking of the free wheel, and the occasional screech of the front brake awakens a strange nostalgia in him. He feels as if he has been through this before. Yet, Freddy realises that he could not have had this experience before; such a feeling of happy fulfilment occurred only in his childhood dreams, at the age when he was trying to assemble a bicycle, tormented by despair that his gang of classmates might escape from him on their bikes forever. Finally Freddy is now experiencing those happy moments in reality, too: a feeling of camaraderie mingling with the intoxication of cycling at speed. These are a few fleeting seconds of real bliss.

When the party is back at the Wooden Village, Feri and Eržika hide the bicycles in the broom closet.

"Who are we going to sell them to?" Piggybank asks Bartaloš.

"I have a man who'll take anything," says Feri. "He comes to the Wooden Village for beer. I'll take a look, he could be here."

"A collector?" Freddy asks.

"No," Feri says, "he has a second-hand shop. He buys anything."

Freddy Piggybank is amazed. That's how he had imagined it. To be a criminal without a twinge of conscience! Let them all see! The whole of society can suffer Freddy's vengeance for his horrible humiliation.

To celebrate his successful fall, he queues for a Montenegro steak.

* * *

A week later Eržika is once more patrolling the wooded park with her *Algida* on her chest. Bartaloš, Piggybank, and Fčilek crouch in the bushes and listen out for the familiar clicking of a bicycle free wheel.

A child comes towards Eržika on a mountain bicycle. He has trouble turning the pedals, since he can barely reach them. His expression is serious, as he's sure that everybody is looking at him. At this precise moment, the child is quite right.

Proud Feri Bartaloš gestures from his hiding place to Eržika.

"Have an ice-cream, young man!" Eržika calls to the child.

The child stops and gets off his bicycle. He turns round, as if he is waiting for someone.

However, Feri and Fraňo have already burst out from the thicket. The child tries to shout, but Fčilek's giant hand has gagged him. Freddy stands nearby; he likes being evil, very evil. He gets pleasure from seeing a child terrified. He hates children.

Just then, where the path bends, the child's father and mother come riding on two more bicycles.

The gang immediately scatters. Eržika has already vanished; now Feri and Fraňo run for it, too.

Only Freddy Piggybank is slow to react. He notices that the man is braking and jumping off his bicycle. Not until then does he decide to run. Wheezing, he makes a run for it, but the vengeful child trips him up with his foot, and Freddy's mouth hits the ground.

The man takes a leaps at Freddy. With his last ounce of strength, Freddy recovers and hurls himself into the darkest and thickest bush. The man jumps after him and grabs him by the shoulder. The fat man almost shits himself with fear. He throws himself to the ground like a big, plump weasel and slides under some branches and roots. He quickly slithers a few yards through the thorny undergrowth, hugging the ground and holding his panting breath, and plays dead. The blood pounds in his ears and he feels he is about to faint.

The child's father seems to have taken the wrong direction. He is beating the bushes close by, but the sound recedes in the opposite direction. Piggybank's face is dug deep into the soft moist black soil. He doesn't breathe.

The man furiously combs the bushes for a while and then gives up. Silence reigns.

Freddy can't believe his luck. For a long while he stays motionless, hugging the ground. The adrenaline level in his blood slowly goes down. His genitals start to hurt from the stress. He can feel ants crawling over his hands and the back of his neck. He shakes them off. Finally, he finds the courage to emerge cautiously from the bushes. Only now does he feel burning pain on his face and hands, scratched by rushing through the thorny undergrowth.

The wooded park is abandoned. Freddy dusts the soil off his trousers and jacket and sets out for the trolley-bus stop.

When he arrives in the Wooden Village, he finds Bartaloš, Eržika, and Fraňo Fčilek sitting with their heads mournfully bent over their beer.

"What's going on?" Piggybank asks, when he joins them.

"The bastard boss came," Feri Bartaloš says. "He says he doesn't need us anymore. He says we can pack up and go."

"He fired you?" Freddy asks.

Proud Feri Bartaloš nods. Yes, the bastard boss fired Feri and Eržika. He says he's not satisfied with them. But Freddy can say: was there ever any mess? Wasn't the lavatory always clean? And the sink, too? But the bastard boss didn't fire them because of the mess. When they had Lady, Feri and Eržika paid him huge sums of money. Now Lady's dead. How can they get as much money as the bastard boss is demanding?

Freddy nods, pretending to be concerned.

The bastard boss appears at the counter.

"Are you still here?" he asks Feri Bartaloš sternly.

Proud Feri Bartaloš keeps a dignified silence and avoids his gaze.

But Eržika is outraged. What business is it of his? Eržika and Feri are customers, if you don't mind. They're as good as anyone else. They are sitting here having a beer. By the way, the beer is foul. And warm. Kindly bring the Customers' Complaints Book at once!

The bastard boss can't believe his ears. He clenches his tiny fists and his eyes pop even more than before.

"The Customers' Complaints Book?" he asks. "I'll show you the Customers' Complaints Book. Get out of here right now!"

The manager arouses the attention of everyone around. The permanently drunk and stinking Majerník and his parasitic band of savages are only mildly entertained. The hairy poets with rucksacks on their backs are amused: Feri had often drenched them with a bucket of dirty water when he wanted to stop their competitive recitals. The stokers and the other beer drinkers are, however, upset. They quietly mutter in protest. Feri and Eržika are their friends: why can't they sit here?

The bastard boss motions to Four-Eyes who is standing by in his white coat, following everything that is happening. Four-Eyes is glad to help; he's been sick of Feri and Eržika for a long time.

"Throw them out!" says the manager and points to the Bartaloš couple. Four-Eyes nods.

"Get moving, you stinking bastards!" he says and grabs proud Feri Bartaloš by the neck.

Eržika begins to scream in a shrill high-pitched voice.

The whole of the Wooden Village follows the quarrel at their table.

Four-Eyes drags Feri off his bench and won't even let him finish his beer. Bartaloš is quite submissive, he's afraid of the tall bony man. But Eržika is not afraid. She takes a beer mug and smashes it from behind over Four-Eyes's bony round head. Four-Eyes turns round. Behind the lenses of his black glasses his one eye fills with blood.

"You stinking turd!" he says and slaps Eržika's face.

It would have been better if killer Fraňo Fčilek hadn't seen that. Whatever he may be, he's still a gentleman. He gets up and taps Four-Eyes on the shoulder. The tall man turns and offers his face to Fčilek's withering blow.

The dark glasses fly all the way to the pavement. Something cracks, like a branch snapping, and Four-Eyes's white teeth fall onto the asphalt. Four-Eyes silently collapses to the ground.

Eržika's screams are drowned out by a much louder sound, as if a circular saw and a siren were switched on simultaneously. Four-Eyes's wife, sitting by the lavatories, has seen what Fčilek did to her husband.

Four-Eyes is lying motionless on the ground, and a puddle of blood spreads round his head.

They all quieten down; only Four-Eyes's wife throws herself down on her husband, wailing.

Fraňo Fčilek smiles proudly. He is showing everyone his right fist.

"Did you see that?" he asks. "Every hit's a knockout!"

They all seem paralysed. Nobody moves.

A police car stops by the curb and two policemen get out. One of them is on his radio, the second approaches the motionless Four-Eyes.

The stokers hurriedly finish their beer, wipe their mouths and go back to work. The poets don't hang about, either. Their rucksacks are full of aromatic cannabis leaves they use to roll cigarettes and get high; they prefer to clear off. Only the stinking and permanently drunk Majerník has no fear of the police. He is sitting surrounded by his band of savages, soulfully singing a Russian *chastushka*.

The only witness of Fčilek's intervention is the bastard boss. There are no other witnesses. Feri Bartaloš was then under the table, gathering his change which he'd dropped. By the time he got up, everything was over. Eržika was looking the other way at the crucial moment. Freddy Piggybank was wiping his eye with his handkerchief; he saw nothing.

An ambulance soon comes. They put Four-Eyes on a stretcher and drive off.

The policemen handcuff Fraňo Fčilek.

"Let's go," they tell him.

When the police car takes Fraňo away, the bastard boss looks at Feri and Eržika.

"You still here?" he screams wildly. "I'll give you twenty seconds! One... two... three..."

Feri Bartaloš and Eržika reluctantly leave. They don't want to go. They mumble something, but they are too afraid to dig their heels in.

* * *

Freddy Piggybank now sits on the chair in front of the toilets in the Wooden Village and sadly watches his old car park. He collects money, sells pieces of toilet paper and, with a sigh of reluctance. occasionally gets up to unblock a lavatory bowl or overflowing urinal.

When the bastard boss sacked Feri and Eržika, Freddy offered his services. He has to live off something, after all.

After the golden era of the car park and a decent income as Lady's assistant pimp (the beer drinkers preferred the expression "mack", which is so obviously a Czech expression that the fastidious author resists using it in this modest piece of writing, however much it may be the work of a pseud and graphomaniac), Freddy is now facing poverty. There's not a lot of money to be made at the lavatories. Only occasionally can he sell at a modest profit a stolen watch, or a leather jacket brought to him by thieves smarter and less asthmatic than he is.

Freddy is now even stingier than he was at the car park. He won't lend anyone the price of a beer and denies himself the pleasure, too. He is saving up. His parents keep asking him for money, but he gives them nothing; he has a purpose. To get some peace from them, he lives in his trailer. He bought Majerník and his companions a beer each to help him drag his cosy fibreboard caravan closer to the Wooden Village from what was the car park. This is Freddy's home now.

The only joy in his wretched life is knowing that soon he'll have saved enough money for a visit to Silvia's *Perverts' Club*. When Freddy imagines all his desires being fulfilled there, he begins to tremble with impatience.

That is why, when D-day arrives, he can't wait for the end of his shift. Instead, he closes an hour early, changes in his trailer, perfumes himself and sets off to the *Perverts' Club*.

Silvia's business is located in a villa not far from the main railway station. Its well-lit entrance is marked by a shining neon girl, whip in hand, and a sign: *Private Club Justine*.

Freddy stops and swallows hard. His excitement is at its height; the veins on his temples are pulsing wildly. He approaches the entrance and hesitates whether to ring the bell or not. He would prefer to run away, but the excitement is stronger. His shaking hand presses the bell a few times.

A spy-hole in the door opens and a man looks out. He carefully inspects Freddy. "Are you a club member?" he asks. "No," says Freddy, "but I'd like to join." The man gives him another thorough inspection. Then he unlocks the door and lets him in.

Piggybank stops in the doorway. He just has time to take a look around when the man tells him: "Please follow me," Piggybank follows him in great excitement. The man knocks at a door and lets Freddy in. It is a tastefully decorated office. At the desk is a neat-looking, made-up black-haired girl who flashes the obligatory smile at him.

"Good evening, sir," she says. "So you're interested in our services?"

"Yes," says Piggybank.

"Please take a seat," the pretty girl shows him to an armchair in front of the desk. Freddy sits down.

The young lady gets up and her long legs carry her towards Freddy. She hands him a piece of paper. "Here is a form to tell us your preferences," she says and offers the fat man a pen. "Write down your name, or whatever name you want to be called, and fill in the rest as frankly as you can, so we know what services to offer you. We're here to help."

Freddy takes a look at the paper. He doesn't understand some words. For example: what does the word "preferences" mean? He is supposed to underline which of the following are of interest to him: *oral, anal, vaginal, mammal, manual, masoch., pedoph., geronto-, copro-, uro-.* Freddy can't understand, and, just to be sure, he underlines the lot. Then he gives the form he's filled to the young lady. She runs her eyes over it and looks at Freddy. "But you must have some preferences," she says, disappointed. "Yes," says Piggybank. "So what do you prefer?" asks the young lady. Freddy blushes. "Take this," says the beauty and hands him back the form he has filled. "Write on the back, if you're too embarrassed to tell me." Freddy is trembling with excitement and fear. Pen in hand, he hesitates like someone about to leap from a high tower. He finally writes the following:

"I want a woman to tie me up and whip me while I'm completely naked and to scream at me as if I'm being punished."

The young lady reads Freddy's request and nods with understanding. "I see," she says. "Whipping. Should she end by urinating on you, too?" she asks to be sure.

"She doesn't have to," says Freddy. He is relaxed now. He makes himself more comfortable in his seat and as far as his fat legs allow him, he crosses them.

"Very well," says the young lady. "I suggest you move to the lounge and have a drink. It's all in the price, of course. A member of our staff will be with you shortly."

Piggybank sits down at the bar in a room which is both bar and reception room. Nobody takes any notice of him; everything is submerged in semi-darkness. Over the bar is a bright monitor on which a huge black man is copulating with two white women. Freddy orders a glass of red wine for courage. The pornographic film excites him.

"Borský?" a deep female voice conditioned by hundreds of strong cigarettes calls behind his back.

Freddy turns round. Borský is the name he put on the form. A woman in a black leather corset, stockings and tall boots is standing behind him. She has something akin to a bathing cap on her head and she wears elbow-length black satin gloves. A thick layer of make-up covers her face. The exaggeratedly painted lips, demonically painted eyebrows and lots of mascara round her eyes give her a cruel and dangerous look.

"Come on, you perverse fat pig!" the woman orders, grabs Freddy, and with surprising strength pulls him off his bar stool.

"Keep going, keep going!" she says and pushes him into a corridor. To emphasize her words, she gives him a lash with a riding whip.

A sharp pain runs through Freddy from his brain to his genitals. He obediently lets himself be pushed by his mistress into a small room equipped as a torture cell. The main feature of the room is a torture rack that looks like a prop from a film about Jánošík, the Slovak Robin Hood.

"Get your clothes off!" the mistress screams at him and casually selects a few of the various whips and other instruments of torture decoratively arranged on a low table.

Freddy Piggybank sits down and with shaking fingers begins to untie his shoelaces.

"Faster, you fat worm!" the mistress urges him. "In a moment you'll curse the day you were born," she adds. "You'll be begging for mercy and a *coup de grâce*."

Perturbed, Freddy looks up from his shoes and searchingly gazes at his torturer. He's heard those expressions before, he just can't recall where.

"Get on with it, get on with it!" shouts the woman and lashes him with a horsewhip.

A sharp burning pain floods Piggybank's back, and his fingers feverishly try to move faster. After his shoes come shirt, trousers and socks.

"And underpants?" the torturer screams at him, when she sees him hesitate. "What about your underpants?"

Freddy takes a cowardly look at his red boxer shorts and pulls them down too.

The whore touches his crotch with her whip and lifts his genitals. She looks with disgust at his semi-erect member. She takes a condom from a drawer and throws it to him.

"Put it on!" she orders him. "I don't want you making a mess here. And get to the rack!"

Piggybank obeys and lies face down on the rack. He notices a sizable hole that the carpenter has made in the middle of the rack for the penis.

The prostitute ties his wrists, ankles and waist firmly to the rack. "So how would you like it?" she asks bored. "Any special request?"

Freddy restlessly fidgets on the rack. "I've got gauntlets in my trouser pockets," he says. "Put them on your hands."

"Who are you ordering about?" the whore shouts at him and lashes him with the whip. Nevertheless, she then takes from Freddy's trousers the big leather gauntlets used to protect brickyard workers' hands. "What do I do with them?" she asks sternly.

"Put them on your hands and you can punish me," says Freddy, delighting in the restraints that immobilise him.

The torturer puts the brickyard gauntlets over her black gloves and takes a different little whip from her varied assortment and, without warning, starts to whip him. Freddy jerks his body, and the burning pain makes him see stars in front of his eyes. A wave of clandestine delight runs through his entire body. His lower lip begins to tremble from the suffering and fierce pleasure. His spine arches back. Freddy moves his round head from the board of the rack and lifts it higher and higher. He shouts: "Aah!"

"Shut up, you fat slob!" the woman bawls. "Get your head down!"

"Aah!" moans Freddy Piggybank. He can now feel everything below, belly, thighs, behind, and genitals contracting abruptly and all of it together working up towards a mighty, blinding ejaculation of sperm.

"Get your head down, I said!" the prostitute repeats, comes up to Freddy's head and with her thighs squeezes it between her legs, pushing it to the rack with all her weight. Freddy's back is on fire. Firmly squeezed by the torturer's black-stockinged booted legs, he presses his face onto the rough board of the rack. Two more lashes of the whip and Freddy is done. Rhythmic moaning and sighs of relief betray him.

The whore stops whipping him and releases his head. She releases the metal buckles on the straps and takes off the gloves. "OK, fat boy," she says. "We're done."

Freddy collects himself and sits down. His back is still burning; he tries a few times to touch it.

"There's nothing to see," says the prostitute and takes a sip from a beer can. "Not a scratch, you fat pig! You'd have to pay me more to turn your back into a bloody steak. You can take a shower over there and *arrivederci*!" The whore points at the door to the bathroom. "You're not the only one. I've got more perverse swine like you waiting."

Freddy gets up and, the condom still on his member, goes to the bathroom. He is still shaking.

When he returns, he begins to dress. He watches the whore disinfect the used torture instruments with eau-de-cologne.

"Excuse me," he dares to ask, buttoning up his shirt. "Didn't you live in Nová Ves once?"

The torturer looks at him. Her morbidly painted face shows no change of expression. "So?" she asks.

"Well, you remind me of someone I knew when I was a child," says Freddy. "Sida Tešadíková."

The prostitute is startled. "It's me," she says.

Freddy stares at her. He doesn't know what to say. "And I'm Alfred Mešťánek," he finally says. He licks his lips and smiles.

"Really?" the torturer reacts. "I seem to remember. You mean that retarded little fat cretin who burned down our secret camp?"

Freddy Piggybank throws up his hands and nods with a sour smile.

"But we got you for that," says Sida. "Near the station, didn't we?"

Freddy clears his throat. "Yeah," he says.

"Who helped you escape then, anyway?" Sida asks, sits down and crosses her legs. I remember we went to untie you in the morning, but you weren't there any more. We were worried the rats might have bitten you in the night."

"The knot wasn't tightened properly," says Freddy. "I untied myself."

Even under the demonic make-up Sida visibly smiles at the memory.

"Those were terrific times," she says. "Afterwards, every time we met you stared at me like an idiot. You probably wanted to screw me, didn't you? Maybe you even wanked, didn't you? But I was never into sex much. I lost my virginity at university. Want a Budweiser?"

The torturer takes a can and throws it to Freddy.

"And what about you?" Piggybank asks, gratefully opens the can and takes a sip. "How did you get here?"

"Well, how…" Sida shrugs. "I was teaching, and when…"

"You're a teacher?" Piggybank stares at her.

"I used to be," says Tešadíková. "I taught primary school Russian and civics. I'd hardly begun and suddenly came that revolution of theirs. And after the revolution those democratic swine just kicked me out of the school. So what was I supposed to do? I didn't know anything else… For a while I worked at a massage parlour, but they wanted me to have sex with the customers. And I don't want to do that, if I don't feel like it."

"And normally?" Freddy asks. "Are you married?"

"No," Sida says. "You know, I'm not much into men…"

Freddy fidgets: he's never seen a real live lesbian, only in dirty magazines.

"Are you a lesbian?" he asks.

"No," says Sida and gets up. "Oh well," she sighs. "I've still got work to do, if you don't mind," she says, apologizing.

Freddy gets up, too. He has another erection. Sida notices. She touches his trousers with her satin glove.

"You'll come back again, won't you?" she asks in a friendly way. "Always ask for me," she advises him. "They call me Teacher, here. I'll beat the shit out of you," she adds, smiling encouragingly. "It was great to chat with someone from Nová Ves. I haven't been back since I don't know when."

Freddy doesn't even know how he found his way out of the *Perverts' Centre*. He feels relaxed. He'll come back, why not? As soon as he's saved up the price. Now he's a club member, it will all be easier.

* * *

Freddy's joy at finding somewhere to realise his painfully suppressed inclinations, and especially at meeting Sida, soon passes.

The money has gone and Freddy has no chance of getting more soon to pay for another visit to the *Perverts' Club*.

Now he sits by the lavatories like a body with no soul. He keeps thinking about the *Perverts' Club* and tries to imagine what Sida is probably doing right now. He is not racked by jealousy, but anger at not being there as well, at lacking the money for these delights.

If Feri Bartaloš finally gave Freddy the money he owes him for the stolen bicycles, he would at least have something. But Feri is rarely to be seen in the Wooden Village. He comes only rarely and quickly drains unfinished glasses of beer and chews on leftover pieces of chicken on the plates. Eržika does the same, working from the opposite side. Both cast fearful looks at the snack bar counters lest the bastard boss see them.

The eternally drunken and stinking end user of unfinished plates, Majerník, reacts to their competition by incoherent shouts of protest, but neither he, nor anyone in his gang, has the energy to stand up to the more solidly built Bartaloš and his loud and hysterical wife.

However, Feri avoids the lavatory. He knows that Freddy Piggybank will stop him and claim his money from the sale of the stolen bicycles, so why would he go there? Freddy is furious: he could use the money.

Even the beer drinkers don't pay after using the lavatory; they simply run away from Freddy. Freddy can't catch them and even if he did, he wouldn't dare say a word to them. He is a coward. He only dares to challenge the hairy poets, but they ignore him; they usually urinate against the fence of the construction site, Freddy's former car park.

Constant sexual excitement and general apathy lead Freddy Piggybank to neglect his work duties; he does not disinfect, sweep or clean the dirty lavatories, nor change the towels and soap, and he doesn't sell lavatory paper. Soon the lavatory looks like Freddy's mind.

At possibly the least opportune moment, the bastard boss shows up. After the inspecting the lavatories, he runs out with a handkerchief over his mouth, as pale as a ghost. He leans against the wall and the jerk's dark angry look settles on the seemingly unconcerned fat slob sitting by the lavatories.

A few seconds later, Freddy is fired and out on the street.

"You miserable homeless scum!" rages the bastard boss. He's the manager but can't rely on anyone any more. Some of them turn the place into a whorehouse and steal bicycles; another one gets into fights and gets himself killed. This one just doesn't move a bloody finger. There is mess and dirt everywhere! This just can't go on any longer! Piggybank can pack up and get out of here right now! Did Piggybank hear what he's just said?

Freddy unwillingly gets up. He reaches for the change at the bottom of the bowl.

"Leave the money right there!" orders the bastard boss. Piggybank needn't think that it's his money. The manager won't let him sit by the lavatory acting as cashier, collecting an entrance fee. No. Customers pay this money to shit, piss and vomit into clean bowls and urinals. Clean enough to eat from.

Freddy moves his hand away. He is silent. The bastard boss is basically right. Freddy took his eye off the job. He was thinking too much about Sida Tešadíková. Suddenly, he sees that now he won't be able to save up the money to visit the *Perverts' Centre* again.

He sadly locks up his trailer and leaves the Wooden Village.

* * *

After a long time, Freddy goes home to get something to eat. His parents welcome him as if he's come from somewhere in Africa. Freddy eagerly accepts the food he's offered, and politely but monosyllabically answers his parents' inquisitive questions, while his eyes constantly scan the interior of the family house; he is searching for something to sell profitably, or at least pawn.

Once he has finished the bean soup, stewed beef and dumplings, sausage and mustard, horseradish, and bread rolls, and five different sorts of pastry, he puts on a weary expression and announces that he is going to bed. He goes upstairs to his room and pricks up his fat ears. When he is sure that his parents are out in the orchard behind the house, he gets out of bed, goes down to the ground floor, where his fat scrounging fingers open the drawers of his parents' sideboard. He finally finds what he is looking for: family jewellery — engagement rings, a thick gold necklace, and a cross. He puts the loot in his pocket, quietly leaves the house, and hurries to the bus stop.

In the city he finds a pawnshop and offers them the stolen gold. What he's paid barely suffices for one visit to the *Perverts' Centre.*

He drops in at the Wooden Village and discreetly, avoiding the bastard boss's eyes, crawls into his trailer. There, in the musty cold, he sits, waiting until five o'clock, when the *Justine* club opens.

Piggybank is one of the first visitors. As a club member, he doesn't have to waste time with entrance formalities and immediately asks for the Teacher. He takes a seat in the bar, and soon Sida Tešadíková comes to pick him up.

After an hour of whipping, wild riding on his back, being bound to a wheel, hanging by his wrists and similar voluptuous delights, Freddy is happily tired and satisfied. He is getting dressed. Sida sits and smokes a cigarette.

"Listen, Sida…" Freddy says. "Don't you need an assistant?"

"What do you mean?" asks Sida.

"Well, an assistant," Freddy explains. "Someone to tie up the victim, hand you the torture instruments, and so on. Like an altar boy, if you see what I mean."

Sida nods and takes a sip from the can. "I've never given it a thought," she says. "But if I did, it ought to be a woman, shouldn't it? We do get gays here, too, but I only service men who are into women."

"Mediæval executioners had helpers," says Freddy. "Imagine the effect…"

"What's all this about?" Sida asks. "Are you so bored that you want to be my altar boy?"

"It so happens I don't have anything to do right now," says Freddy. "I'd be a good altar boy. I'd be your slave. You could humiliate me as much as you want. I'd put up with anything."

"Seriously?" Sida can't believe it.

She finishes her cigarette and stubs it out in the ashtray.

"But it wouldn't be much fun being my slave," she says. "Lots of suffering and no reward. And you'd make peanuts. I'd have to pay you out of my own earnings."

"That's all right, Sida," Freddy says eagerly. "Glad to be of service."

"I can get angry and ratty sometimes," Sida warns him. "I'll whip you until you bleed for no reason at all. How will you like that?"

Freddy almost faints from joy and excitement.

"I could handle that," he says.

"Very well, then," Sida agrees. "I'll try you out. But first we sign a contract."

"A contract?" Freddy doesn't understand.

"Yes, a contract," Sida says. "A slavery contract, get it? And you'll sign in your own blood."

Sida opens a door and lets Freddy into her dressing room.

"If you want to start today," Sida says, "get ready. Some of this stuff might fit you."

She points to a cupboard full of leather, rubber, latex, and metal accessories that Silvia, her boss, bought by the ton in Austria.

Freddy rummages through strange contraptions, gloves, chokers, boots, armour of various shapes, and black rubber stockings. He ends up putting on a mask with holes for his eyes and mouth, leather trousers, which leave his genitals and buttocks generously exposed, and a complex system of leather straps which criss-cross his fat chest and belly in a chaotic grid. Once he is ready, he shows himself to Sida.

"Very handsome," says Sida. "Now come here, porky, here's your contract."

Freddy approaches Sida and reads:

I, the undersigned repulsive and perverse fat worm, Alfred Mešťánek, hereby pledge that I shall faithfully and obediently serve my mistress, Sidónia Tešadíková, as her vilest slave. My fidelity and obedience will be unlimited and I shall gladly suffer at my mistress's hands the greatest privations, torment, humiliation, and even shameful death.
Signed: pervert Alfred Mešťánek, a.k.a. Piggybank

"You'll get a hundred crowns a day from me," Sida says. "If I'm satisfied with you, then, in time, you'll get two hundred. If I'm not, you'll be out of here in a flash. You take the job?"

Freddy enthusiastically agrees. A hundred a day is not much, but for a start, it is better than nothing. Besides, Freddy will be doing the sort of work he likes.

"Then sign it!" Sida orders him. "In your blood."

"Sorry?" Freddy doesn't understand.

Instead of a lengthy explanation, his newly appointed mistress lashes his thigh with a little whip. A few drops pour from the cut in his skin.

"Put your thumb in the blood!" Sida orders. "Print it on the paper."

Freddy, stunned by the sudden pain and pleasure, obeys.

"So," Sida says, rolls up the contract and puts it away in a drawer. "You're mine. We can begin. Today is just a training day. Pay attention. I'll tell you everything that you'll have to do."

Freddy nods. His round face reflects his eager devotion.

* * *

As they agreed in advance, Martin Junec comes to Nová Ves to be exorcised by Hruškovič. He comes, as Hruškovič insisted, on an empty stomach.

Hruškovič welcomes him in his surgery. He is dressed in simple white clothes.

"Where are your patients?" Martin wonders, pointing to the empty yard.

"I've sent them all home," says Hruškovič. He has once before dealt with something like what Martin is suffering from. He was exorcising a seventeen-year-old girl to rid her of the jealous ghost of her present boyfriend's late former girl friend. The ghost came to her at night and tormented her in all kinds of ways. The girl was psychically at her lowest ebb when she came to see Hruškovič. Hruškovič got rid of her ghost, and in the afternoon went on to treat other patients. But the treatment was useless; nobody got better, and some unfortunates even ended up worse. What's more, Hruškovič fell into a coma and slept without a break for two days and nights. However, when he got up, everything was all right again. "You know," Hruškovič concluded, "maybe I was coming down with something. Flu, I suppose, or something. But it really shook me."

It's raining outside; the leaves on the trees are yellow, red and brown. Everything, the yard and the orchard, is covered by a creeping layer of mist. The drain pipes tinkle with the water running off. Hruškovič's surgery is kept nice and warm by a gas fire.

"Frankly, I don't have much experience of this sort of thing," says Hruškovič hesitantly, squinting at a big book filled with various magic symbols. I have helped a few patients with similar problems... I really don't know how...."

"You have the ability," Martin interjects. "Please, get rid of that arsehole for me."

"I have shit-all ability," says Hruškovič. "It's all coincidence."

"Okay, okay," admits Junec. "Let's say you're a charlatan. I'm asking you then to help me get rid of Žofré the same way as you'd help a stranger, an ordinary client of yours. Don't tell me you've never performed an exorcism."

"Well," the healer admits, "I've tried now and then to do something like one... you know, since the books are there anyway... It'd be a pity not to have a go..."

"Well then," the American Slovak reacts victoriously.

Hruškovič is not too keen to start casting spells. He leafs through the book and clears his throat. "Well," he says and lifts his eyes, "we can try something. Sit here!"

He gets up, opens the door to the yard and calls his wife who is feeding the chickens.

"Veruna's my best medium," Hruškovič says. "I just put my hand on her head and she goes straight into hypnosis."

Mrs Hruškovič looks straight ahead with wide-open eyes.

"Of course, she's just fooling us and herself," whispers Hruškovič to Martin, "but that's the way you wanted it."

Hruškovič puts a white cloth on his head and then a complicated wire hat: his round peasant head with its full carefree face reminds you of a picture of the sun, as children draw it, with straight rays radiating out all round.

"What on earth are you up to, for God's sake?" Junec asks in amused disbelief, but when he sees Hruškovič opening a cupboard, taking out a cape decorated with stars and various symbols and putting it on, he becomes serious.

"Woman," says Hruškovič in a strong voice brooking no resistance. "What spirits can you see in our proximity, spirits that appear in beautiful human form with no deformities? Give me their astral names!"

Mrs Hruškovič begins to speak in a quiet voice, as if asleep: "Namamiah, Uniabel, Leabiah, Zezael..."

"Continue, woman!" Hruškovič insists.

"Zeiriel," continues his wife. "Lehemiel, Firásek, Melahel, Cachetel..."

At the word Firásek, Žofré's surname, Martin jumps from the chair, but Hruškovič calms him down with a movement of his hand. "Enough, woman!" he commands. "Wake up!" He claps softly a few times and she wakes up. "You can get back to your work," says Hruškovič, and his wife leaves the surgery.

Hruškovič goes back to reading his book. "Spirit by the name of Firásek!" he shouts after a while. "Are you here?" he pauses for a moment. "Spirit Firásek, I'm talking to you!" he continues solemnly. "I invoke against you the high powers of Adonai and Agla, the general clavicle of Solomon, the Saturnine Kabbalah key, the keys of Ieve, Adni and Aehieh that explain the Universe and that focus on the Earth. I invoke against you the lunar esoteric key and the new cosmological key: leave this world and go in peace where you belong!"

The astonished Junec notices in a corner of the surgery the outline, vague and blurred, of Žofré's astral body.

"What?" shouts Hruškovič and puts his hands to the wire hat as if adjusting earphones. "Message?" he asks. "What message?"

Martin can see that Žofré's outline is still unable to materialise; the spirit remains in the form of glittering fog.

"In the name of Ieve-Zebaoth, I free you from bondage to your mission, spirit Firásek!" says Hruškovič in a solemn voice. "In the name of Elohim Ghibora, I free you from the promise you gave a mortal person called Edna Gershwitz. You have paid enough for your guilt. Stop visiting the mortal Martin Junec! Leave this world in peace and go where you belong! To put it briefly, Žofré, clear off and leave Martin alone! He's not family to you any more, he means bugger-all to you. Go and pester your stupid sister Marfa!"

Hruškovič intones the last words angrily. Then he walks to the door leading to the yard and opens it in one sweep. Žofré's outline dissolves and the apparition vanishes. Martin detects a strange smell that reminds him of ozone, or overheated dust. From outside comes the cold, the sound of rain, the tinkling of drain pipes, the cackle of hens, the distant noise of a circular saw and the barking of dogs.

"That does it," says Hruškovič, takes his wire hat off and carefully puts it in the glass case.

"He won't come back?" Junec asks with hope in his voice.

"Look, uncle," says Hruškovič. "I think I can tell you that I don't believe in this bullshit. I've done exactly what I do with my patients. It helps most of them. Maybe it will help you, too."

Martin gets off his chair. Actually, deep in his soul he feels a refreshing relief. "How much do I owe you?" he asks.

"Are you trying to insult me, old pal?" Hruškovič retorts, putting his cape away in the cupboard. "How long have we known each other? We're good friends, aren't we? Am I so poor my friends have to pay me? Just buy me a beer and a shot of rum in *Konzum*, and we're quits."

* * *

Feri and Eržika find themselves on the streets without a job or a roof over their heads. The manager takes the keys to the lavatory from them and they can't rely on Freddy Piggybank letting them sleep in the lavatory. Anyway, Feri is avoiding Freddy; he owes him money for the stolen bicycles.

"We can't touch the bank account!" Bartaloš says firmly every time Eržika suggests that they take a sum of money out to improve their wretched standard of living. "What an idea!" he adds. "If we ever touch that money it will all be lost. We've got to hold out."

Eržika grumbles, because at night she feels cold despite the sleeping bag and inflatable mattress. On the other hand, she believes that their suffering in the alien, hostile city will soon have its reward.

Some of the night Feri and Eržika spend in trams, for example, in the number 5. They get in at one terminus and get out at the other. Between the two, they get an hour's uninterrupted sleep in the warm. After midnight, when the trams stop operating, they move into the underpass below the Central Square. They take out their sleeping bags and mattresses from plastic bags, make themselves comfortable and sleep. Sometimes they talk before they go to sleep. Eržika is quite clear what to do with their hard-earned money. They'll go back home, to their native village, and open a boutique. Eržika can see herself as a boutique owner; wearing elegant clothes, she'll stand in the middle of a fashionably designed room and welcome customers with a smile. She often fantasizes about her ideas for hours before she falls asleep.

Feri gets a better look at her in the underpass's dazzling neon light. Eržika has a dreamy gaze and a smile plays on her lips. When she looks into some happy, prosperous future she doesn't feel the cold or see the damp dripping off the broken and defaced wall tiles, nor does she notice the silhouettes of the nocturnal drunks stumbling through the underpass.

It is hard for Feri to join Eržika's fantasy world; their bank account doesn't exist any more, he's lost the lot at cards. He doesn't know how much money was in it, anyway. But he'd rather hang himself than let his wife ever find out about it.

Naturally, Eržika has as yet no inkling. She can't understand why they're still in the city and not returning home, to the village, to live on their hard-earned money.

Feri finds it increasingly difficult to persuade his wife that they still have to wait a while.

In the morning they are awakened by the first passers-by. Feri and Eržika get up. A new day, a new opportunity. The struggle continues.

For a time, Feri and Eržika collect old paper. They steal a cart, a collector's most important equipment, from someone as poor as them. They follow him for a while as he hurries to the recycling depot in a green quilted jacket with his cart loaded to the brim, and then they track him furtively as far as the pub, where the poor man decides to refresh himself before his next trip.

He leaves the cart on the pavement. Feri grabs it and runs like greased lightning.

In the courtyard of the Hotel Ambassador, they repaint the blue cart red, and as soon as the paint is dry, they set off looking for business.

The best sources for a paper collector are fruit and vegetable stalls. Feri and Eržika make rounds of all the fruit and vegetable stalls and haul a big bundle of cardboard to the depot.

But a few days later someone steals their cart, parked and hidden in the courtyard of the Hotel Ambassador, and their income is gone.

"I've had enough of this!" Eržika screams at Feri. "Why stay in this bloody city where they rob you blind? People are buggers: they steal anything that isn't nailed down. Thieving gangsters!" On the other hand, Eržika and Feri have certainly saved up enough for that boutique. They have to take their money out of the bank and go back home. She'd like to have a bath, anyway.

It's harder and harder for Feri to pacify his wife. Finally, he has to stoop to deception.

One night, just as they're getting to sleep on the floor of the underpass, a masked robber appears above them.

Eržika is scared and starts to yell like someone out of their mind, but the passers-by don't even slow their pace as they walk by.

"Don't scream, you *gadjo* cunt!" the masked robber, a toy gun in his hand, hollers at her and turns to Feri. "And you, you give me your money, you *gadjo* shit!"

Feri checks his pockets with trembling hands. As if by accident, his savings book falls out on the pavement. The masked robber grabs it.

"Look at that!" he says, pleasantly surprised, when he opens the book. "A nice little bundle! I see you used to be rich, ha, ha, ha! Used to be, but not any more! Now I'm the millionaire! My regards!"

With these words, the gentleman robber bows out and runs towards the escalator.

Eržika begins to scream again, and her whole body is shaking. She completely failed to notice the masked robber's schoolboyish, amateurish performance, as well as the fact that he declaimed his lines unnaturally, as if someone had written them in advance and he'd had some trouble learning them by heart.

"Our money!" Eržika yells, as if out of her mind. "Our money!"

Feri pretends to be angry and bitter, too. With clenched teeth he curses and occasionally looks at Eržika out of the side of his eye.

Now Eržika's rage turns on Feri. Yes, Feri should have done something. If he weren't a coward, they wouldn't have been robbed. That was everything they owned. All that effort wasted!

They argue long into the night about who should have done what and how. They finally tire and fall asleep.

The next day they decide to go to the bank to report a stolen savings book.

The cashier checks their account and tells them that it is empty.

Eržika gets upset. "What do you mean empty? That savings book was only stolen last night."

The cashier just shrugs. She looks through the glass partition at the two dirty smelly individuals with frank revulsion. She knows nothing about it. The account was cleared. There's just twenty crowns left in it.

Eržika begins to laugh bitterly, hysterically. "Well, of course!" she shouts. Eržika Bartalošová knows how it is done. That's why the bank is so rich. Eržika and Feri worked day and night and suffered privation. And there's only twenty crowns left? That account wasn't empty. There was a lot of money in it.

Eržika stops for a second in amazement.

"There could have been a million crowns there! A million Slovak crowns! Empty account, my eye! That's a lie! A swindle! This bank is a nest of swindlers. Poor people are robbed of their honestly earned money. How about the rich? Nobody would tell Rácz that there were only twenty crowns left in his account. They're all afraid of him. But nobody hesitates to rob the poor."

Everyone in the bank stares at Eržika. Feri is standing next to his wife, a little embarrassed by her. He was the only person who robbed the account, since he took out the last bit of money to pay his card debts. And the masked robber was Šípoš, whom Feri paid to do the job. Only now, seeing Eržika's despair, Bartaloš fully realises what he has done. Shame begins to mingle with remorse in Feri's soul.

Two armed security men appear in the hall.

One of them gets a polite but determined hold on the enraged Eržika and leads her out. Eržika fends him off wildly, but it's no use. Feri gets the same treatment; the other sheriff in black grabs him.

On the pavement Eržika yells even louder. All her despair gushes out in an uninterrupted flow of tears, words, and inarticulate screams.

She has nothing! This bloody city has robbed her of everything. If she'd married Rácz, she could have been lounging in a big villa overlooking the city. But she was stupid: she married that idiot Feri Bartaloš instead, and this is how she's ended up.

The passers-by pause near this odd couple, listen for a while and then, fully entertained, hurry off.

She has lost everything, Eržika continues. First, they were mugged by the masked robber and now by the bank. They had about a million;

now they have nothing. The bank claims that the account is empty. Eržika will show them "empty". She will complain. She will write to the President of the Republic. She will write to the Prime Minister, too; he, at least, is on the side of the poor. Everyone will see what she can do.

Feri drags Eržika away, but she wriggles frees of him and hammers the smoked glass entrance to the bank with her fists. Feri tries to pull her away from the building. The two sheriffs in black run out and push her away from the glass. Feri gets a blow from a truncheon as well.

Eržika runs round the pavement and tugs at the sleeves of passers-by. Did you see that? She's been robbed by this society. She has nothing left; she's reached the bottom. And she was once almost a millionaire!

Feri, too, begins to rage. The truncheon blow on his back hurts, even though he's wearing a thick jacket. He shouts something about injustice, fascism, and communism. A brickbat that he picked up off the pavement is suddenly in his hand. He swings his arm a few times, and soon a giant pane of smoked glass on the bank's façade shatters with a roar.

The sheriffs in black run out of the bank again, but by now Feri and Eržika are round the corner on the other side of the street.

After running for a while, Feri and Eržika get tired and slow to a walk. Eržika is whimpering and wiping away her tears. Her voice is faltering. Feri puts a hand round her shoulders. He, too, feels like crying. He feels he is the lowest treacherous swine on the planet. Feri Bartaloš is responsible for everything that has happened.

Pangs of conscience bother him and eat him up. He presses Eržika to himself even tighter and silently swears to give her back everything a thousand-fold, even a million-fold!

* * *

When Sida gets bored waiting for a client, or is in a bad mood, she commands her slave Piggybank to entertain her. He has to sing her happy songs in his mooing voice, or make silly faces, or she simply orders him to wank in front of her. The faces that he pulls while he does it are always certain to make her laugh.

That's how it is now; Sida has a headache, she is in a foul temper and wants to torment someone. Freddy is handy and utterly defenceless.

"What kind of a man are you, Freddy?" she goes for her slave. "You never get a decent erection. Show me! See, you can't get it up. I want you to get it up. I give you three minutes. Get on with it! If you don't get it up by then, I'll torture you with my lighter."

Sida lights up, sets the lighter to produce the longest possible flame and measures it against Freddy.

"I'll scorch you like a hog," she says lubriciously.

Freddy tries to do as his mistress demands.

Sida watches him. When she notices that his breathing has quickened, she firmly grabs his moving hand with a torturer's smile on her thickly painted face.

"Enough!" she says. "You're my slave and you'll come when *I* want you to. Right?"

"Right," says Freddy and takes his hand off his engorged member. He feels his genitals jerk two or three times like an engine running out of petrol. Coming like this is unpleasant, but a job is a job.

Sida takes a whip from a stand and tries it for quality on Piggybank's fat back.

"Sit!" she shouts at the fat wretch. For mysterious reasons, Sida shouts her monosyllabic and disyllabic commands in Czech. Even now. "Good boy!" she says and scratches Piggybank under his chin.

She inserts her finger-tip into her crotch and lets him lick it. That is the sweet she rewards him with. Then she puts a pear-shaped wooden gag in his mouth and fixes it to his head with leather straps. Now Freddy can produce, instead of words, only a variety of slavish screeches.

"Let's see if anyone is interested in our services," Sida says, takes the leash and attaches it to Piggybank's collar. "Let's go!" she commands in a low voice and gives Freddy's behind, almost bare in his special leather underpants, a lash with a whip.

Freddy moans with gratitude. He obeys his mistress's every word. He is glad to serve. If he had a tail, he would wag it madly.

When they enter the bar, Sida orders a can of beer. Freddy stands next to her, but he cannot drink: he has a wooden pear in his mouth. He would endure anything, even thirst, for his mistress. He knows that when their shift ends, to reward his suffering, his mistress will have quenched a thirst that even a thousand cans of beer wouldn't have quenched.

The club members slowly assemble. Some already know Freddy and greet him with familiarity. Freddy politely bows and, mumbling as best he can, returns their greetings. He is happy to be among his peers. He is happy to serve.

The working evening in the *Private Club Justine* is beginning.

* * *

For along time Silvia has been plotting revenge on Rácz for what he did to her, an emancipated and reserved young lady.

It is clear as day that there's no sense reporting Rácz to the police. Rácz has the police in his pocket: they'd laugh about it.

Then Silvia considers having him beaten up, or even killed by the underworld, but realises right away that this wouldn't work: Rácz has at his service a numerous and well armed security squad that accompanies him everywhere and patrols outside his villa even at night. Besides, Silvia doesn't actually know anyone in the underworld.

Burning with hatred, Silvia considers the possibility of kidnapping Rácz's wife, drugging her, smuggling her to Austria and selling her to a brothel. Finally, she decides against it: she realises, first of all, that an innocent person would suffer; secondly, this wouldn't provide tangible evidence of her suffering that she could send Rácz to make him suffer.

The idea of tangible evidence surfaces again later on, when she recovers from the unpleasant memories of violent coitus with the savage hotelier and when all the negative emotions in her mind are displaced by her cold desire for a sophisticated revenge.

It begins one morning when a courier brings to Silvia's freshly renovated villa below the railway station a giant bouquet of a hundred orchids. In the bouquet, Silvia finds Rácz's business card. On the back is the following note: "Rácz remembers times spent together and hopes for more. Best wishes, Your Rácz."

Silvia is almost felled. She goes momentarily blind, and when she remembers Rácz's enormous sexual organ wildly moving inside her, she feels like vomiting. She re-reads a few times the brazen note written in Rácz's hand, so energetic but as crude as a schoolboy's. She cannot believe her eyes. The arrogance!

A desire for revenge begins to quicken again. Silvia lies down on the sofa and gets up only when she has thought up a plan. She puts on her most seductive dress and then goes down to the ground floor, the *Perverts' Club*. From her office there she takes some up-to-date technical equipment and puts it all in her bag, to make her revenge perfect. Then she calls for a taxi and drives to the Hotel Ambassador.

"I urgently need to talk to Mr Junec," she tells the receptionist. "Is he in?"

"Yes, he is," says the receptionist. "Mr Junec is asleep. He came back late last night."

"I have to speak to him," says Silvia. "Call him, please, and tell him I'm here."

"Sorry," says the receptionist. "I have strict orders not to disturb him."

Silvia pulls out a thousand-crown note. The receptionist looks at the ascetic face of Monsignor Andrej Hlinka, Father of the Nation, on the note and, after an inner struggle, shakes his head.

"I'm sorry, I can't ..." he says.

Another note joins the face of Andrej Hlinka, all spirituality, on the marble counter.

"Mr Junec is going to kill me..." says the receptionist and reluctantly reaches for the phone, while his other hand discreetly slips the banknotes into the pocket of his dark-red uniform.

"Mr Junec is expecting you," says the receptionist after a polite quiet conversation on the phone. "It's what we call the Presidential Suite, on the sixth floor..."

"I know where it is," Silvia interrupts him and strides to the lift. Still in the lift, she turns on a Dictaphone with a highly sensitive microphone and a miniature video camera which can record through a tiny opening in the bag everything within a radius of two hundred and twenty degrees.

Martin opens the door at the first knock. He is wearing a silk dressing-gown and he smells of toothpaste: he has quickly cleaned his teeth.

"Silvia," he says surprised and almost afraid.

"Good morning, Martin," says Silvia. "I hope I haven't woken you."

"Oh, no," says Martin. "I've been up for ages."

"Are you going to let me in?" Silvia asks.

"Of course!" Martin says and moves away from the door. "Sorry."

Silvia enters the living room and looks around. The suite hasn't changed since the time she lived there with Rácz. Silvia makes herself comfortable on the sofa and puts her bag to one side. She crosses her legs, ensuring that her narrow skirt shows as much of her divine shapely thighs as possible.

"Can I offer you anything?" asks Martin.

"A glass of mineral water," says Silvia unconsciously running her fingers over her knees. She notes with pleasure that the crotch-high lump under Junec's dressing-gown has begun to swell considerably.

"A glass of mineral water," Martin repeats. "I'll have dry sherry, he says. "It always wakes me up."

"I'll wake you up, just you wait," Silvia thinks.

When Junec puts the drinks on the table, Silvia pretends to be scared and looks at the door.

"What is it?" Martin asks. He does fancy Silvia, but can't forget Rácz's well-meant advice.

Silvia presses a finger to her full lips and silently points at the door. Martin approaches the door and opens it wide. He looks left and right down the corridor, and then closes the door.

Meanwhile Silvia has dropped a white, highly soluble powder in his drink.

"There wasn't anybody," says Martin. "You were imagining things."

He sits down and takes a sip.

"We haven't seen each other for ages," he says.

"I came to tell you that I am very sorry about..." Silvia says.

"About what?" Martin asks.

"Our interrupted evening," says Silvia. The owner of the hotel had me locked in his office and only let me out after you'd gone."

Silvia tactfully omits the fact that Rácz had also raped her. She felt that this would make her less attractive in the American's eyes and thus endanger her plans.

"He did that to you?" Martin pretends to be amazed.

"Yes," nods Silvia. "Didn't you wonder why I took so long coming back?"

"I thought you and Mr Rácz might have something going," says Martin in his defence. "I didn't want to interfere in your affairs."

"I'm sure Mr Rácz told you nice things about me," Silvia remarks.

Martin has loosened the knot on the cravat round his neck under the dressing-gown. He is sweating profusely. His pulse has become very rapid. The sight of Silvia's legs is driving him mad. His member hardens and stands to attention against the inner side of his right thigh.

"I bet," says Silvia coquettishly, "that most of it wasn't true."

She throws Martin a kittenish look.

"Rácz told me that you had a relationship," Martin says carefully, though he longs to throw himself at Silvia and thrust himself into her. "That you were..." he adds in confusion.

"That we were having sex?" Silvia helps him out.

"Yes, having sex," says Martin, and sweat starts trickling down his left temple.

"That's not true," says Silvia. "We were lovers, yes. But that was a long time ago. I was very young and stupid then. Rácz is a coarse, vulgar man. A criminal. As a lover, he's useless. Today I don't often choose men for sex and I'm much more careful. I have strict criteria."

Martin is quiet. He knows he should say something, but nothing suitable comes to mind. His throat is dry and his heart is beating somewhere in his throat. A sharp pain in his erect penis signals that almost all his blood is being pumped to this particular spot.

"Aren't you interested in knowing if you meet those criteria?" Silvia asks provocatively and gets up. She comes to Martin.

Martin gets up, too, and puts his sherry glass on the edge of the table.

Silvia passes her long index finger over his chin and wipes a trace of toothpaste off. "Aren't you?" she asks.

Instead of answering, Martin, drugged by a horse-size dose of aphrodisiac, hurls himself hungrily at her, throws her onto the sofa and starts making love to her compliant and passionate body, which she has positioned in the field of vision of the mini camera hidden in the bag.

* * *

The rickety old bus stops on the village square and the door opens with a hiss.

The dust raised by the bus slowly settles, and out come old ladies in headscarves, sweaters, full skirts and black polished shoes. Some carry wicker baskets in their hands, others bundles knotted from chequered tablecloths on their backs: they are returning from a district town market.

The old ladies get off, and behind them proud Feri Bartaloš leaves his footprints in the dust of the little square, as he drags a blushing Eržika by the hand.

They set off across the little square with heads raised high, touching and ridiculous in their dignity.

The old ladies stop at the local council building. They give the comical couple ironic looks and from time to time hide their sly smirks behind hands as wrinkled as squeezed lemons.

For Feri and Eržika, the road to the impressive house of Kišš the butcher is the stations of the cross.

The villagers stop to look at them and whisper to each other. Windows open. There is the sound of laughter from somewhere. Somebody says: "They failed…"

Feri grabs Eržika's sticky hand all the more firmly. Over their shoulders they carry their sleeping bags and inflatable mattresses, their only possessions, in plastic bags. They are grimy and in rags. The battered high-heel shoes that Freddy Piggybank sold them hurt Eržika's feet. Feri Bartaloš's feet are wrapped in towels tied in plastic bags; his shoes were stolen last night in the Central Square underpass.

Kišš the butcher is sitting on a chair in the kitchen, enjoying a smoke with one eye closed. This is his day off; every other day he stands behind the counter from morning till evening. Today, Saturday, he closed at one.

When Eržika and Feri Bartaloš appear in the doorway, Kišš gets up, noisily pushing his chair back; his cigarette and holder fall out of his mouth.

His blood-shot staring eyes inspect his daughter and his son-in-law. He can see it all. They've failed. They've come back as poor as beggars. Hatred seethes in Kišš's primitive mind, hatred of that *nyomorult* (as the Hungarians call a wretch) Rácz: he made it, but these two, though they had all the advantages, did not. The wealthy village butcher had believed in them. Not even in his dreams did he suspect that Eržika, his daughter, and proud Feri Bartaloš, his son-in-law, would fail in the city.

"*Apuci!* Daddy!" Eržika shouts and weeps, as she throws herself at her father.

Old Kišš pushes her away.

Feri Bartaloš stands there, his eyes stubbornly focused on the floor.

"Eržika!" shouts Mrs Kišš, running in from the yard. She embraces her daughter with both arms and her son-in-law with her eyes. Then she fixes her husband with a searing look. "Antal!" she shouts at him sternly. "Welcome your daughter!"

The old man stands in the middle of the room, trying to put the cigarette in its holder. His big belly and trembling hands make it impossible.

"Antal!" Mrs Kišš shouts.

"*Apuci!*" whimpers Eržika.

Kišš puts the cigarette holder in his mouth.

"Run them a bath; they can get washed," he orders his wife in a voice that is harsh, but just a little moved. "They stink. Give them something to wear. Feed them. And then they can sweep the whole yard. I won't feed them for nothing."

Old Kišš walks past his old wife and Eržika as if he was walking past a group of statues.

Feri is still standing in the doorway.

"If you don't mind," says the butcher harshly, averting his gaze.

Proud Feri steps aside, and Kišš walks outside.

"Thank you, Father!" Feri says quietly.

Startled, Kišš gives Bartaloš a hard, silent gaze. Then he goes out.

"Where's he gone?" asks Eržika.

"He's gone out riding," says Mrs Kišš. "Whenever anything bothers him, he saddles the horse that Rácz gave him and rides over the fields. But come, you must both be hungry!"

* * *

In the evening the Kišš family goes to bed. The old man lies down and covers himself with the eiderdown. He closes his eyes and stubbornly refuses to talk.

"Aren't you interested in what they've been through in the city?" his wife asks him.

The old man keeps quiet and pretends to be asleep. Only his trembling eyelids give him away.

"They even had a daughter," said the old woman. "As beautiful as a picture. Her name was Lady…"

"What?" the old man asks and opens his eyes.

"Lady," says the old woman, glad that he's showing interest.

"Odd name," says Kišš. He immediately regrets being caught out and closes his eyes again.

"That was the name of a woman friend Eržika had," the old woman says. "Later, her friend died," she adds, but the old man doesn't react this time. "And Lady was kidnapped by some Germans," the old woman continues, watching old Kišš's eyelids quivering. "They both suffered a lot. And you're as hard as nails: hard, and unbending. And unfair." Old Mrs Kišš sighs. "My heart bleeds when I think that my granddaughter, whom I haven't even seen, was kidnapped!" she says. "Eržika's suffered a lot. Why can't you forgive her? Why won't you accept her?"

"They failed," the old Kišš says, without opening his eyes, as if surfacing from deep sleep. "They failed. Why didn't they make it? That stupid Rácz made it. So why couldn't Feri Bartaloš and my daughter?"

"How do you know they didn't make it?" the old woman retorts. "They made lots of money; they meant to open a boutique here…"

"What's a boutique?" Kišš stops her.

"It's a sort of shop," says Mrs Kišš. "Like our clothes shop *Spring* over here. They made a million. But they lost it. They were robbed."

"Ha! A million?" Kišš laughs condescendingly, as if to himself. "Is that what they told you?"

"I believe my daughter," says Mrs Kišš. "She's never lied to me."

"Go to sleep now," says Kišš. "We'll see what use they are. If they made a million, then so be it."

Old Kišš gets up, feels for his slippers with his feet and with a heavy step leaves the bedroom. He heads for what used to be Eržika's bedroom. A light is shining under the door. Kišš knocks loudly and enters. Stern and huge in his nightgown, he stands in the doorway. Eržika and Feri are lying next to each other, their hands bandaged: the broom handles have taken the skin off.

"Eržika, on Monday you start in my butcher's shop," says Kišš. "Selling at the counter. That will be your boutique: pork neck, tenderloin, sirloin."

His turbid gaze moves to his son-in-law.

"And for you, Ferenc," says Kišš, "I have a place at the pig farm that I've just set up You'll start at the bottom. We'll see what you're made of. If you try hard and show you're smart, maybe in time you'll work your way up to being chief swineherd!"

Eržika jumps out of bed and covers her father's hard hand with kisses of gratitude.

* * *

It gets light early. Around five, when the shift ends in Justine, day has usually broken. Sida sits down, throws her wig off, discards her tall boots and puts her long black-stockinged legs up on the rack. She lights a cigarette with pleasure. "Would you like one?" she asks Piggybank and moves the pack to him. She concentrates on detaching the artificial nails, blood-red and as long as talons, from her real ones. Freddy lights up and, with one eye closed, tidies up the torture room equipment.

"What a night!" says Sida, gets up and goes to take a shower.

While Tešadíková is in the bathroom, Freddy cleans the torture room, carefully wipes the instruments and gets everything ready for the evening. Then he, too, takes a shower. The hot aroma of Sida's shampoo lingers in the cubicle. Freddy soaps himself, showers, and puts his everyday clothes on.

"Are you coming?" asks Sida, now dressed in patched jeans and a thick leather jacket. She wears hand-made cowboy boots and has a motorcycle helmet over her shoulder. Her short ash-blonde hair is freshly combed and her face has no trace of make-up. Freddy still hasn't got used to this morning transformation. In her everyday clothes his mistress reminds him very strongly of the old Daughters of Death times and the camp sites in the woods, so much so that only with the greatest effort can Piggybank suppress the painful emotion and excitement.

"I can drop you off at the New Bridge ,where you can catch the 101, if you like," says Sida, and Freddy, as always, gratefully accepts.

In the courtyard of the *Perverts' Centre* Tešadíková's Honda *750 Magna* is parked. Sida lowers the stand, straddles the huge fuel tank and starts the engine. "Coming?" she asks her slave and puts on her helmet. Freddy doesn't keep her waiting, mounts the high seat behind her and embraces her firmly around the waist with both arms. This, their sole non-professional intimacy, always makes him feel odd. Sida's waist radiates pleasant warmth and Freddy can't believe that it is the same person with whom he spends entire nights whipping, burning, hanging, impaling, racking, crucifying and otherwise tormenting dozens of randy perverted customers.

Sida revs the engine and the powerful motorcycle rushes wildly onto the street. Freddy has to hold on to her waist tighter if he is not to fall onto the pavement. He is looking forward to his bed.

* * *

Freddy's father, his face yellow from cigarette smoke, sits in the kitchen chain-smoking. The window is closed; Freddy's parents hate draughts. They air the place by equally distributing the smoke everywhere. You can smell the tobacco that infuses the carpets, curtains, tablecloths and every item of furniture. The Mešťánek house by Nová Ves pond announces its presence from afar by its striking tobacco smell.

Old Mešťánek worries about his son. He can't understand why he has to have an abnormal offspring. Everyone else nearby is quite normal, only Mešťánek's son has to be a pervert.

And yet, when Freddy was a child, he was interested in quite normal pastimes: he collected postage stamps, flags of football teams, and had a herbarium. All his childhood hobbies were modest; they had to be, since the Mešťáneks were building a house and every crown went on buying bricks, and so on. If Freddy got a modest gift for his birthday, name day, or Christmas — handkerchiefs, wool for a pullover, shirt, or shoes — he was overcome by joy. He ran around the living room with an expression of disbelief and then ended by trying to crown his joyful and stormy amazement by rolling on the floor and doing clumsy somersaults.

When he was about seven, a problem cropped up: he began stealing toys from the children in the brickyard area. Freddy's father found it suspicious that little Freddy spent so much time in a tool shed on the building site of their house. A thorough search of the tool shed revealed a hiding place where Freddy concealed all the stolen toys and where he played with them. In the evening, Mešťánek and Freddy did the rounds of the brickyard barracks, and in each flat where there were children a blushing Freddy had to return a toy and apologize, using words that his father forced him to learn. All the families, except for Freddy's father, took a humorous view of the matter. But when they got home, Freddy was thrashed by his hysterical mother, who had just got back from work and found out about everything.

He always had technical inclinations. Once, he assembled a bicycle. One that worked.

Old Mešťánek reminisces as he smokes. It was those blasted tarts from the brickyard that ruined Freddy. Those forward, precocious young girls who ran around all day dressed in tee-shirts and shorts, always giggling at various immoral things that they learned from the adults. Their parents knocked back the drink in the factory buffet and the girls had no other entertainment but to ruin normal little boys like Freddy. Mešťánek's son fell victim to those monsters. It certainly wasn't quite like what old Forgách said. And anyway: who knows what old Forgách saw? Those blasted tarts from the brickyard must have seduced Freddy, if he masturbated in front of them, if he had masturbated at all!

Afterwards, when Freddy was a student at Hodonín, he behaved quite normally. True, of course, Freddy's father saw him only at weekends, but then Freddy behaved quite normally. Indeed, he was even more normal than his classmates: no beer, no cigarettes, no discos, and no girls. He preferred roaming the woods round Nová Ves, alone, or in a group. Every now and again younger friends would come to see him. They would play nice games: cowboys and Indians, and so on. It's odd that Freddy had no girl-friend; not at home in Nová Ves, nor in Hodonín. But that was OK, too. Freddy was in no hurry.

What his parents missed were his explosions of happiness when he got his gifts: his right shoe on his birthday and his left shoe for his name day a few weeks later. Or when he got the wool for a pullover at Christmas and the knitted pullover for his birthday. Freddy seemed uncommunicative and didn't talk much any more. Most of the time he spent outside, with his younger friends.

But let's face it, what could he do at home? His attic room was furnished like a room in the worker's dormitory: a bed, table, chair, a chest for bedding, wardrobe, carpet, and a dusty palm grown from a date seed which (together with another two dates) Freddy got for Christmas. The only thing you could do there was lie on the bed and stare at the ceiling for hours, your hands under your head, or do your homework.

For his secondary school matriculation evening Freddy's father lent him his wedding suit. It was a bit tight on Freddy, but otherwise it was fine, so his unhappy parents never understood why Freddy refused to go to the party and preferred to stay sulking in bed under his eiderdown.

Even after secondary school, when Freddy worked in the brickyard as a shift foreman, nobody saw him with any girl. He wasn't conscripted into the army, since a vein in his brain had ruptured when he was a child. Nothing serious, at least he could stay at home. He wouldn't have liked the army anyway; he liked his comforts.

Old Mešťánek would have never thought that his only son was a pervert. They always got along well. But ever since Freddy became a businessman and started to work at the car park, his father could never find a way of communicating with him. Perhaps, this was because Freddy rarely came home; he mostly slept in his trailer at the car park. His uncomfortable bachelor room was left empty most of the week. One day his mother was cleaning up and unwittingly opened the bedding chest. She discovered such terrible magazines at the bottom of the chest that she started to scream like a woman demented, until old Mešťánek ran in. Horrified, they both browsed through these well-thumbed colourful picture magazines with horrifying covers, names, and even more terrible contents and tried to tell each other that what they were seeing couldn't be true. The magazines specialized in one or other narrow field of unusual sex, so unusual that Freddy's parents, who had a simple education, couldn't even understand what was going on when they looked at some photographs. The sight of some pages in one of the magazines, depicting a live schoolgirl being quartered, forced old Mrs Mešťánek to go outside and vomit. Freddy's father was tougher; he packed up the magazines, took them behind the house and ritually burned them in the garden incinerator. He looked at the fire and used a long poker to ensure that all the pages were burned, watching the hungry flames consume the squashed or tumescent female, male, children's, or animal genitals and turn them into grey ashes. He was wondering what to say to Freddy when his son came home, but could not think of anything.

Usually, Freddy didn't come home for days on end, and when he finally came, nobody said a thing to him. His parents were silent about burning his magazines, and he asked no questions when he opened the chest and found his expensive magazines gone. Everything carried on as if by silent mutual agreement.

"He should find a girl; that would calm him down," his mother used to say. After all, he was thirty-five now, she would add. And old Mešťánek nodded in agreement. "For a catch like our Freddy," his mother went on, "an only son with a family house and a large garden, girls would do anything."

But Freddy didn't even want to hear the word marriage. He worked hard, day and night. When he came home, he only wanted to eat and sleep and didn't want to hear any talk of marriage. He was always in a bad mood. He realised that the perverted magazines, for which he'd paid an extortionate amount while still working at the car park, had been discovered and removed by his parents. However, he had no idea what to do about it, and so he did nothing.

Several times now, old Mešťánek has climbed the stairs to see him. He knocks at the door of Freddy's room, enters and sits down, his eyes open wide and full of paternal understanding, asking his son if he had any problems. "No, thanks, there's no problem," Freddy would always respond. "Do you need any help with anything?" his father would ask. "No thanks, I don't need any help," Freddy would say. "If you have a problem, tell me about it," said his father. "We can find a solution together," he added. "Thanks, I don't have any problems," Freddy said politely, but firmly. Old Mešťánek felt as if his son was throwing him out. He sighed, rose reluctantly to his feet, and went towards the door. "But still, if there is anything…" he said with his hand on the handle. "Thanks, everything's okay," Freddy would answer, and old Mešťánek would leave the uncomfortable room in a huff. Mrs Mešťánek would wait downstairs and look enquiringly at her husband. "Well, what is it?" she would whisper. Old Mešťánek only waved his hand. "Maybe he's in love," said Mrs Mešťánek and her face shone with hope and inner light. "Freddy should be married by now. All his classmates got married a long time ago. And Freddy isn't a bad match; with a house like this near the pond and a big garden full of fruit trees, any girl would take him. I hope he doesn't shack up with some city tart with a face plastered in make-up; an ordinary country girl with a school-leaving certificate would be best." Old Mešťánek sat down in the kitchen, picked up the newspaper for the umpteenth time and lit a cigarette.

He's still smoking, one after another. He never stops.

Around eleven, Freddy wakes up, gets dressed and goes downstairs. He gobbles up lunch and gets ready for work.

"You're going a bit early," remarks his father, shrouded in clouds of yellowish pungent smoke.

"Mmm," says Freddy.

"Will you be back in the evening?" Father asks.

"I don't know," says Freddy, meaning no.

"We're having doughnut balls with vanilla custard for supper," Father mentions as if in passing and watches his son out of the corner of his eye. This is his son's favourite dish.

Freddy Piggybank quivers and then freezes for a fraction of a second, but very soon he looks indifferent.

"I'll probably have to work at night, too," he says.

"What kind of job is this," Mrs Mešťánek butts in, "if you don't even know whether or not you'll be working at night?"

"Well," Freddy mumbles. "It's a job…"

"If you'd stayed in the brickyard," his mother says, "you'd work eight and a half hours, and no more"

"This is more interesting," says Freddy, "and I make more."

That argument stops his mother in her tracks. Money talks.

"Still, I'd like to know exactly what you do there," says his father.

"What I do?" says Freddy, blushing. "You know what: I'm a car park attendant…"

"But what does an attendant do?" Mrs Mešťánek persists.

"He attends," says Freddy.

"Don't be rude to your mother!" old Mešťánek jumps up, sending a vortex of pungent smoke round the kitchen.

"You were a car park attendant before," says his mother, "but you didn't get so exhausted!"

"The situation has changed," Freddy lies.

"It's not one of those car parks where streetwalkers go, is it?" worries Mrs Mešťánek. "If it's in the centre…"

"No," Freddy energetically shakes his head. "Only customers with top IQs go there…"

Freddy is glad to get his shoes on and be off to work.

The old Mešťáneks are on their own.

"And he didn't take a snack with him," says his father sadly. "If he goes on like this, he'll ruin his stomach and health."

They both become even more downcast. Finally old Mešťánek takes a decision.

"Make those doughnut balls for him, too," he tells his wife. "I'll take them to the car park for him. He'll enjoy warm food, you'll see. And I'll give the place a look-over; something's not quite right with the boy."

* * *

Even outside opening hours, Freddy has a lot to do in the Perverts' Centre. Sometimes he goes with the manager and the driver Eugen to fetch the linen from the laundry; sometimes they go to the warehouse to stock the bar. An impressive amount of alcohol gets swilled in the bar, evening after evening, night after night. Sometimes they send Freddy to the post office to collect or send a parcel. Freddy's glad; he likes to feel useful. The disgust he felt when he last worked as a car park attendant and later a lavatory attendant has been supplanted by the euphoria of his new, interesting employment.

Freddy arrives at work, stores his things in the dressing room that he shares with Sida, and goes to the bar. He orders mineral water and reaches for a new issue of *Bondage Fantasies* which Silvia's *Perverts' Centre* subscribes to, as well as other specialised magazines. Freddy immerses himself in reading. More precisely, he peruses the pictures. He tries to keep abreast with world-wide advances in his field, like any other person who loves his work.

Soon his boss, Silvia, enters the bar. They've known each other for a long time, from the old days. Silvia asks Freddy to take invitations to some evening do to the post office. On the way back, he has to buy her the evening paper and, if it's out, *Reflex* magazine.

Freddy is glad to be of service. He happily gets up, takes the envelopes and goes to the post office. The closest one, he believes, is at the main railway station, so that's where he decides to go.

The city has put on its autumnal garb. Freddy walks along the Jaskov Row and smiles. Gold coins rain down from the birches in villa gardens. A flock of sparrows flies over the garden fence right in Freddy's face, like a handful of stones swiftly launched low over the ground. Freddy feels an intense love of life and the world, at least for the moment.

His chores done, he returns to *Justine*, his half-read magazine and cold mineral water.

At about four the male and female staff assemble. The men don't look male, since their clothes, looks and behaviour are female. They have real breasts and slim legs that they like to show off in miniskirts. Only their deeper voices might give them away, otherwise they are indistinguishable from women.

Finally, Sida Tešadíková arrives. The sight of her makes Freddy tremble with servility and devotion. Sida sits next to him; she is wearing a leather jacket and trousers. She puts her helmet on the bar and orders a beer. Bored, she leafs through *Bondage Fantasies* which Freddy has put down, as he awaits her latest commands.

"So?" Freddy asks.

"So what?" Tešadíková asks.

"Are you satisfied with me?"

"You'll do." Sida takes a Marlboro from the breast pocket of her motorcycle jacket and lights up. She blows the smoke at Freddy. "Why do you ask?"

"Well, you did promise to raise my salary," Freddy says shyly.

"I did?" Sida says sceptically.

"Yes," says the fat man with a blush, but then continues calmly, like anyone sure his cause is just. "I coped with hanging and immobilising perfectly," he begins to itemize. "Crucifying, too; I hand you the instruments without your having to say a word; you only have to think about them. And the tidiness? Tell me: did you ever have such an well-organized torture room before?"

Sida silently drinks her beer.

"I've pawned my family's gold," Freddy confesses. "I have to get it out of hock and put it back before my parents find out…"

The owner of the business appears.

"Ladies and gentlemen, finish your cigarettes and drinks, and get your work clothes on," she says and claps her hands sharply. "We open in ten minutes."

"Let's go," Sida tells Freddy, stubbing out her cigarette. "I'll think about the rise. Well, why are you gawping at me? Move, you perverted pig!"

Freddy obediently follows his slave-owner into the torture room to get ready for the evening.

* * *

His eyes bulging, hotelier Rácz is sitting at his desk, hammering it monotonously with his fist. His cruel lips are covered in yellowish foam dripping down his chiselled chin. Rácz doesn't wipe the foam off. His bloodshot eyes look at the photographs he got in the morning post. The pictures are of poor quality, taken from a television monitor, and they all show Silvia with Junec, that Slovak American: Silvia under Junec, Silvia on top of Junec, Silvia with Junec in her mouth, Junec with Silvia in his mouth, Junec in Silvia from the front, and Junec in Silvia from behind. The hotelier swears furiously, and sweeps the photographs off his desk with one wave of his arm. So the American ignored Rácz's warning. He didn't dump Rácz's girl friend. Quite the opposite, he went ahead and slept with her: so he insulted Rácz and humiliated him.

Rácz is so upset by a sudden flood of jealousy and hatred that he is trembling all over. Silvia ought to have been happy at the mighty Rácz taking an interest in her. Instead, she is rebelling, and refusing Rácz. Fame in Austria has turned her head. She's acting the grand lady. First she stabbed Rácz's arm, then she bit his palm, and finally she nearly gouged out his eye with a piece of ice. And now, these photographs.

Rácz gets up, gathers up the photographs strewn all over the floor and studies them attentively once more. No, Silvia wants Rácz. It's just that she won't sell herself cheap. She wants to torment Rácz a bit. That's why she's done all this. This, too, was one of her tricks to get him all hot and horny. Rácz smiles. He'll get her one of these days and then he'll punish her severely for cheating on him with other men. He'll punish her and then he'll shower her with kisses, flowers, jewels, and presents: that's the kind of man Rácz is.

But as for the American Junec, that's a very different matter. Rácz gave him a friendly warning, even offered him an indemnity, if that was what you could call his bribe. Junec the American accepted it and seemed to have got the message. He seemed to have known what kind of game he'd got involved in. Rácz looks over the American's trim figure and his taut genitals ravaging Silvia's pudenda. Yes, the hotelier decides, the only way he can wash away such deep humiliation is with blood. American blood.

He presses the button of his intercom.

"Get me Mozoň, Šolík and Tupý," he orders his secretary. "At the double!"

The trio of ex-secret policemen appears in an instant. They line up in front of their boss and stand respectfully to attention.

Rácz doesn't acknowledge their presence. He is working hard at something with scissors, his tongue protruding between clenched lips as hard as leather. Finally, he has finished. The result of his efforts is two clumsy likenesses of a man, only too obviously cut out from larger photographs. The man's face shows excitement, sensual ecstasy in the extreme. Mozoň's men would rather like to have seen the rest of the photographs, but these have ended up shredded into tiny fragments in Rácz's wastebasket.

"Who is he?" asks Mozoň.

"He's staying here in the hotel," says Rácz. "The Slovak American. Mozoň saw him when I had a meeting with him."

"So what's up with him, boss?" asks Tupý. "Why are you giving us his photo?"

Noisily, but with all the dignity he can muster, Rácz gets up from his chair, walks round the gigantic desk, and starts pacing the room with his hands behind his back.

"What's up with this American?" asks Tupý.

Mozoň kicks him on the ankle.

Rácz paces the room a little longer and then stops. He looks at his bodyguards. He doesn't want to know anything. He pays his men royally; in exchange he supposes he can express a wish not to be involved in anything, right?

Mozoň nods. "We understand, boss," he says. "Don't you worry."

"I hope you haven't lost your touch yet," says Rácz, looking the trio over.

"No worries, boss," Mozoň assures the hotelier. "His life insurance is about to be cashed in," he says with a vicious smile.

Rácz theatrically covers his ears. The ex-secret policemen respectfully leave the office.

* * *

Old Mr Mešťánek stops at Freddy's old car park, where construction is in full swing. He is carrying a string shopping bag and in it is a two-section lunch-tin. The upper part contains freshly made doughnut balls and the lower part is filled with vanilla custard.

Dismayed and puzzled, Freddy's father surveys the huge construction site, but then his face brightens up. In a corner between the construction site and a busy fast-food stall he spots Freddy's trailer. Old Mr Mešťánek walks across the Wooden Village and knocks on the trailer's fibreboard door. Nobody answers, nobody opens the door.

"What do you want over there?" some arsehole sticks his head out of the snack bar and asks Mešťánek's father. "There's nobody there!"

The old Mešťánek turns to the arsehole.

"Hey mate, do you know where I can find the man who works here?" he asks.

The arsehole loses his temper.

"I threw him out," he says. "I'm the boss here."

That makes no impression on Freddy's father.

"Do you know where he works now, mate?" he asks.

"I don't, and I don't like you calling me mate," the bastard boss takes offence. "I don't remember saying you could take liberties."

"Why would I want to be mates with a runt like you?" asks old Mr Mešťánek and, thwarted, strides to the exit from the Wooden Village.

"Hey," an unkempt, short man reeking of beer addresses him. "You looking for Fweddy? Fweddy Piggybank? He's working now somewhere called a *Perverts' Centre*, it's a bwothel. It's called *Justine*. Below the main railway station. Ask the taxi dwivers, they'll know!"

The man went back to his beer.

Old Mr Mešťánek is so shaken that he forgets even to say thank you. In utter horror he approaches the parked taxis. The first one in the rank flashes its lights. Freddy's father goes up to it.

"Could you tell me, please," he asks shyly, for he has never in his whole life spoken to a taxi driver, "Do you know of an establishment called… ah, *Justine*?"

"Of course I do," the cabdriver smiles in amusement. "Get in, we'll get you there!"

Stunned, Mr Mešťánek submissively gets into the taxi. For the whole journey he is very tense, gripping in his hand the string bag with Freddy's snack.

"Going to let your hair down?" The taxi driver tries to get a conversation going, as he spins the steering wheel.

Old Mr Mešťánek feels very tense and awkward sitting there. He now regrets taking a taxi; he could have taken a tram and then walked.

"Well, here we are, sir," says the taxi driver and puts a finger on the taximeter's digital screen. "Eighty four," he says.

Old Mr Mešťánek takes out his purse and reluctantly pays off the driver.

"Have really good fun," says the driver politely.

Freddy's father stops on the pavement, his head flung back, examining the neon girl and a sign which is alternately bright and dim and says "*Justine*." Then he knocks hard at the door of the villa.

A little window opens and two penetrating eyes stare at old Mr Mešťánek. Old Mr Mešťánek politely says hello, takes a breath and tries to explain why he has come.

"Are you a club member?" the man at the entrance asks him.

"No, but…" says old Mr Mešťánek.

Obviously, the bouncer has decided that this scraggy old man, his skin yellow from nicotine, presents no danger, and lets him in.

"I'm only visiting," says Piggybank's father. "To see my son... I've got his supper here..."

Old Mr Mešťánek lifts up the string bag with lunch-tin and scones.

"Oh, I see," says the bouncer. "And which one is it?"

"Alfred Mešťánek," says the father. "He's quite a big fellow."

"Freddy?" the bouncer asks. "Freddy Piggybank?"

"That's what they call him," Freddy's father nods unwillingly. He has never liked that nickname, though he's heard it a few times before.

"I don't think he's free at the moment," says the bouncer. "He's with a client."

Mešťánek's father is dumbfounded with horror.

"You mean?" he says, puzzled.

"Well, he's got a client," says the bouncer. "Don't you know what your son does? Come and sit down in the bar for now. I'll get him to come and see you when he's finished."

In the course of a few minutes old Mr Mešťánek aged ten years and shrank four inches. He followed the tall brute into a bar elegantly lit by spotlights.

"That's Freddy's dad," the bouncer told the barmaid who was wearing a tight knitted miniskirt. "He's brought him his supper."

They both smiled knowingly.

"What will you have, Mister Piggybank?" the barmaid twittered. "Cola, Fanta, coffee? Or perhaps a little cognac?"

"Cognac, please," old Mr Mešťánek sighs. "Make it a double."

Freddy's father hurriedly downs the cognac and looks around the room. His gaze falls on the half-naked females working for the house: they are dressed, or rather undressed, in provocative outfits that we who have had a classical education call *dessous*. They're waiting for clients and whiling away the time talking almost inaudibly.

"When might my son be available?" old Mr Mešťánek asks the barmaid.

"It's hard to say exactly," says the young lady. "It depends on the client..."

"You see, I don't have much time," says the old man. "I wanted to catch the news on TV. I don't suppose you'd let me watch the news here."

Old Mr Mešťánek points to a huge cinema-style screen showing two young girls copulating with a huge dog.

"I'm afraid not," the barmaid says. "Here in *Justine* we don't have the stomach for politics..."

The barmaid picks up the phone and calls a two-digit number.

* * *

The client is lying face-down, his hands and feet tied to a rack. He's an elderly gentleman, an Austrian, and he's naked. Sida stands in front of him, her legs splayed, her bare genitals roughly level with the client's face. She is holding a whip. Freddy, dressed in leather underpants, leather apron and a black face-mask, turns the wheel a few notches tighter and then puts on the catch.

"So what's it going to be, you swine?" Sida screams at the client. "Are you going to tell us, or not?"

"Pliss, pliss," the client pleads first in broken Slovak, then in German. "Ich weiss nix! Nix wissen! Gnade! Gnade!"

"Speak Slovak!" Sida orders him, lashing the client's back with a whip. She fixes her bleary eyes on her underling. "Molten lead!" she says tersely.

"No, not the lead!" the client whines. "Um Gotteswillen, no lead!"

Freddy goes up to a cauldron, takes a ladle and dips it into the lead. Of course, the molten lead is ordinary water dyed silver and heated to a high, but bearable and safe temperature. All Freddy's actions are orchestrated so that the client can follow them with his bloodshot eyes.

Freddy comes up to the client and slowly and carefully pours the liquid between his shoulder-blades, onto his back and behind. The client howls and writhes, as if it really were molten lead.

The telephone rings.

"Yes," Sida answers the phone. "Good," she says and hangs up. She looks at Piggybank. "You've got a visitor," she says.

Freddy takes fright. What sort of visitor? Could it be the police, about the bicycles? Or suppose it's because of what happened to Lady?

"Who?" he asks, his eyes goggling with terror.

"Your dad," says Sida. "He's brought your supper."

"You're joking," says Piggybank incredulously.

"Who's joking?" Sida is enraged and with a few well-aimed lashes, whips Freddy's bare thighs. "Who's joking, you stupid fat slob? How dare you talk like this to your mistress? Down on your knees! Ask for forgiveness!"

However, Freddy is beyond all that. His gaze switches nervously from side to side.

"Jesus Christ!" he says.

"You've got five minutes!" Miss Tešadíková tells him. "And come straight back. I'll finish him off," she points to her shackled client. "Just go."

Freddy gratefully turns his gaze to her who must be obeyed and runs to the dressing room. With trembling fingers he rips off his leather garb and searches for his XXL jeans, the biggest you can get.

In the meantime, Sida continues torturing her client. She is still trying to torment him into giving her the secret code-word which they have agreed in advance. When the client gives the code-word, it's a signal that he has had enough pain and that the client has been serviced. Sida goes on with great gusto; the Austrian is a regular client and pays as if there's no tomorrow.

* * *

When Freddy, dressed in his everyday clothes, gets to the bar, his father has already gone.

"He cleared off two minutes ago," said the barmaid. "His nerves couldn't take it, poor man. He ordered a double cognac, so I put it on your tab."

"A double cognac?" Freddy couldn't believe his ears. He just couldn't get his mind round the thought of his father, a notorious kill-joy and teetotaller, drinking cognac in the city's most perverted brothel.

"He left this for you," the barmaid handed Freddy the two-compartment lunch-tin in the string bag.

Looking flabbergasted, Freddy takes the lunch-tin, and carries it like a treasure into the torture chamber. He puts it down in the dressing room, changes into his working leathers and goes back to help Sida.

"These doughnut balls are good," says Sida, her mouth full, a few hours later, before daybreak. "Divine," she adds. "And the custard!"

"Hmm," says Freddy sadly, as he sweeps the floor.

He had shared his food with his mistress like a brother and now he wondered where he could lay his head. He would probably have to sleep here, in the dressing room. He would never be able to face his parents, particularly his father, again. For how could he ever explain his job in such an establishment? How, indeed?

"Is something wrong," Sida asked, wiping the bottom of the lunch-tint with the last doughnut ball.

"It's nothing," Freddy said. He put the broom away and sat down next to his slave-owner. "Listen, Sida…" he starts with embarrassment.

"Yes?" Miss Tešadiková asks him.

"Do your parents know what you do for living?" Freddy enquires.

"What do you think? Of course not," says Sida. "They think I teach in a private school. I told them it was a Catholic grammar school. Good, isn't it?"

Freddy gives a wan, completely joyless smile. He looks at Sida.

"Why are you gawping at me like that?" Sida asks brusquely and averts her eyes from the fat man's unusually piercing and serious gaze.

"Sida, I'm up shit creek!" says Freddy. "How do I explain to my father and mother that I'm working in a brothel?"

"You're the best judge of that," says Sida. "Why do you order supper from home?"

"What do you mean order?" Freddy explodes. "I can't even understand how my father found this place! If only he'd waited a bit..."

Sida goes off to take a shower. Freddy makes up a bed on the dressing room couch.

"What's this?" Sida asks when she comes out of the shower cubicle, wiping her ears with a towel. "Are you sleeping here?"

Freddy nods.

"You really are scared shitless of your old folks," Sida says bitingly.

"And what am I supposed to tell them?" Freddy asks.

"What? Nothing!" advises his slave-owner. "Aren't you an adult? You are. Are you in charge of your life? You are. Did I lend you the cash for the rings? I did. Did you pay me back? You did. So what do you have to account for to anyone?"

"So why do you keep it a secret from your people?" fat Freddy counter-attacks.

"I've got no secrets," says Miss Tešadíková, "I'm grown-up, I have my own flat. I live my own life. I see my parents once in six months, why should I throw anything in their face? But if they find out anything, nothing will change. Not in MY life it won't. But you, you old layabout, still live with your parents, and their opinion is scripture for you. It's shameful in this day and age to depend on someone else's opinion."

"Me? Depend?" Freddy objects.

"You certainly do," asserts Sida. "If you didn't, you wouldn't care what your father thought about your job."

Freddy says nothing. The sky in the narrow cellar window is bright now. Sida changes into jeans and leather jacket.

"Good night," she says to Freddy, who is stretched out on the couch.

"Good night," says Freddy.

* * *

Martin wakes up with the persistent feeling that he is being watched. He shakes himself fully awake. Through the window shutters the neon signs' obtrusive pulsating splendour penetrates his hotel room. Martin reaches out and turns on the bedside lamp. The dimmed light reveals the massive figure of Žofré standing dithering by the window.

"Oh, shit!" Martin cries desperately in English, and quickly tries to reach for something to throw at the ghost that was once his brother-in-law. So Hruškovič was right to say he was a charlatan and couldn't really do exorcisms, he realises in horror and grabs a slipper.

"Stop it, man," Žofré says with dignity.

The effect of his measured and somehow alien voice is such that Martin's hand holding the slipper freezes in mid-throw.

"I was at one point relieved of my mission," says the ghost, "but now I've been allowed to come and warn you for the last time."

"No need, thanks!" says Martin and his arm drops in resignation. "If you have no more to do on earth, then what are you doing here?"

"The All-Highest is letting me visit you one more time," says Žofré.

"That's nice of Him," says Martin, and takes his watch from the bedside table and looks at it. It's three in the morning. "So what have you got for me, Žofré?" he asks with an ostentatious show of patience.

"In a moment you're going to be murdered," says Žofré.

"Get on with you," Martin bursts out laughing, "Who'd want to murder me?"

"The hotelier Rácz," says the ghost.

"And why?" Martin says sceptically.

"Because you screwed that slut of his," says Žofré.

"Don't be insulting, okay?" Martin objects. "How did he find out?"

"She sent him photographs of you both naked..." says Žofré and blushes. "I've seen them, too," he adds pointedly.

"Damn dirty bitch!" Martin swears in English and leaps out of bed.

"She sent him the pictures to hurt him," says the ghost, "and at the same time to get back at you."

"At me? For what?" Junec is at a loss. He visualises Silvia, all lust, desire and passion, screaming in ecstasy.

"Because you slept with her, that's why," says Žofré. "She hates men and hates you, too. But no more talk, Martin! In a few minutes Rácz's three killers will come in and throw you out of the window. It's supposed to look like suicide."

"How do you know?" Martin refuses to believe it.

"I heard them a while ago in the car when they were driving here. At the moment they're walking up the stairs. They won't use the lift, in case the liftboy sees them."

Martin clutches his head. He is seized by a moderate degree of panic.

"What am I to do?" he asks. "I don't have a gun, or a knife on me. I can't fight off three hit men with my bare hands."

"Not even one," says Žofré. "You're crap; they're professionals."

Martin makes a dash to the phone, listens for a while, and then slams the receiver down in fury.

"They've cut the line," Žofré explains. "I did say they were professionals. They've thought of everything," he adds, almost in admiration.

"So, what am I to do?" Martin asks in desperation and feverishly starts to get dressed.

"Well, now even old Žofré comes in handy, doesn't he?" the ghost laughs maliciously. "You, the pride of the American establishment!"

"What am I to do, Žofré?" Martin repeats the question as he puts a sock on. "This is no time for kidding."

"What am I to do, Žofré?" Žofré apes Martin's begging, whining tone. He smiles. "They've reached our floor now," he reveals with a smile. "Now they'll take a short rest. You're the one running out of time, my old pal. I've got all the time in the world..."

"Well, Žofré!" Martin insists and, now he has his shoes on, gets up.

"Pick up your chequebook and passport," Žofré says.

Martin opens the bedside table drawer, takes his chequebook out, then his US passport and a wad of credit cards. His eyes spot a Spanish switchblade he always uses to clean his nails. He puts it in his pocket.

"Open the window," the ghost orders.

Martin goes up to the window and opens it. Six storeys beneath him the street and pavement glisten in the rain, and in the distance the muddy river glimmers. From the port comes a tugboat horn's prolonged call.

"Jump!" says Žofré.

Martin steps back from the window and looks at Žofré reproachfully.

"I mean it, jump," says Žofré. "You won't get killed, I'll help you. Seriously. Boy scout's honour!"

"I don't trust you, Žofré," says Martin and once more looks into the abyss. He is trembling with fear.

"Now they're opening the door to your suite," says Žofré. "They'll be here in a few seconds."

Martin is resigned and puts one leg over the window ledge.

"You'll fall like swan's down," says Žofré. "Trust me. I've got everything under control."

Martin looks down beneath him and his guts convulse with a spasm of unspeakable horror.

"It's too far, Žofré!" he says desperately, in English.

He hears a noise and jerks round. His gaze falls on the door handle. He can see it moving. But his horror of the abyss and his mistrust of Žofré are too strong. Martin gets off the window ledge and freezes in helpless panic.

The door opens and three dangerous-looking men walk into the bedroom.

"Is that him, chief?" one of them asks excitedly.

"No, it's his old mum," the other one counters dryly.

The men hurl themselves at Martin, grab him and without further ado drag him to the window.

"Be careful," orders the oldest, evidently in charge. "We don't want to leave any traces."

Martin fights back desperately, he tries to shout, but one of the hit men gags him. Martin's eyes desperately search for Žofré. Like a host seeing his guests out, Žofré slowly and with resignation follows the group of men to the window.

Martin frees his mouth and shouts: "Žofré!"

In no time they gag him again.

"It'll work that way, too," says Žofré calmly, watching Mozoň opening the other pane of the window, too, and the two underlings throwing Junec into the vertiginous abyss.

"Get away from that window!" Mozoň shouts when he sees Tupý and Šolík watching the American Slovak's fall.

The secret policemen obey unwillingly, but quickly.

"You pricks!" Mozoň rages. "Somebody might have seen you."

The secret policemen remove all traces of the struggle and in the middle of a rainy night Martin Junec descends as gently as swan's down from the sixth floor. Eventually he makes a soft landing on the pavement. Žofré is there by his side.

"Ooff," says the ghost. "I didn't know you were that heavy."

Martin pinches himself on the cheek to wake up from this weird dream, but it doesn't help.

"I do think I deserve at least a thank you," Žofré mumbles.

Martin shakes his head incredulously. "Thank you, Žofré," he says.

"Don't mention it," says the ghost. "Let's say goodbye now, Martin. I've finished here. We won't see each other again. I suppose we will meet some day, but there's plenty of time for that."

"Where are you going?" Martin asks.

Žofré laughs and points his finger upwards. "And you?" he asks. "What are you going to do?"

"Well, what else?" says Martin. "I'm going to the police to report an attempted murder. I'll show Rácz what's what."

"Nobody's going believe you," says Žofré. "How are you going to explain to them that you're alive after falling from the sixth floor?"

"Hmm, that's a fact," Junec admits in English.

"Besides, Rácz has the police under his thumb, too," says Žofré. "And when he finds out that you're still alive, he'll have you killed again. He wants to make an impression on that hooker."

"That dirty whore!" Martin adds, now that he remembers whom he has to thank for all this.

"Leave the country," Žofré advises him. "You simply have to disappear. Go and find Edna. Marry her. Love is the best cure for everything. Real devoted love. And never come back here; this country belongs to the Ráczes of this world. After all, an American, a real American, doesn't need to do business in Slovakia."

Martin stops to think. "I think you're right, Žofré," he says.

Žofré stretches his hand out to him. "Let's say our good-byes," he says. "That Hruškovič business was a blow below the belt from you, but screw it! I realize you must have had it up to here with me. Now that my mission is finished, I'll leave you. But don't ever be unfaithful to Edna. If I find out that you're seeing other women, I'll come and make myself known to you. Good-bye!"

Martin tries to shake the hand that Žofré is offering, but his fingers pass through immaterial, slightly warm mist.

"Good-bye, Žofré," says Martin, "and forgive me."

Žofré smiles and closes his eyes… and dissolves in front of Martin.

Martin sighs. Then he puts his hands in his pockets and nervously looking around, heads for a night hamburger stall whose lights are flashing in the distance near the taxi stop. There he buys two cheeseburgers and a paper cup of chips with ketchup. He washes his meal down with a can of Pepsi. After his vertiginous fall from the sixth floor, he feels hungry. He eats and reflects on what he's going to do with his new lease of life.

The vision of a future with Edna at his side makes him quite enthusiastic. So much so that when, with a full stomach, he gets into a taxi that will take him to Vienna, he smiles contentedly.

* * *

It seems like a good idea to take the taxi to Vienna, since it is the closest civilised city and it takes less than an hour to get there. He needs to feel safe: only when he is at Vienna airport does he feel he is beyond the reach of Rácz's tentacles.

From Vienna, Martin takes a jumbo jet to Hong Kong; from Hong Kong he flies to Manila, spending a night in a hotel, and in the morning he hires a Lear jet from a small charter company. From Manila he flies to the southern Philippines and from there, after taking on more fuel, he makes it as far as Port Moresby in New Guinea.

In Port Moresby, Martin takes a taxi to the local branch of the Smithsonian Institute, the address Edna left him.

"I'm sorry," a polite institute employee tells him, "at the moment Dr Gershwitz is on the island of…" the employee consults his documents, "Kalalau."

"Where's that, for God's sake?" Junec asks in alarm.

The employee takes the map of Oceania and turns it so Martin can see. "Here," he says and points a finger, "It's north of the Wallis Islands between Funafuti and the Tokelau Archipelago."

"There's nothing there," says Martin, disappointed.

"But there is," says the employee. "It's just not visible on the map."

"How do I get there?" Martin asks.

"You fly to Fiji and then take a boat to Futunu. From Futunu there's a mail boat to Kalalau."

"How often?" Martin asks.

"Quite often in summer," says the Smithsonian Institute employee. "Every month."

"I need to speak to Miss Gershwitz right away," insists Martin.

"I'm afraid that won't be possible," the employee smiles politely.

Martin runs out of the building and stops a cab. "To the airport," he orders. "Hurry!"

The chartered Lear jet is still parked, taking on fuel. Martin runs up the steps into the cockpit. The surprised pilots look round nervously.

"I'm glad you're still here," says Martin. "I've got another job for you."

Soon they're crossing the wide ocean.

"The Solomon Islands," says the pilot, pointing to forested land below.

"How much further?" Martin asks.

"Another eighteen hundred kilometres. That gives you two and a half hours," says the pilot.

Martin nods and leaves the cockpit. He takes his seat. A nice slant-eyed flight attendant brings him coffee and a dessert. Martin eats the cake, drinks his coffee and falls asleep.

A tactful hand on his shoulder wakes him. The flight attendant is over him. "It's time, sir," she says.

Martin follows her into the cockpit. The pilot shows him a tiny speck on the map and then points at the window. There is a small green island below.

"Kalalau," he says.

"Are you sure?" Martin asks.

"A hundred per cent," replies the pilot.

"Okay," says Martin and pulls out a cheque book. "How much do I owe you?" he asks.

When Martin has paid the crew of the Lear jet, the co-pilot brings a parachute. With the help of the crew, Martin puts it on. He moves towards the exit.

"You don't have to do anything after you jump," the co-pilot tells him. "Just count to ten and pull this firmly." He points to a metal ring hanging on the left shoulder strap. "And then you can steer with the two strings you'll see when the parachute opens."

"Don't be afraid," the pilot tells him.

"I'm not," says Martin. "I had a go at something like this recently."

He smiles at the slant-eyed attendants. The co-pilot turns a wheel and noisily opens the cabin door. The wind enters the cabin together with the roar of the jet engines. Martin makes for the door. He firmly grabs the handle. Below shines the sea. Land is looming up somewhere on the right.

"Now!" shouts the co-pilot. Martin takes a deep breath and throws himself into the void. He counts to ten and pulls the ring. There is a sound of folded silk opening, and Martin is jerked up in the air. The fast dive has shaken him up. The roar of the passing aeroplane soon dies away. He can see tiny figures, natives running along the blindingly yellow beach towards the place they reckon he will land.

Junec lands in warm shallow surf. He immediately stands up and unbuckles the straps. He heads towards the natives. Some children quickly try to pull the soggy parachute out of the water. From the crowd of local natives an old man sets out, dressed like others in a flowery sarong, but with an amulet hanging round his neck. When the old man comes closer, it turns out that the amulet is an empty flattened can of Fanta.

Martin realises that he is dealing with the village chieftain. He puts his hand on his chest and says: "Martin Junec."

The chieftain smiles.

Martin points significantly to the sky. "I..." he says, "fly... big iron bird..."

Martin accompanies each word with a pantomime, solemn, but easy to understand, together with grimaces copied from films about Indians.

"My wife... here... A white wife... from far away... Doctor Edna Gershwitz... Here... Kalalau... I've come to get her... I love her..."

Martin points at his heart.

The old man spits out the betel he is chewing and smiles broadly, showing teeth blackened by the betel.

"I fully understand your predicament, sir," he says. "It's just that you are not in Kalalau. This is Aumaoua. My name is Tioka the Third: I am king here. Kalalau is about one hundred and fifty kilometres that way."

The king points his brown hand with its glittering bracelets to the open sea.

"God Almighty!" Martin curses and his gaze wanders murderously to the sky. Then his eyes rest in despair on the horizon. The flaming orange sun is slowly setting, making a lovely picture with the line of foaming surf and rustling palms. "What a bloody business," says Martin.

"Do me the honour of being a guest in my modest dwelling," suggests the king. "Tomorrow, I'll let you have a man and a catamaran to take you to Kalalau. No problem, as they say. Do you agree?"

Martin sighs and shrugs his shoulders. The king takes this to be consent. He claps his dry hands twice and two beautiful native girls come up to Martin and hang wreaths of aromatic flowers around his neck. Another native woman with thick black braids and a flower in her hair gives him half a coconut with some yellowish drink.

"Piña colada with Bacardi on ice," says Tioka III, noticing him hesitating.

The procession, led by Martin and the King, walks from the beach to the trees, and then the roofs of the palm leaf dwellings come into sight.

"You may be curious to know where I learned my English so well," says the king proudly. "I went to the local mission primary school," he boasts, before Martin can react.

Martin knows that he should pretend to take at least a polite interest in the king's education, but he still hasn't got over his unpleasant surprise. He stares at the neat huts that look like huts in tourist brochures.

"I know Dr Gershwitz," the King informs him when they sit down on a clearing among the huts. "She was here, too, a few weeks ago."

Martin looks askance at Tioka III.

"She showed an interest in our... well, love customs," says the king. "Especially in our custom of offering a guest the company of our women."

Martin finishes his drink and a pretty native beauty gives him another coconut.

"You know," says the king, "on our island this tradition has been kept for centuries... when a stranger comes here, we offer him all our women. The stranger can take his choice. How many women he makes happy with his company is up to him, but it shouldn't be less than ten... Well, in a nutshell, it's our tradition here, you understand."

Martin nods. "It's an interesting tradition," he says.

"A female stranger is offered our men," says the King. "The most handsome and the youngest ones. And this was the custom that your wife studied here. She bestowed her company and made twenty-eight of the best fishermen of our island happy. One after another, including myself. She is a very good woman. I am sure you are very happy together..."

Martin absentmindedly nods. "She isn't my wife yet," he mumbles. "But we are happy, indeed."

"And so, dear friend, I am asking you to make your choice," says the king and claps his dry hands.

Several native beauties line up in front of Martin with seductive smiles on their lips.

Martin's mouth turns dry. He looks around nervously. The king and the elders in his suite observe him intensely. Martin knocks back the piña colada and puts the coconut down.

"This ancient tradition applies to you, too, my friend," says the king. "And all the more because you are the man who flew down from the sky. I know, I know," the king assures Martin, "we all saw the aeroplane and we know that the Americans have landed on the moon, too. But from the point of view of folklore, you are, whether you like it or not, Ahuhuai Tahuhuneui, the Man from the Sky."

Martin begins to explain. He is unbelievably tired. He is no Ahuhay-Tahuhay. Bratislava-Vienna-Hong Kong-Manila-Port Moresby, and so on. All of it with little rest. His body desires anything but sex. He wants to sleep, sleep, sleep. He doesn't want to offend the honourable Tioka III, but he really is in no state to perform as local tradition prescribes...

"Our tradition can cope with that, too," smiles the king. He claps his dry hands twice and a pretty girl brings a wooden box. The king opens the box and shows the guest its contents, a green powder.

"What is it?" Junec asks.

"It's the extract of a plant called ramaateua," says the king. "When you rub it into your genitals, you'll have no problem favouring a hundred, what do I mean by a hundred, TWO HUNDRED of our women, one after the other! I can't see any problem here."

Martin's glazed eyes inspect the beauties paraded in front of him. They are all gorgeous, well built, with smooth milk-coffee complexions, long legs and shoulders as broad as competition swimmers'.

"Is there no way of refusing this honour in a way that doesn't offend anyone?" he asks after a certain inner struggle.

"But certainly," says the King. "If you are determined not to honour us with your favours, all you have to do is get up and shout aloud: 'Uouiauaue!' That means you are rejecting it. In that case," Tioka III claps his dry hands twice, "a different destiny awaits you..."

After hearing the king clap, the natives stand aside and behind them Martin spots a huge cauldron blackened by smoke and years of use.

"This is traditional, too," says the King. "As a mission primary school graduate and believing Christian, I am not very proud of it, but the mission is far away on the island of Tokelau, and we and the kettle are here. An old superstition says that when you eat human flesh, it passes all the good features of that person on to you. You are Ahuhuai Tahuhuneui, the Man from Sky. Your good features will pass on to us whether you sleep with our women, or we eat you for supper..."

The king's face is friendly and good-natured. Thunderstruck, Martin looks now at the king, now at the kettle.

"Hang on," he says. "Are you telling me that you'd kill me and boil me in that cauldron?"

Tioka III shakes his head with a kindly smile. "No, my friend. We wouldn't kill you. We'd boil you alive. Don't you know that brains of people slowly cooked alive happen to be this region's greatest delicacy?

A man who goes mad from horrendous pain has everything addled in his brain. That gives the brain meat an excellent taste."

Martin is trembling with horror. He averts his gaze from the cauldron that is so menacingly close. The beautiful native women, full of suspense and excitement, dance.

"And it really has to be at least ten of them?" Martin asks Tioka III.

"It does," nods the king.

"And if it were fewer?" Martin cautiously enquires.

"In that case I'm very sorry," says the king, pointing to the cauldron.

"I see," says Martin.

The king shakes the box of powder. "With the help of ramaateua you'll have no problem making the entire island happy," he says.

Sighing heavily, Martin gets up and heads for the hut. The beautiful women, twittering enthusiastically, follow him.

"Hey!" Tioka III, lifting up the box of aphrodisiac, calls after Junec. "And apply it generously," he advises him amiably. Martin takes the box and turns it in his fingers. He goes to the hut, dimly lit by a flickering fire in the hearth and by the naked bodies of native beauties, ready to receive the favours of Ahuhuai Tahuhuneui, the Man from the Sky.

* * *

Day is breaking by the time that Ahuhuai Tahuhuneui gets round to the last native beauty. Despite the extract of ramaateua, things didn't go all that smoothly. When the Man from the Sky finished his last bout of lovemaking, he collapsed onto the mat and fell into a deep sleep, oblivious of the throbbing, searing pain in his badly abraded genitals.

By the time he awakes, the sun is high. The rippling surf makes him want to sleep, so he spends more time in sweet slumber. His gold Rolex stopped when he landed on the beach, so he has no idea what time it is.

When he wakes up again and sits up on his primitive bed, someone in the dark hut says a few words and a beautiful native girl enters, carrying a bowl of rice and spicy vegetables. The girl smiles radiantly at Junec: he assumes that she was one of thirty to whom he dispensed his manly favours the previous night.

Into the hut steps Tioka III, accompanied by several elders.

"How did the mighty Ahuhuai Tahuhuneui sleep last night?" asks the King and sits down on a low bamboo seat.

"Very well, thanks" says Martin. "You promised me a catamaran to Kalalau. Will that be possible?"

"Well," Tioka III says, "events have taken a different direction…"

"What am I to understand by that?" Martin asks, displeased. He has fulfilled his duty. He acted like a real Ahuhuai Tahuhuneui and screwed not ten, but thirty women. The mighty Ahuhuai Tahuhuneui even noticed that some came back for a second, and even a third bout. So Tioka III should now keep his promise.

The king smiles. "You don't give me credit, my friend," he tells Martin. "This morning we contacted Kalalau Island by radio. Why should you bother with a catamaran? This afternoon Doctor Gershwitz is coming here by seaplane to pick you up."

Martin trembles. The mention of Edna arouses the most tender emotions in him.

"I hope that will be acceptable to you," says Tioka III.

"Oh yes," says Junec. "Very acceptable."

The monarch claps his dry hands and a native girl enters the hut carrying a clay bowl on a tray. Behind her stands another girl holding a folded piece of fabric. Martin looks at them and suspects that their slender milk-coffee bodies have, as local custom requires, accepted his favours.

"I imagine that your honourable genitals have had quite a seeing-to," says the King. "So let this girl soothe them with uiopeniauieaua, a healing ointment. It works almost instantly. Also, I think a light sarong will suit you better in our climate than uncomfortable European dress."

Despite being somewhat embarrassed, Martin gets up and lets the girl treat him. The ointment stings mildly, then cools. The girl's fingers are very nimble and sensitive. She spreads the ointment into the skin and does not miss a single square centimetre of Martin's aching genitals. The other girl waits, then wraps the florid fabric round his lower body.

Ahuhuai Tahuhuneui, accompanied by the king and his elders, walks out of the hut.

"By the time Doctor Gershwitz arrives," Tioka III says encouragingly, "you'll be fine."

And indeed, when in the afternoon a small dot appears above the sea and the village hears the sound of a piston engine, Martin gets up and nothing hurts any more.

The whole village gathers by the lagoon to watch the Cessna come down on its floats. Several men launch their long narrow boats and quickly paddle towards the plane, which is rocking on the waves.

Martin shades his eyes from the sun, watching a few passengers get out of the plane into the boats.

"Well, go and meet her," the amiable king encourages him, and propels him towards the lagoon.

Now Martin can already see Edna sitting in the first boat in her white shorts and blouse. He gets into the water and walks until it is waist-deep.

"Martin!" Edna shouts from the approaching boat and jumps into the water. Up to her breasts in salty, foamy water, she rushes to Junec.

"Edna!" shouts Martin, embraces her, lifts her up and turns her round a few times.

"How did you find me?" wonders the gorgeously fresh, suntanned and fragrant Doctor Gershwitz. "How did you get here?"

"Oh, Edna!" Martin presses her friend to his body and covers her face, neck, and hair with passionate kisses.

"Don't be silly, Martin!" Edna laughs, freeing herself from his passionate embrace.

"I came to ask you to marry me," Martin says fervently.

Edna laughs.

"So what will it be," says Martin seriously. "Yes, or no?"

"Is that why you've come all this way?" ask Edna.

"Yes, that's why," says Martin. "I've had enough of modern lifestyles. Enough of time spent apart." Martin Junec will never leave Edna. He will go where she goes. And vice versa. He knows it can work. Each will have to adapt a bit. Each will have to make a few allowances. He worries about Edna and will never again let her go away on her own.

Edna becomes serious. The waves tickle her suntanned thighs. She looks Martin straight in the face.

"Well, what's it going to be?" Martin would like to know. He's had enough of his dubious freedom. He wants to marry the woman he loves, yes, loves, and he wants to live with her, sleep with her, eat with her, have children by her, the lot! He'll be forty in a year and then in ten years fifty, and so on. He wants to experience a little bit of happiness. Can Edna understand? Everything passes, you're not even aware. Nothing can make up for lost time. Every moment that Martin lives without Edna will be lost forever. Time flows into a great drain and never comes back. He loves Edna as he's never loved any other woman in his life. And Edna has never been loved as much as he loves her. So what is it going to be? Yes, or no?"

"In that case, yes," Edna agrees, and for Martin, the whole world begins to whirl crazily round and round.

Then they walk through the shallow surf to the shore. Hand in hand, a handsome couple, like a sculpture of lovers.

"What was it like in your country?" Edna asks him. "Tell me!"

Martin sighs. He'd love to tell his future wife everything. About Žofré's ghost and Hruškovič; about Rácz and Silvia; about visiting his native village; about his miraculous escape from the Hotel Ambassador and his mad journey to Hong Kong, and further. But he doesn't know where to begin. Suddenly he realises that his command of American English is not good enough to make her understand everything that he'd been through in his old country, or even how he'd got here, to Aumaoua Island.

"I survived," he finally says and takes a breath as if he wanted to add something.

Edna turns to him, awaiting another sentence, but Martin is silent again.

Together they walk along the beach to the native village looming in the distance. The sea ripples and white albatrosses hover in the air.

From the village comes the melodious sound of Hawaiian guitars.

* * *

It takes Freddy a long time to find a good moment to remind Sida about raising his salary. Finally one night, as they sit at the bar, waiting for a customer, Freddy starts harping on again about money. Sida is in a bad mood, staring dully into her glass. Freddy explains that she had promised to raise his salary to two hundred a day if she was satisfied.

"Yes, if I'm satisfied," Sida remarks.

That does it for Freddy. "What do you mean?" he snaps. What did his mistress mean by that remark?

Sida grabs the leather strap attached to Freddy's collar and gives it a sharp tug.

She didn't mean anything. She only said, "If I'm satisfied."

Freddy tosses his head in a gesture of resistance; he won't let her pull him closer. But Sida's tone suggested she wasn't satisfied, he says. Could Sida possibly be dissatisfied with him? Could she find anyone else like him? Certainly not!

Sida has no desire to haggle with the fat slob. She just reminds him that she didn't need anyone; it was Freddy Piggybank who offered her his services. And he knew what he was letting himself in for. Well then?

Freddy lowers his voice. Everything can be settled amicably. He has no objections, the work is fine and he likes it. But he can see how much

Sida makes. Not that he envies her, but with takings like those, his slave owner should have no problem giving him another hundred a day.

Sida explodes. She should have seen that coming! People are swine; they get used to living in clover. And Freddy's no different. When she remembers that only a few weeks ago Freddy was happy enough to be completely prepared to be her assistant completely unpaid! But now it's just a boring routine to him. At first, he was happy just to lick her arse. Today he wants two hundred, and tomorrow he'll ask for three hundred. All right: she's no bitch. She says, "A hundred and fifty a day."

Eyebrows raised, she looks at her slave.

Freddy mulls over the new offer and something in his tiny brain commands him to accept it. In the end, however, he digs his heels in.

"No," he tells Sida. "It's all, or nothing. Two hundred."

"Are you bored with your job?" his mistress asks.

"I'm not bored with my job," says Freddy. "I love my work, really. But everybody around me is making big money, and I'm not. So I say, give me two hundred! It's not that much. I was making a thousand a day at the car park."

"Well then, go back to the car park, if you're so clever," says Sida.

They sit for a while silently and watch a perverted porno movie, which they've seen a hundred times, projected on the wall.

Sida is disgruntled. She's not bothered about the money; it's the principle of the thing. Freddy Piggybank pushes himself in, forces himself on her as her slave and even signs a contract, and now he's got too big for his boots. He should be purring with happiness every time his mistress looks at him.

Freddy shrugs. For him it's not the principle so much as the money that counts. He hasn't enough to live on. He can't save. "Two hundred a day!"

"It didn't take you long to get bored with me," says Sida bitterly. "Money means more to you than obedience and devotion to your mistress! Right, pack your bags and clear off, you perverted pig!"

Freddy can't understand; he can't believe his ears. He smiles hesitantly.

"Didn't you hear?" Sida says. "Bugger off!"

Freddy shakes his head. This isn't what he wanted. Not ending like this. After all, it can all be sorted out peacefully.

Sida nods. "Exactly. Peacefully." So Freddy Piggybank can peacefully fuck off. Sida Tešadíková has just finished with him. She doesn't need Freddy Piggybank; he needs her.

Freddy gets up. He may be fat and have weird tastes. But he's not a fat pig. He won't take any more insults. If Sida tells him to go, he will.

He proudly turns round and marches out of the bar.

He sits in the dressing room, changing his clothes and waiting for the door to open and his mistress to come in and say that she didn't mean it that way. Nobody enters. Freddy puts on his ordinary clothes and just sits there for a while. Then he decides to go home, regardless of whatever's waiting for him there.

As he walks out of the *Perverts' Centre*, Sida deliberately pretends not to see him. Freddy comes out on the street, rolls up his collar and, in the face of a cold wind, heads for the number 34 bus stop. As he passes the YMCA cinema, the audience is just leaving. Freddy waits by the bus stop, surrounded by satisfied, cheerful, even happy people. The adventures experienced in the cinema have left them with wide-open, radiant eyes. They discuss the film animatedly, with occasional bursts of laughter. Freddy hates them at this moment. How can they be so happy at a time when Freddy is so miserable?

It gradually dawns on him that he has made a mistake. He shouldn't have pressed Sida so hard; Sida is no Feri Bartaloš! And besides: oh, Sida! Sida!..

* * *

Freddy Piggybank unlocks the gate of his parents' house, enters the veranda and tries to unlock the door in the dark. He can't: a key is in the lock inside. Freddy turns his key, and suddenly the door opens and his father appears in the doorway. He gives his perverted son a stern look.

"Is that you?" Father asks.

"It's me," answers Freddy, blushes, and lowers his eyes.

"Have you brought the lunch tin and string bag?" asks his father.

This question is a painful reminder to Freddy of his father's visit to the *Perverts' Centre*: it takes him a while to give a positive answer.

"Did you at least like it?" old Mešťánek asks when tears gush from Freddy's eyes.

"Well, come in then," says his father in a conciliatory tone, and lets his son in.

"I haven't said a word to your mother," the father whispers, as Freddy, breathing hard, puts on his slippers.

Freddy greets his mother, but politely and firmly declines her offer of food and cake. He is suffering too much to want it.

He enters his uncomfortable room, undresses, turns off the light and lies in bed in the dark. He stares at the ceiling with wide-open feverish eyes.

There's a knock at the door; his father enters. He clears his throat; he doesn't know how to start. "May I?" he asks and sits down on the bed. He sits for a moment in silence and Freddy doesn't say a word either.

"I went to where you work," says Father. "I saw it all. Why did you lie to us?"

Freddy doesn't know what to say, so he says nothing.

"That door-keeper or bouncer, or whoever he was, told me that you had a customer," Father continues. "What kind of customer was it?"

"Well, a customer..." says Freddy.

"What do you mean?" Father asks. "Are you saying you are a ... pervert? A homosexual?"

Old Mešťánek pronounces the last word in a way that suggests that he's scared of it.

Freddy blushes, unseen in the dark.

"I'm not," he says.

"Then what sort of a customer was it?" Freddy's father insists, undeterred.

"Well," Freddy says, "it an old man, you know. People who come to us like to be whipped..."

"To us?" Father focuses on a word. "Who is this 'US'?"

"Well, it's us...Sida and me."

"What Sida? Who's Sida?"

"Sida Tešadíková," says Freddy. "From Nová Ves."

"Oh, from Nová Ves, is she?" old Mešťánek nods. "And what about this Sida? I mean, what is it she does?"

"Well..." Freddy reflects. "She whips people who pay her for it."

"And you?"

"I help her," says Freddy. "I hand her the instruments, assist her, clean up... that kind of thing."

"And what else?"

"Nothing," says Freddy. "Just that."

"So you just help her," his father checks. "You know, Alfred, how can I put it... in a word, there are men who... you see... go with other men... Are you sure you're not one of them?"

Freddy is so embarrassed he wishes the ground would swallow him.

"Who do you think I am?" he shouts indignantly. "Of course, I'm sure!"

"You know," his Father says. "I thought you were one of them."

"I never have been one of them," says Freddy.

His father sighs with relief. His mood gets noticeably better; the burden weighing for days on his mind has been removed.

"And that Sida?" he asks. "What kind of a girl is she? She probably hasn't much going for her, if she works in a place like that, has she?"

"She used to be a school teacher," says Freddy. "She went to university. She's clever."

"Really!" his father is incredulous.

"Really," Freddy insists. "She used to live in Grb. Now she lives in Petržalka."

"Oh well," says his Father and stands up. "If you like it... The main thing is you're not one of those... faggots."

His father heads for the door.

"And I won't tell your mother anything," he promises. "I don't want her to worry. She probably wouldn't understand... I mean times have changed. It's not like in our day... Aren't you hungry?"

Freddy shakes his head. On the one hand, he's happy that things have gone so smoothly at home; on the other hand, when he thinks of Sida his heart aches.

His father goes downstairs to the living room. Freddy is lying in bed, imagining what it would be like if he died. He would lie in an open coffin. They'd all cry over him. First of all his grieving parents and then... and then who? Freddy has no friends who'd come to the funeral. Maybe, the neighbours would come and people his parents know. And then there would be a rustle: Sida would appear, all in black: black dress, black kid gloves, black stockings, and black veil. She'd have a bouquet in her hand. She'd throw it into his grave, onto his coffin, and cry. She'd be crying disconsolately, but it would be too late. All she could do for Freddy by that time would be to kiss his arse.

Freddy ponders the right way to commit suicide. Should he hang himself? No, he'd suffer for too long. Cut his veins? Freddy gets shivers from the unpleasant thought. Shivers run down his spine when he imagines the cold razor-blade silently, but all the more treacherously slashing his wrist. Anyway, he might damage his tendons and end up a cripple for life. Sleeping pills? He doesn't have any. Gas? Gas stinks. And his parents never leave the house.

Freddy jumps out of his bed, opens the wardrobe and takes out a plastic bag. He climbs back into his bed, puts the bag over his head and ties it round his neck. Now he is breathing in his own microclimate, his own atmosphere. Death by suffocation might not be so hard. Maybe he'll fall asleep without even knowing.

Freddy's heart beat speeds up. The oxygen level in the small volume of the plastic bag has fallen drastically. Freddy is getting a bit hot. He starts to weep for his cruel fate; tears flow down his fat cheeks. He fights back his survival instinct and the urge to rip the bag off his head and, wheezing, humbly inhales almost pure carbon dioxide and nitrogen. Black circles form in front of his eyes; interestingly, Freddy can see them clearly even against the absolutely black background of his little room. The plastic bag inflates and deflates to the rhythm of his breathing.

Suddenly Freddy becomes terribly disgusted with himself; he has no will power. In one brusque movement, he rips the bag off and hungrily inhales the cooling fresh air.

* * *

Sida ties the hands of the first customer of the day to a cross laid over two wooden trestles and cracks her whip a few times over him.

"Forgive me, countess!" a customer shouts. "Forgive me! I didn't mean to offend you!"

"I never pardon anyone!" Sida shouts at the customer. "Especially when they offend me!"

Sida begins to whip the customer's chest and thighs, but more symbolically than in earnest. The customer, prone on the rough wood, writhes, and his fingers are bent like talons. The condom placed on his erect member soon begins to fill with liquid.

"Ah! Ah!" cries the customer. "Ah! Ah!"

Sida puts down the whip and unties the customer's hands and legs. The customer gets up and goes to the bathroom. He comes back soon and gets dressed.

"I won't be able to come next week," he says, putting in his cuff-links. "I have to attend trade negotiations in Japan with the minister. Can I bring you anything from there, Miss Sida?"

"Why should you bring me anything?" Sida smiles modestly, sipping from her beer can.

"I'd really like to bring you something," says the customer, unrolls his collar and puts a knotted tie over his head. "I really would," he adds.

"Then choose something from their sex shops," Sida concedes. "Anything to make you happy, too."

"I'll find something," says the customer. "And where is Mr Freddy?" he asks.

"Freddy's on leave," Sida lies.

"That's a pity," says the customer. "When he tied me up, I couldn't even move. No hard feelings, Miss Sida, but you don't have the strength in your hands."

"Are you saying that you weren't satisfied?" asks Sida.

"Oh I was," the customer tries to mollify her. "Of course, I was. But I was even more satisfied before. It was as if you were a bit distracted, or something… Your thoughts were somewhere far away. Customers notice that sort of thing, don't delude yourself."

"I'm very sorry," says Sida.

"Maybe you've got something on your mind," says the customer. "Could I be of any help, Miss Sida?"

"No thanks," says Tešadíková. "Everything's fine. I have a slight headache, that's all…"

When the customer leaves, Sida opens another beer and lights up a Marlboro. She scratches her thigh through a hole in her net stocking. She sits on the rack and smokes. She doesn't feel like doing anything. Her gaze falls on Freddy's mask hanging on a rack.

The internal phone rings. Sida answers it.

"There are two more customers waiting for you in the bar," the bar girl informs her. "Come and get them."

"Get Dagmar to take them," says Sida. "I'm done today."

"And what do I tell the boss if she asks?" the bar girl enquires.

"Tell her I'm ill and I've gone home."

"Fine," the bar girl agrees and puts down the phone.

Sida puts her cigarette in the ashtray and starts taking off her make-up.

* * *

Freddy lies on the bed of his bachelor room and browses through a new issue of *Latex Persuasion* that he's borrowed from the *Perverts' Centre*.

"ALFRED!" his Mother shouts from the living room downstairs. "YOU HAVE A VISITOR!"

Freddy tucks the magazine under his pillow and sits down on the bed. He waits a few seconds for his erection to disappear under his track-suit bottoms, then gets up and opens the door to his little room.

Up the stairs walks Sida Tešadíková.

"Sida!" Freddy shouts in surprise.

Sida also looks at Freddy in surprise; during his involuntary leave, Piggybank has been depressed and off his food. The result is that he has lost over thirty pounds and his formless figure has taken on a more masculine and human shape.

Freddy invites Sida into his little room. Sida walks to the window and looks at the pond in the twilight and at the flaming pink sky. This kind of sunset can only be seen in Nová Ves.

"Nice view," says Sida. "Can I smoke here?"

"Of course," says Freddy and searches for an ashtray.

Sida wearily sits down in the armchair and taps her cigarette ash onto Freddy's much-loved date palm.

Freddy sits down on the couch opposite her.

"Look, Freddy," Sida begins. "I think I went a bit too far last time. I know, you may feel offended, but I think you should stop sulking and come back to *Justine*."

"Do you?" Freddy Piggybank shows interest.

"I've had a word with the owner," says Sida. "She doesn't object to your becoming a permanent employee of the *Perverts' Centre*."

Freddy nods.

Sida can't take her eyes off him. Freddy's somewhat emaciated face, dark, sunken eyes marked by suffering and the four-day stubble give his face a completely new expression.

"I know that you miss the work," says Sida. "And if you want me to apologize to you, then here goes: forgive me."

Freddy smiles. He gets up and strokes her soft, short hair.

"I had an inkling you'd come," he says.

He opens a drawer and takes out a longish object wrapped in silk paper.

"It's for you," he says and hands it to her.

Sida tears off the paper and takes out a beautiful, hand-decorated leather whip. She weighs it in her hand and cracks it a few times. Its sound is full and heavy.

"Is it really mine?" asks Sida in disbelief, her eyes wide open.

"It is," says Freddy.

Sida places the tip of the whip under his chin.

"It's genuine hippo leather!" Freddy stresses.

"It must have cost a fortune," says Sida. "Where did you get the money?"

"I've sold my trailer," says Piggybank.

"Thanks, Freddy," says Sida and her voice softens. "You've no idea how happy you've made me. But I can't accept it. Strangers don't give each other such expensive gifts."

"We don't have to be strangers," says Freddy and blushes.

"What do you mean by that, Freddy?" Sida asks and blushes, too.

Freddy can no longer hold back.

"I love you, Sida!" he blurts out and throws himself onto his knees. "I know that I'm not good enough, but just say the word! Give me hope! I know that you don't like men, but if you don't want me to, I'll never even touch you all my life. Just be mine, Sida!"

Sida looks at him. "You don't say," she says. She grabs his hair and pulls him towards herself. "And will you go on being my slave?" she asks him.

"I will," Piggybank blurts out without thinking.

"And will you obey me in all things?" Sida asks, drawing on her cigarette.

"I will," Freddy promises.

"And you'll put up with all the torments, injustices and humiliations that I devise for you?" Sida enquires. "As our contract states?"

"All, all, every one of them!" stutters Freddy.

"And you'll let me treat you like the vilest dog?" asks his mistress.

"Yes," says Freddy as he quivers from pure sincerity, obedience and fidelity. His eyes shine like a dog's by a groaning Sunday dinner table.

Sida pulls him by his hair even closer and purses her unmade-up lips for a kiss. Freddy tries to respond passionately. He quickly shouts with pain and astonishment. He pulls back sharply and touches his lips. Blood is pouring from his lower lips which she has bitten.

"Very well then, you'll be my dog," Sida decides and begins to kiss Freddy's mouth.

Freddy feels her slippery hot tongue in his mouth.

"I'll drink your blood like this every day," says Sida, her mouth full of blood, when she detaches herself from him. "You might quickly lose your strength and die from that," she adds. "What do you say?"

Freddy is trembling at the sudden onset of happiness and excitement. He doesn't care. He breathes in, preparing to say more or less that life without Sida doesn't interest him anyway. But his mistress's stern gaze silences him. Rather than speak, he obeys her silent command and throws himself down at her feet. He takes off her boots, first one and then the other. With one small foot, free, but clad in a sock, Sida imperiously and capriciously pushes Freddy away. Freddy loses his balance and rolls on the floor. He is silent. He feels his lower lip still bleeding slightly. He touches it.

Sida gets up and stands over him, her long legs spread over him. Her crotch, in tight ragged jeans, is thrust forward. Slowly, like a music video, she takes off her thick, well-worn leather jacket and throws it at Freddy, who is stunned, without taking her solemn gaze off him. Then, equally slowly, she takes off her white cotton socks and throws them at her slave, like a stripper making her audience happy by throwing her stockings at them.

Freddy's heart rises to his throat. His mouth is dry, but he swallows and flaps his heavy tongue. His burning blood races faster and faster.

"SIDA!" Freddy's mother calls from downstairs. "WILL YOU HAVE SOME COFFEE AND CAKE?"

"Later," says Sida barely audibly, continuing to fix her trembling slave with her pitiless snake-like gaze.

The thread of Freddy's slowly growing excitement is abruptly cut. Piggybank is outraged. He gets up and opens the door of his small bachelor room.

"NO, SHE WILL NOT!" he roars downstairs, ignoring the pain in his bitten lip. "I HAVE TO SOLVE AN IMPORTANT WORK PROBLEM! DO NOT DISTURB ME!!!"

"Can't you lock the room?" asks Tešadíková, wrestling with her trouser zipper.

Freddy blushes. He turns the key in the lock. Twice.

When he turns away from the door, Sida is wearing only knickers and a tee-shirt. She puts her cigarette for a moment into the flower pot and pulls the tee-shirt over her head. Piggybank can see that his boss has no bra under her everyday clothes. He can't stop looking at her smooth, almost boyish, breasts. Sida strokes them very slowly for a while with visible pleasure. As if she were trying to gain time before the final and crucial unveiling. At last, without taking her eyes off Freddy's face, she takes off her knickers and kicks them into the corner.

Freddy stands opposite her. He has never in his life seen her completely naked, free of textile, leather, rubber, and metal accessories, without wigs, artificial nails and eyelashes, long gloves, fake tattoos and a wildly made-up face. Her small, slender body with little tits and her sparse, groomed pubic hair impress him, without all those awe-inspiring accessories, as defenceless, almost touchingly childish.

"Well, what is it, wanker?" Sida asks, and her voice rings with the intimately familiar impatience and strictness of a dominatrix. The momentary tenderness has vanished. "What are you staring at? Let's get on with it!" she orders him roughly. "Off with your clothes!"

Freddy obeys. He is undressed in a seconds. Naked in the presence of his naked slave owner, he feels strange, but agreeably so.

Sida comes up to Piggybank; her cruel eyes seek out a place on his bare chest, she takes her cigarette out of her mouth and stubs it out there.

The searing, delicious pain makes Freddy close his eyes, but he doesn't step back even an inch. His nose registers the stench of burned hair and flesh. He knows that this time it's for real. He realises that this act is Sida's way of showing clearly that she, in turn, has feelings for Freddy Piggybank.

Sida pulls out a pair of coarse leather brickyard gauntlets from her jacket and puts them on. Freddy almost faints with excitement. "Let's go, you fat wanker," says Sida and grabs him by his tumescent organ. "Now I want you to service me properly, get it?" Sida leads Piggybank, stupefied by excitement, to the bed and pushes him onto it. She uses her hand to straddle his erect member. Freddy begins to breathe heavily. The burning pain on his lip and chest turns into pulsating delight.

Sida briefly, but painfully, presses his scrotum.

"Now you do it to me, but heaven help you if you come before I say you can," she hisses threateningly and bites his fleshy ear. "I'll decide when you come. You'll never get rid of me, porky."

When Sida notices Freddy's eyes filling with tears from the sudden pain, she mercilessly twists his nose with her gloved hand.

"Never, you understand?" she repeats.

Freddy lies as obediently as a dog under his mistress and holds her waist with both hands, as he always dreamed of doing while she drove him on her motorbike to the New Bridge. His mistress moves on top of him with a savage lack of concern. Freddy is forced to focus all his thoughts on something else so as not to come prematurely and make himself liable to severe punishment. But even so, it is hard to say what he'd like most: to come, or to be punished.

* * *

Freddy Mešťánek's and Sida Tešadíková's wedding turns into a popular event in the city's erotic underworld. Silvia takes on the organization and half the financing of the wedding; it is the first and perhaps the last, at least for some time, wedding of two staff members at the Perverts' Centre.

The wedding ceremony itself takes place in the church and then everybody moves to *Justine*. Freddy looks rather good in a white suit, but the real star is, naturally, Sida: pale, wearing black, with a train, her arms in long black gloves and with a crown of blood-red orchids on her head covered by a black veil. Perhaps for the first time in her life, Sida is in feminine attire, and she looks wickedly beautiful in it — like the evil black queen from Disney's *Snow White*.

Freddy's parents are beside themselves with happiness. Mother particularly likes Sida's bridesmaids. Old Mešťánek likes them even more. They would certainly be astonished to learn that one is called Dárius, another Otmar, a third Radúz and the fourth, Vratko.

Before the reception, the old Mrs Mešťánek gives the newlyweds a wedding present: wool for Freddy's and Sida's pullovers. She will never find out what son and his bride do for a living; her husband won't tell her and she'll never guess. She simply doesn't want to think about it.

* * *

Ten thousand miles away, another wedding is taking place. Doctor Edna Gershwitz and Martin Junec say "Yes, I will," to each other, and soon set out on a honeymoon trip to Israel, Edna's parents' ancient homeland. Martin's firm *Artisania Lamps* is doing better and better, and soon he'll manage to set up a European branch. Understandably, Martin doesn't come to Europe in person; he'll never ever do that again. He sends his manager and a lawyer. In a little village, fifteen miles from Dresden, they buy cheaply a site with commercial buildings and after the necessary reconstruction begin producing the famous plywood lamps. After some time, Martin gives up his job as the CEO, leaves the firm, buys a ninety-foot yacht and sails with Edna and an eight-men crew on a round-the-world cruise. We should add that Žofré will keep his word and, ever since he left Martin outside the Hotel Ambassador, nobody will ever see him again.

Hruškovič devotes a few more years to his patients, but then retires. He has enough money and doesn't need to lift a finger for the rest of his life. But he has to devote this remaining life to seeing doctors to cure him from diseases that he seems to have caught from the patients he's cured. Hruškovič bears it humbly: he sees it as a punishment from God for being a charlatan and a fraud. Until the day he dies he is one of the most respected residents of Nová Ves. More than ten thousand people from all the corners of Slovakia and from abroad, mostly his former patients, attend his funeral, and it's on the evening television news.

Rácz finally exploits the real estate property he bought in the port area and buys a couple of tug boats and a few barge towers and, in addition to all his business activities, he throws himself into the river transportation business, as well. He finally understands that he will never get Silvia back. He takes it like a man and finds another mistress. Of course, he won't stop passionately and jealously loving his wife Lenka. The Chamber of Commerce votes him Businessman of the Year, the Association of Hoteliers and Restaurateurs votes him Hotelier and Restaurateur of the Year, the Alliance of Private River Shippers votes him River Shipper of the Year, and one women's weekly magazine even names him Man of the Year.

Eržika Bartalošová works in her father's, the butcher Kišš's, shop as a sales woman. Her husband, proud Feri Bartaloš, rears pigs on old Mr Kišš's farm. They make good money. Soon Eržika gets pregnant and they have a baby boy. They name him Antal, after his grandfather. They go on living in the Kišš house. Proud Feri spends his evenings in the pub, telling the men about his life in the city. They have all by now had enough of his bragging stories, but they keep listening, since they too feel, at least temporarily, somehow illuminated by the big city lights. When old Mr Kišš comes into the pub, Feri goes quiet. He knows that his father-in-law would instantly stop his bragging with a pointed poisonous remark. So he prefers to stand Kišš a shot of apricot brandy, keep his peace and patiently wait for the old man to kick the bucket.

Fraňo Fčilek, suspected of murdering Four-Eyes, was arrested and investigated. He soon had to be released for lack of evidence, as my more observant readers will have noticed. Fraňo Fčilek now collects beer mugs in the *Hunter's Inn*. As for Four-Eyes, the official verdict on his death is that he slipped on a mustard-covered plastic sausage tray and fractured his lower cranial bone.

The Heilig spouses manage to deceive everyone. As soon as they get back from holiday they move to Berlin. None of their new colleagues and acquaintances ever suspect little Felicitas to be anyone but their own daughter. Felicitas grows quickly. In the future she will be a talented pupil and a good athlete. People will all be amazed how much she resembles her mother.

Silvia's *Perverts' Club* prospers. Silvia spends most of her time in her spacious attic flat. Only occasionally does she venture outside, looking about in case Rácz's men are lurking; she worries that she might be kidnapped and thrown to the hungry and bestial savage hotelier. She lives like this for a long time, but then, at a gallery opening, she meets an intelligent young woman who wins her heart and soul. As it turns out, the young woman quite fancies Silvia, and so a little bit of simple happiness and love moves into the attic of the pretty villa by the main railway station, where a neon girl with a little whip in her hand shines into the dark night.

Freddy and Sida Mešťánek use their savings to buy a comfortable flat on Björnson Street, less than five hundred yards from the *Perverts' Club*. Sida soon becomes pregnant, but works until the last moment: the advanced pregnancy gives her services a certain perverse cachet. After all, it is a *Perverts' Centre*. After the birth of their child, named Silvia, in honour of their boss who acts as godmother, Sida stays at home. She sells her motorcycle and buys a car, to avoid the hassle of a pram in the packed buses and trams. Freddy stays in the *Perverts' Centre*. Since he no longer has a partner, Silvia invents a new role for him: devising new programmes, small perverted plays for *Justine's* basement theatre. Freddy throws himself into his work with verve and soon turns out to have a great talent for putting together pornographic one-act plays. Later, when Silvia begins to cooperate with the Danish company *Colour Climax Corporation* in producing deviant pornographic films locally, Freddy becomes its sole scriptwriter. Of course, his income goes up accordingly. He is no longer dependent on Sida, quite the reverse.

Only occasionally, at night when their little girl is asleep, Sida enters Freddy's study, almost unrecognizable in her make-up, in leather corset and gloves, the whip he gave her in one hand, a studded dog collar and leash in the other, and demands her due. Work or no work, script or no script, the contract that Freddy once sealed with his own blood is still in force and always will be. Freddy has to serve. And he likes serving.

Soon Sida talks him into studying, despite his advanced age, film and scriptwriting at the Academy of Arts. They accept him onto the programme because of his great talent: so Freddy Piggybank spends his mornings at lectures and his afternoons on film and theatre scripts for Silvia. He's off medication: regular sex has cured his brain condition.

Occasionally he treats himself, sits down at the café outside the Academy and with a whimsical gesture orders a Becher. He sits alone; he's still a skinflint. He's not friends with anyone. He can't understand his classmates and they in turn can't understand him. There is almost a generation gap between them. Besides, they find their older classmate a bit pedestrian and stupid, even though he tries to cover it up with a few terms that he's picked up from the lectures. Freddy downs his Becher and a pleasant warmth spreads inside him. He recalls his wife and daughter, the two beings he loves most in the world and his heart is seized by a sudden surge of love. He gets up and hurries home.

In the evening he sits at the computer, writing a new piece for the small theatre. The little girl is playing in the living room with her children's puppet gallows set. Sida watches the video of a new film produced by Silvia to a script by Freddy.

"What do you think, Sida darling," Freddy shouts into the living room, without lifting his eyes from the screen. "Could we get a live elephant on stage in *Justine*?"

Sida thinks about it and takes a sip straight from the can.

"Not likely, you stupid fat pervert," she tells her slave.

"I see," says Freddy, disappointed. "Then I'll have to think of something else."

He turns round and through the open door his eyes catch the view of his dominatrix and their child. He suddenly realises that some time ago even for him, Freddy Piggybank, the sky became cloudless.

His days will be as lovely as a field of flax.

also available from the Garnett Press

Д. Рейфилд, О. Макарова (ред.). Дневник Алексея Сергеевича Суворин (*Dairy of Aleksei Suvorin, the 19th C. Russian magnate, in Russian*). 1999, pp xl+666 ISBN 0 9535878 0 0 £20.00

D. Rayfield, J Hicks, O Makarova, A. Pilkington (editors) *The Garnett Book of Russian Verse. An Anthology with English Prose Translation* 2000, 748 pp. ISBN 0 9535878 2 7 £25.00

Donald Rayfield, editor in chief (with Rusudan Amirejibi, Shukia Apridonidze, Laurence Broers, Levan Chkhaidze, Ariane Chanturia, Tina Margalitadze) *A Comprehensive Georgian-English Dictionary*, 2006. 2 vols. pp xl + 172. ISBN 978-0-9535878-3-4   £75.00
(*a few seconds [8 replacement pages inserted in volume 2] are available at £40.00*)

Peter Pišt'anek, translated by Peter Petro. *Rivers of Babylon* 2007. pp 259. ISBN 978-0-9535878-4-1. £12.99

Peter Pišt'anek, translated by Peter Petro *The End of Freddy* (*Rivers of Babylon 3*) 2008. pp 320. ISBN 978-0-9535878-6-5 £13.99

Nikolai Gogol, Marc Chagall *Dead Souls* , a new translation by Donald Rayfield, *with 96 engravings and 12 vignettes reproduced from the 1948 Tériade edition* 2008. pp366. ISBN 978-0-9535878-7-2 £29.99

forthcoming
in 2009:

Otar Chiladze *Avelum* (the fifth novel by Georgia's greatest living novelist)
Donald Rayfield *The Literature of Georgia — A History*, the third revised and expanded edition

in preparation

a full translation, the first into English, of Avicenna (Ibn Sina) *The Laws of Medicine* (*Al Qanun fi at Tibb*)

for enquiries, or to buy any of our books, contact:
d.rayfield@qmul.ac.uk
or write to:
Garnett Press, School of Languages, Literature and Film, Queen Mary University of London, Mile End Road, London E1 4NS, UK